INHERITANCE TRACKS

INHERITANCE
TRACKS

Catherine Aird

This first US edition published 2019
in the USA by
SEVERN HOUSE PUBLISHERS LTD of
Eardley House, 4 Uxbridge Street, London W8 7SY.
Trade paperback edition first published
in the USA 2020 by
SEVERN HOUSE PUBLISHERS LTD.

British Library Cataloguing in Publication Data
A CIP catalogue record for this title is available from the British Library.

ISBN-13: 978-0-7278-8932-4 (cased)
ISBN-13: 978-1-78029-619-7 (trade paper)
ISBN-13: 978-1-4483-0234-5 (e-book)

All Severn House titles are printed on acid-free paper.

Severn House Publishers support the Forest Stewardship Council™ [FSC™],
the leading international forest certification organisation.
All our titles that are printed on FSC certified paper carry the FSC logo.

Typeset by Palimpsest Book Production Ltd.,
Falkirk, Stirlingshire, Scotland.
Printed and bound in Great Britain by
TJ International, Padstow, Cornwall.

For Harvey and Oscar Christopher
Mytton Thornycroft
With love

ONE

The first person to arrive at the solicitors' office that particular morning was a trim, grey-haired woman with a neat hairdo.

'If you would come this way, please, Mrs Port,' said Miss Florence Fennel, leading the way to the waiting room of Puckle, Puckle and Nunnery, Solicitors and Notaries Public, of Berebury in the County of Calleshire, 'and I'll tell Mr Puckle that you've arrived.'

'I'm a little early, I'm afraid,' the woman said diffidently, looking round the empty waiting room, 'but I didn't want to be late.'

'Of course not,' murmured Miss Fennel, who was never late herself.

Mrs Port sighed. 'And getting into Berebury here from out Bishop's Marbourne way can be very difficult on market day. The traffic is really awful first thing in the morning.'

Miss Fennel, who didn't own a car herself, nodded as sympathetically as if she did.

'So,' the woman went on, 'I thought I'd rather be early than late. Especially since I'm not really sure what all this is about.' Sue Port took a letter out of her handbag and held it up in front of the secretary.

Florence Fennel made no reply to this. She did not normally act as the firm's receptionist as she was in fact the personal confidential secretary of Mr Simon Puckle, the senior partner in the firm, but today was different.

Very different.

The next client to arrive already had his letter in his hand as he came through the door. He announced himself in a businesslike manner as he approached Miss Fennel, waving the letter in front of him. 'Clive Culshaw of Culshaw's Bakery, Berebury,' he said importantly. 'I have an appointment to see a Mr Simon Puckle here at ten o'clock this morning.'

'Yes, of course, Mr Culshaw. If you would just follow me . . .'

He continued to hold the letter in front of her. 'And he hasn't said what this is all about. Just that it's a matter that might be of some potential interest to me, which isn't exactly specific.'

Miss Fennel, who had in fact written the letter and knew exactly what it was all about, said nothing to this either. She simply ushered him into the waiting room. Mrs Sue Port, its only other occupant, glanced incuriously at the newcomer, showing no sign of recognition. Instead she returned her gaze almost immediately to the glossy magazine she had been studying.

'I do hope Mr Puckle won't keep me waiting long,' said Clive Culshaw. 'I'm a very busy man.'

'I'm sure you are,' said Miss Fennel soothingly. As it happened she knew a great deal more about Clive Culshaw and his business than the man realised – including that he was also a very impatient man. 'I'll tell Mr Puckle you're here,' she promised, closing the door behind her.

The two in the waiting room had been sitting in silence for some five minutes when the door opened again, and a flustered youngish woman hurried in, talking over her shoulder to Miss Fennel as she did so. 'So sorry to be late,' she said. 'I am late, aren't I? I nearly forgot and then I remembered and thought I would come along and see what's up.'

Giving a polite nod in the direction of Sue Port and Clive Culshaw, she settled herself into a chair. 'Morning, everybody, I'm Samantha Peters,' she introduced herself cheerfully, plonking herself down on one of the hard chairs and looking round. 'Oh, what lovely magazines!' she exclaimed. 'They don't have these posh ones at my hairdresser's.'

Neither of the others in the room spoke and so she buried herself in the colourful pages of a well-known weekly devoted to the antics of the newly very rich and therefore famous.

The next person to arrive was definitely late and totally laid-back about it. 'Don't know what this is all about,' the young man said casually to Miss Fennel, pulling a crumpled letter out of his jacket pocket, 'but I thought I'd better come along and see, just in case there's anything in it for me. I'm Martin Pickford, if you need to know.'

'Of course,' murmured Miss Fennel, who didn't need to know and, in any case, had documented a great deal more about young Mr Pickford than he could ever have supposed.

'You never know with solicitors,' he went on, suggesting that he had already had some unfavourable interaction with them. He sniffed. 'Slippery fellows, if you ask me, and never on the side of the innocent motorist.'

Since Miss Fennel, loyal member of Berebury's longest-standing legal firm, could not possibly agree with this sentiment, she again said nothing.

'Don't usually get out and about as early as this either,' he added unnecessarily. 'I mostly work from home and I over-slept. Flexible hours and all that.'

Miss Fennel had already realised this since the young man was unshaven and his hair tousled. Whether he was also unwashed was something about which she was keeping an open mind so far. There was a livid bruise down one side of his face and one of his front teeth was missing. 'But needs must, I suppose,' he said, shrugging his shoulders. 'I admit it doesn't happen often.'

'If you will just wait in here, Mr Pickford,' she said, opening the waiting-room door. 'I'll let Mr Puckle know that you've arrived.'

Whilst all of the existing occupants had looked up as the man entered the room, limping slightly, none of them spoke or appeared to recognise the new arrival, although Clive Culshaw, still making it quite obvious that he was a busy man, did look first at his watch in a meaningful manner and then at Miss Fennel as she closed the door behind her. Even so, it was a little while before Miss Fennel reappeared.

'Mr Puckle will see you now,' she announced. Since she had looked at none of them in particular when she spoke, all four people sitting there looked up expectantly. Clive Culshaw had even started to rise from his seat when she added, 'All of you.'

'All of us?' echoed Samantha Peters uncertainly, waving a hand round the room. 'I mean, I don't know any of these other people.'

'Me neither,' said Martin Pickford, the dishevelled young

man who had been the latest to arrive. He peered blearily round at the others and then added uncertainly, 'At least, I don't think so.'

'I'm quite sure I don't,' said Clive Culshaw decisively. He brandished the letter he had brought with him again. 'And the writer of this didn't say anything about any other people being involved when he wrote.'

'Nor to me, either,' said Samantha Peters.

'I'm sure Mr Puckle will be able to explain everything when he sees you all,' said Miss Fennel.

'The operative word being "all", I suppose,' mumbled Martin Pickford, clambering to his feet rather unsteadily, the fact that he had a limp becoming more apparent.

'If you will please come this way,' said Miss Fennel, not deigning to respond to this, 'you will find Mr Puckle is waiting for you in his room.'

Mr Simon Puckle was indeed waiting for them in his room. He rose with an old-fashioned courtesy as they entered and shook hands rather formally with each of them in turn.

'I expect,' he began pleasantly, 'you are all wondering why you have been asked to come this morning.'

'Yes, indeed,' said Clive Culshaw, nevertheless casting another furtive glance at his watch.

The solicitor indicated a large folder on the desk in front of him. 'And how it comes to be that, although I can advise you all that you have a common interest in what I have to say, you don't, as far as I am aware, know each other.'

'We don't,' said Clive Culshaw flatly, looking round. 'Not as far as I am concerned, anyway. I don't think that I have ever seen any of these people here in my life before.' He didn't sound as if he regretted this.

'Nor me,' said Samantha Peters.

Mrs Sue Port looked round curiously at the other three and then shook her head. 'I don't think I have, either.'

'Can we get on?' asked Martin Pickford plaintively. He was holding his head in his hands now.

Simon Puckle gave a little cough and cleared his throat preliminary to saying, 'You and one other person who has been delayed and another man who cannot for the time being be traced have all been invited here as a consequence of the recent death of an old lady called Clementina Henderson.'

'Who?' asked Samantha Peters.

'Never heard of her,' mumbled Martin Pickford. 'Or, come to that, anyone else called Clementina.'

'Me neither,' said Samantha Peters, looking mystified.

'Actually,' admitted Martin Pickford, 'I thought Clementina was an orange.'

'That's a clementine,' the woman called Susan Port informed him kindly.

'Perhaps he was thinking of a clementini,' suggested Clive Culshaw, who had noted the other man's bloodshot eyes and slight tremor. 'Martini's big brother,' he explained. He had shaken his head at the first mention of the other man's name and scribbled it now on the back of his letter.

'Good heavens!' exclaimed Mrs Sue Port, the older of the two women there, sitting up suddenly. 'I've heard of her. I remember now. I came across the name when I was working on my family history. Clementina Henderson – I don't believe it. I didn't even know she was still alive.'

'She isn't,' pointed out Martin Pickford. 'Didn't you hear what the gentleman said?'

'I thought she must have died years ago,' said Mrs Port, ignoring this. 'She was so very old.'

'She was indeed. I can tell you that she was nearly a hundred when she did die almost three months ago,' said Simon Puckle. 'In a nursing home in Calleford, as it happens.' Calleford was the county town of Calleshire and some distance from the market town of Berebury.

'But who was she?' asked Clive Culshaw, who obviously prided himself on getting unerringly to the nub of any matter as quickly as possible.

Mrs Port turned to him and said slowly, 'I suppose she would have been my great-aunt. I think,' she added uncertainly, 'that she was my late grandfather's sister.'

'But not my grandfather's sister,' said Clive Culshaw quickly. 'I've never even heard of her.'

'You are quite correct,' Simon Puckle nodded gravely at the pair of them. 'Both of you.'

'What does that mean, may I ask?' asked Martin Pickford truculently. 'I'm not with you.'

'It means,' said Simon Puckle, 'that she was Mrs Port's great-aunt but not Mr Culshaw's.'

'How come?' asked Martin Pickford, clearly puzzled.

Simon Puckle tapped the file on his desk. 'The late Clementina Henderson was the cousin of Mr Culshaw's great-grandmother who was called Horatia.'

'Was she really?' Clive Culshaw sat up and began to look quite interested. 'I'm sure I've heard of her – Horatia, I mean. In fact,' he frowned, 'I think I must have seen the name on our family tree at some time. It's quite a strange name, isn't it? After Horatio Nelson, I suppose, and one that you wouldn't easily forget. My son got really interested in looking everyone up when he compiled the tree, but I'm afraid I was too busy to go into it all.'

'Quite so,' murmured Simon Puckle. He indicated the file on his desk. 'Horatia Culshaw predeceased Clementina Henderson many years ago . . .'

'I'm not surprised,' interjected Martin Pickford, 'if Clementina nearly hit a hundred. Not many people do that.'

'But it is a consequence of her death,' carried on the solicitor imperturbably, 'that all of you here have an interest in a residuary trust.'

Martin Pickford lifted his head at this and looked at the solicitor. 'Sounds good to me, but how come? I mean, if we've none of us heard of her.' He waved a hand in Sue Port's direction. 'Except this lady here, of course.'

Simon Puckle pointed to the file on his desk again. 'You are all, one way and another, descendants of the late Algernon George Culver Mayton.'

Samantha Peters, the young woman who had arrived late, sat up suddenly and said that that name rang a bell with her. 'Mayton, I mean. I don't know why, though,' she said, clearly puzzled. 'But it does.'

'Quite possibly,' said Simon Puckle.

Clive Culshaw sat up, too, and looked round at the others. 'Does that mean we all – we four here that is – are all in one way and another related to each other?'

'Distantly,' said Simon Puckle. 'You four are, and also with another relative who, as I said, is on his way here now, and the missing man. The one we can't trace.'

Martin Pickford gave a short laugh. It sounded like a seal barking. 'It's the six degrees of separation that you hear about, that's what it is.'

'In fact, there do happen to be six degrees of separation as far as your family descent is concerned,' said Simon Puckle sedately. 'Six generations from Algernon Mayton to you.'

Samantha Peters was still frowning. 'I'm sure I've heard the name of Mayton before. My mother said my father used to mention it a lot, but I wouldn't know. He died just before I was born, you see, and in any case it was all rather a long time ago.'

'That is more than likely,' said Simon Puckle, opening the folder on his desk. 'I have your birth certificate here, Miss Peters. Let me see now, you are the daughter of William Charles Peters . . .'

She nodded. 'That's right, and my mother was Gladys Ivy.'

'As it happens, Miss Peters, your mother's name is irrelevant since the trustees are only concerned with the descendants of William Peters who are of full age.'

'Men only, is it, then?' said Martin Pickford.

'By no means, Mr Pickford.' The solicitor pointed to the file. 'As it happens, your involvement comes through your mother – your late mother, that is. It is your father who doesn't come into it.'

'Alive and well and living in the south of Spain,' said the young man. 'With my stepmother, as it happens. God help him.'

Simon Puckle, like a coachman gathering the reins of a four-in-hand, came back to his narrative. 'Your father, Miss Peters, would have been Algernon Mayton's great-great grandson.'

'Really? I don't remember my father, of course,' said Samantha Peters, looking up, a little surprised. 'He died very suddenly, asthma, I think it was – but before I was born. He was a bit older than my mother, too.'

'That is so.' Simon Puckle opened a file. 'His death certificate, a copy of which I have here, has the cause of death down as status asthmaticus, with your mother recorded as present at his death.'

Samantha Peters nodded. 'That would figure. That's when my mother came back to live with her parents here in Calleshire and had me.'

'Naturally,' went on the solicitor, 'in the circumstances, extensive enquiries have been made into all of your families . . .'

'What circumstances?' asked Clive Culshaw immediately.

'Anything to ramp the bills up,' muttered Martin Pickford, lisping through the gap in his front teeth.

'The circumstances involved in the winding-up of Algernon Mayton's family trust,' said Simon Puckle.

'And who, may I ask, was this Algernon Mayton?' asked Clive Culshaw.

'I've remembered who he was now,' interrupted Mrs Port. 'My father told me once. He was my great-great-great-grandfather and he was the inventor of "Mayton's Marvellous Mixture". He made his fortune out of selling coloured water in vinegar. At least,' she looked a bit abashed, 'that's what I was always told as a child. I don't know if it was true or not.'

'"What I tell you three times is true",' quoted Martin Pickford, lifting his head. 'That's what it says in *The Hunting of the Snark*, anyway. Lewis Carroll, if you want to know.'

'I'm not sure that I do,' said Clive Culshaw crisply. 'Perhaps we could get on.'

'I agree. This is getting interesting.' Samantha Peters turned back to the solicitor. 'Please do carry on, Mr Puckle.'

Martin Pickford, who had perked up at the mention of the word 'fortune', sunk his head back in his hands again.

'Algernon Mayton left his money to his descendants,' said Simon Puckle, tapping the file on his desk, 'but he put it in a trust that was not to be wound up until the death of the last of his great-grandchildren.'

'This lady's great-aunt Clementina?' divined Clive Culshaw swiftly.

'Exactly,' said Simon Puckle, adding 'wound up *per stirpes*, of course.'

'Sounds painful,' said Martin Pickford.

'That's herpes – shingles,' said Samantha. 'I'm a nurse,' she explained.

'You know, I thought I'd seen your face before,' said Martin Pickford with a certain satisfaction. 'Berebury Hospital? Accident and Emergency Department? Saturday nights?'

'Could be.' She shrugged her shoulders. 'Since it's where I usually work.'

Simon Puckle saw Mrs Susan Port looking up at that, too, and nodding. He made a note.

'But what does it mean?' asked Clive Culshaw. 'That's what I want to know.'

'*Per stirpes* means that the next generation inherits equally but their children inherit only in proportion to their parents' share,' explained the solicitor fluently.

Clive Culshaw lifted his head sharply at that, started to speak and then obviously thought better of it. Simon Puckle made a note of that, too.

Samantha Peters frowned. 'So if one of them has four children and the other has only two, the four children have the same amount to divide between them as the other family's two?'

'That is so, Miss Peters,' said Simon Puckle.

'It doesn't matter to me, as it happens,' said Samantha. 'I'm an only child and so was my father. His parents had been killed in a car crash when he was a little boy and so he didn't have any brothers or sisters either.'

'But naturally,' said Simon Puckle, 'the condition *per stirpes* could be highly relevant to some of you and to what I am about to tell you.'

'I haven't got any children,' said Mrs Port, 'so that bit doesn't matter to me either.'

'That is correct.' Simon Puckle nodded. 'But what does matter to you, Mrs Port, is that you are an only child yourself and therefore you won't need to share your inheritance with any siblings or, failing them, their issue.'

Before he could say anything more, Clive Culshaw suddenly murmured, 'The Mayton money.' He rolled the words round his tongue as if he could taste them and said it again. 'The Mayton money. It's coming back to me now, too. I'd forgotten all about it.'

'What about it?' asked Samantha Peters.

'Something my mother mentioned once.' Clive Culshaw looked suddenly alert. 'She told me that there was money about in the family, but our particular branch wasn't likely ever to get its hands on it. I'm not sure as a child that I really believed her.'

'Sounds to me as if you should have done,' remarked Samantha Peters.

'I didn't believe in Father Christmas either,' put in Martin Pickford. He grinned, the gap in his front teeth now very evident. 'It sounds to me as if I should have done, too.'

'Yes,' went on Clive Culshaw, ignoring this, 'the phrase "the Mayton money" does ring a bell, Mr Puckle, but I just couldn't place the name at first.'

'The Mayton money,' echoed Martin Pickford, latching on to a word he understood even when patently not himself. 'How much money?'

The solicitor put his elbows on the desk and steepled his fingers in front of him. He said, deliberately imprecise, 'Quite a considerable sum.'

'What does that mean?' demanded Clive Culshaw. 'Can't you quantify it?'

'Not at this stage,' said Simon Puckle, 'and certainly not until all the legatees have been found.'

'And divided by four?' asked Clive Culshaw instantly. 'No, five. You said there was someone who was going to be late.'

'Well, not five exactly,' said the solicitor. 'Therein lies the problem.'

'Problem?' Culshaw stiffened. 'What problem?'

'Not with Great Aunt Clementina's death, I hope?' said Sue Port anxiously. 'She was so very old, and I'd heard a long time ago that she hadn't been well. I'd always assumed that she'd died ages ago, but I'd lost touch with her family – I suppose they'd be my second cousins, wouldn't they? They weren't exactly local, either.'

'Quite so,' responded Puckle. 'No, no. There was no problem with her cause of death. We checked, of course . . .'

'Of course,' muttered Martin Pickford, sotto voce. 'More fees.'

Simon Puckle carried on. 'And we established that she died of natural causes, duly certified by the registered medical practitioner in attendance at the nursing home where she died.'

'Problem with what, then?' demanded Culshaw.

'With the rest of the legatees,' said the solicitor.

'The rest?' Martin Pickford looked round at the other three. 'Are there more of them, then?'

'More of us,' Sue Port pointed out.

'There is, as I said, another of Algernon Mayton's descendants who has been delayed by traffic problems on his way here, and yet another one whom we can't trace, as of now.' The solicitor gave another little cough. 'I was rather hoping that perhaps one or other of you might know of him and thus be able to help us in finding him. We've tried all the usual channels, of course.'

'Of course,' echoed Martin Pickford sardonically. 'Well, you would, wouldn't you?'

'But what I have to tell you,' continued Simon Puckle, unfazed, 'is that unfortunately we haven't been able to trace him. Not at this point, but it was felt that, even so, the rest of you should all now be advised of the position.'

'Does it matter?' asked Samantha. 'That you can't find him, I mean.'

'It certainly does,' insisted the solicitor. 'As far as the trustees are concerned, no distribution of the assets – the considerable assets, as I said – in the Mayton Trust can take place until all the legatees are found.'

'Alive and well, I suppose?' growled Culshaw.

'As it happens,' said Simon Puckle unexpectedly, 'that is not so important.'

'Dead or alive, then,' said Martin Pickford, giving a hiccup.

'As far as the winding up of the Mayton Trust is concerned,' Simon Puckle answered him smoothly, 'either will do.'

'Fe, fi, fo, fum, I smell the blood of an Englishman,' said Pickford, his speech a little slurred. 'Or don't I?'

'His name,' said the solicitor urbanely, 'is Daniel Elland, and we haven't been able to find him anywhere.'

TWO

'Ah, Sloan, there you are.' It was first thing in the morning and Police Superintendent Leeyes looked up from his desk at his subordinate, sounding surprised. He had somehow contrived, as usual, to make Detective Inspector C. D. Sloan feel invisible until then, in spite of his standing there in front of him.

'Yes, sir.' Since he hadn't been invited to sit, the inspector stood.

'I thought you were supposed to be tied up with the Faunus and Melliflora case.'

'Not until Friday, sir. That's when it comes to court.' Faunus and his partner in crime were a notorious pair, professional criminals both of them. The court case was the culmination of months of hard police work and Sloan was due to give evidence at their trial.

'Good,' grunted Leeyes. 'That means you're free now. So what can you tell me about a sudden death yesterday over at Bishop's Marbourne?'

'Nothing, sir,' replied Sloan truthfully. 'In fact, I didn't even know that there'd been one.'

'I've had a letter this morning from a solicitor about it, that in my experience is pretty quick off the mark for the legal profession.' Leeyes picked up a piece of paper from his desk. 'Apparently the deceased was a Mrs Susan Port.'

Sloan shook his head. 'The name doesn't ring a bell at all, sir. Nothing's come my way about it this morning. Not yet, that is.' Detective Inspector Christopher Dennis Sloan (always known as 'Seedy' to his friends and family) was the head of the Berebury Force's tiny Criminal Investigation Department and as such all crime in 'F' Division fell within his remit. He asked now, 'Should it have done, sir?'

'I couldn't say – not at this stage, anyway – but Simon Puckle, this solicitor from Puckle, Puckle and Nunnery, seems to have a bee in his bonnet about her death. They've never been ambulance-chasers, have they? That outfit?'

Since the firm had been practising in Berebury high street since long before ambulances appeared on the world scene, the inspector said that they hadn't. 'As you know, sir, they're a firm of long-established family solicitors of good repute.'

The superintendent waved the letter in question in his hand. 'Their senior partner, Simon Puckle, wishes to know if the cause of Mrs Port's death has yet been ascertained since he understands that in some cases sudden deaths are referred to the police.'

'And has it, sir?' asked Sloan pertinently. 'Been referred, I mean.'

'No, not yet,' said Leeyes, the letter still in his hand, 'unless this counts as doing so.'

'Good point, sir,' said Detective Inspector Sloan. In his experience, buttering up the superintendent never did any harm.

'It would seem from this letter,' carried on Leeyes, still waving it about, 'that the woman is said to have died following an attack of food poisoning. Or so the writer of this has heard.'

'Ah,' said Sloan. There was, he knew, quite another meaning to the common expression 'food poisoning'. That was 'eating food that had been poisoned'.

'Exactly, Sloan,' said Leeyes as if he had been reading his subordinate's mind.

'And I take it that the family want to sue someone?' concluded Sloan. 'That is, if they've asked a solicitor to act for them quite so smartly.'

'No, Sloan, on the contrary,' Leeyes came back on the instant, 'it doesn't seem like that at all. Firstly, apparently there isn't any immediate family around the deceased to instruct him to sue anyone – she was a childless widow – and secondly, it is Simon Puckle himself who has a professional interest in her death as,' the superintendent applied himself to the letter again and read aloud, '"a trustee of the estate of the late Algernon George Culver Mayton". Ever heard of him, either?'

'No, sir.'

'Nor me,' said the superintendent.

'And what does the deceased's general practitioner have to say about it?' enquired Sloan, himself interested now. In his experience, solicitors' letters usually followed any action rather than initiated it. 'Unless she died in hospital, that is.'

'That's just what you'll have to find out, Sloan. You'd better make sure everything's in order in case there's anything in it for us.' Leeyes laid the letter back on his desk and leant back in his chair with the air of a man having done his share.

'Or for Simon Puckle, I suppose,' said Sloan slowly.

'Him too,' said Leeyes. 'And you can take that young fool, Crosby, with you.'

'Thank you, sir,' said Sloan stoically. Detective Constable Crosby was not the brightest star in the police firmament – more a hindrance in any investigation than a help, in fact.

'He should have been assisting Sergeant Perkins today,' said Leeyes, 'but she won't have him at any price.'

'Really, sir?' said Sloan warily. The redoubtable Woman Police Sergeant Perkins, always known as Pretty Polly, was considerably outranked by the superintendent but she held a trump card in her dealings with him and he knew it. It was called 'Women's Rights'.

'Extra help is all very well in its way, I suppose,' grumbled Leeyes, 'but of course that's only if it knows what it's doing.'

'Or does what it is told,' supplemented Sloan, who knew the detective constable in question only too well himself.

'Sergeant Perkins,' sighed the superintendent, man to man, handing Simon Puckle's letter over to Sloan, 'said she was a very busy warranted police officer with a full caseload and not a babyminder.'

'What's up, sir?' asked Detective Constable Crosby, easing the car out of the police station yard and into the stream of traffic swirling around in the road outside.

'A sudden death,' said Sloan, telling him to head out to Bishop's Marbourne, one of the smaller villages in the rural hinterland of Berebury. 'We want a Pear Tree Cottage in Church Lane there.'

He brightened. 'Suspicious, then?'

'Too soon to say, Crosby. Much too soon, although,' he

added fairly, 'a local solicitor has written to tell us that he has worries on that account.'

'So who's bubbled?' asked Crosby as he threaded the police car through the main street of the town.

'"Bubbled", Crosby?' Detective Inspector Sloan had long ago decided that one of the signs of early middle age was not grasping the new argot prevailing among the younger element in the force.

The constable translated. 'Spilt the beans, then, sir.'

'If it weren't for the fact that solicitors, like priests, aren't supposed to, Crosby, I would say it was Simon Puckle himself.'

Crosby then used an old expression that Detective Inspector Sloan did understand for all that it came from the racetrack. 'That's a turn up for the book, sir.'

Sloan agreed it made a first for him, too.

The detective constable changed the engine down a gear as the traffic ahead thickened. He pointed out a couple of rough sleepers huddled in the doorway of a derelict building as they passed. 'The woollies have been told to move them on, sir. The mayor doesn't like them.'

'And the uniformed branch doesn't like being called woollies,' Sloan came back smartly. 'Remember?'

'You'd think those two over there would be up and about by now, wouldn't you, sir?' said Crosby, swiftly changing the subject. 'Like us,' he added virtuously. He wasn't at his best early in the morning.

'Rough sleepers have nothing to get up for,' Sloan reminded him absently, reverting to the matter in hand. 'The solicitor has also asked if we would be permitted in due course to give him any information about the death.'

'And are we, sir?'

'No. We wouldn't if we could and we can't anyway,' said Sloan pithily. 'Not at this stage. Not until after a post-mortem or an inquest, either of which there will have to be, Crosby, unless the deceased died of natural causes. And if it's an inquest then the whole caboodle will be in the public domain, newspapers and all. We'll soon find out.'

No one answered the door at Pear Tree Cottage but the sight of the police car in the road and the sound of Crosby's knocking soon produced the next-door neighbour. Detective Inspector Sloan explained who they were.

'I'm Doris Dyson,' said the woman, jerking her shoulder in the direction of the house next door. 'You'd best come along home with me.'

Sitting round the woman's kitchen table, Sloan got out his notebook and asked, 'What happened?'

'Food poisoning, the doctor thought at first,' she began, 'that is to say, we all thought it was food poisoning in the beginning. It had almost cleared up and then poor Sue took a turn for the worse.'

'Did anyone else have it?' asked Sloan.

Doris Dyson shook her head. 'No. Well, not me or my husband, anyway. I never heard about anyone else being ill like Sue was.'

'Funny that,' said Crosby.

'But you ate in her house sometimes?' persisted Sloan.

'Course I did, Inspector. Well, not ate, exactly, but I'd go over to her for a cup of coffee and a biscuit in the mornings every now and then,' the woman sniffed, 'and she'd come over to me for a cup of tea and a piece of cake some afternoons. She was a friend, you see.'

Detective Inspector Sloan nodded gently. In his book that was probably as good a definition of friendship – well, neighbourliness – as you could get these days. 'Tell me about her.'

Doris Dyson brightened immediately. 'Oh, she was ever so nice. She'd come to Bishop's Marbourne to retire two or three years ago. Always wanted to live right out in the country, she said, so she bought herself this little cottage next door to me with a big garden and got really stuck in.'

'Gone native,' muttered Crosby, who wasn't enamoured of green fields himself.

The woman ignored him. 'Started to grow her own vegetables, bake her own bread, take up quilting. You know the sort of thing.'

Sloan did. It was the daydream of many a hard-pressed worker in a city.

'Not that this year has been good for gardens. Too much rain for most of what she'd planted.'

Crosby yawned.

'Then,' said Doris Dyson, 'when she wasn't in the garden, she'd sit in front of that there computer of hers for hours. Doing her family tree, she said she was.' The woman sniffed again. 'Can't understand it myself. If we wanted to do that – hubby and me – all we'd have to do is go over to the churchyard and read the gravestones. We're both Bishop's Marbourne people, you see, and we've all been buried there since for ever.'

Crosby yawned again. Wider this time.

'She got a dog, too, to make sure that she went for a walk every day.' Doris Dyson's face clouded over. 'But that was a mistake. He wasn't properly trained and pulled her over a couple of times. She broke her wrist the last time. Very upset about Todger, she was – that was just about the time when she became so ill all over again.'

'Man bites dog, no problem, dog bites man, the dog it was that died,' said Detective Constable Crosby almost – but not quite – under his breath.

'I reckon having to have Todger rehomed didn't help,' said Mrs Dyson austerely, 'not with her having all those pains in her tummy and being so sick with it all time after time. Not that she would have been in any fit state anyway to take Todger out for his walk, although I would have done that for her if I had had to.'

'I expect,' said Sloan, 'that you did all you could for her.'

'Changed the sheets, anyway – she was perspiring something remarkable for all that she complained of being cold all the time. And of having to run to the bathroom all the time, too. Night and day.'

'I get the picture.' Sloan nodded. 'And then what?'

'I made her go to the doctor and he gave her something for food poisoning – gastric upset, he called it at first. She got a lot better after that and we thought it had all cleared up.' Her face drooped. 'And then, blow me, it all came back again quite sudden and she had to go back to the doctor.'

'Which doctor?' asked Sloan.

Detective Constable Crosby, a young man with a low boredom threshold, muttered, 'They're all witch doctors. They should wear pointy hats.'

Doris Dyson, not understanding, ignored this and replied to Sloan. 'Dr Browne, of course. He sees to everyone round here.'

'And what did he say?' asked Sloan. Dr Angus Browne's surgery was going to be the next port of call for the police, but he didn't say so.

'Like what we had thought – still some form of food poisoning, although he couldn't say what. Not without doing some tests.' Doris Dyson sniffed once more. 'It's what the doctors say all the time these days, isn't it? Won't make up their minds without them now.'

Detective Inspector Sloan nodded gravely. In his book that was an improvement on the past. His own grandparents had lived at a time when pathology wasn't advanced enough for any tests for some dire conditions that exist, let alone be reliable, or for there to be a cure for those same dire conditions, once diagnosed.

'Anyways,' said Mrs Dyson, 'whatever they were he didn't get the results back in time to prescribe anything useful.'

This was something Sloan did understand. Many of his own cases had been held up because forensics hadn't got back to him quickly enough for his liking. The fortnight that seemed commonplace to the police laboratory to report results nearly drove him to despair. The importance of keeping up the heat of an investigation was something those bench-bound boffins just didn't seem to comprehend.

'Then what?' he asked now.

'She got worse,' said Doris Dyson lugubriously. 'Much worse. She started to feel the cold so much that I had to bring some of my own blankets over from my place for her, not that the weather had turned or anything. I piled them on top of her, but even then she still complained of being cold. Then . . .'

'Then?' prompted Sloan.

'She started not being able to sleep. Time and again she went all night without dropping off. The doctor gave her something for that, too, but it didn't work either. That's when I started to get worried. Not that not having slept a wink all night seemed to make her tired. That was the funny thing.'

'I'll say,' said Crosby, himself always notably irritable after a bad night.

'We could none of us understand that,' she said.

'Go on,' said Sloan.

Doris Dyson drew breath and said impressively, 'Then quite suddenly she went into meltdown.'

'Meltdown?'

'She started to see things that weren't there,' said Mrs Dyson.

Detective Inspector Sloan metaphorically sat up. 'What sort of things?'

'Animals, mostly, she told me, and in ever such bright colours. Not,' Mrs Dyson went on, 'proper animals, mind you, but weird ones.'

'Such as?' prompted Sloan.

'Such as lizards with horns in funny places, men with tails and eggs with people's parts sticking out of them. Bats, everywhere, with swords coming out of their mouths, too. She said it was like a painting by someone – I can't remember the name now – it sounded like Bosh, and if you ask me pure bosh it was. But she said it was the colours that really frightened her.'

'On the magic mushrooms, was she?' asked Detective Constable Crosby with an informality that Sloan, officially his mentor, could only deplore. It was no way to begin a delicate line of questioning.

Detective Inspector Sloan might have taken the query amiss, but Mrs Dyson didn't.

'That's what I wondered,' she said frankly, 'seeing as how that was how young David from the pub behaved after he'd been on them for a bit. Don't know exactly what, but David had certainly been on something. He saw elephants.'

'Sounds to me as if she was away in La-La Land,' scoffed Detective Constable Crosby.

Sloan had to make a heroic effort not to remind the constable that his opinion hadn't been sought, deliberately postponing a reproof until they were alone. It was the duty of a police officer to listen, not to pontificate, a fact that it seemed Detective Constable Crosby had not yet grasped.

'They had to stop young David from the pub from jumping off the belfry tower,' Mrs Dyson informed them. 'In fact, I did ask her if she'd been mushrooming. Plenty of 'em in the woods round here – good and bad. Being from the town she wouldn't have known one from t'other.'

'And?' said Sloan.

'She did say she'd gathered some mushrooms but not lately,' said Mrs Dyson. 'I told her next time she had to ask me before she ate any of them.'

'Goes with the territory,' said Crosby, who had not long ago been on a course on the effects of hallucinogenic drugs. 'Jumping off high places, I mean.'

Doris Dyson's face hardened and she said tonelessly, 'Then she took a real turn for the worse and we had to send for Dr Browne in a hurry. She'd climbed up on her kitchen roof – it was one of those cat-slide ones that you can get up easily – and she was talking gibberish. The doctor came straight out here and said he'd get her into hospital at Berebury immediately, but before the ambulance arrived, poor Sue had slipped down off the roof, fallen and died. Just like that, poor thing.'

THREE

'About whom?' Dr Angus Browne asked the two policemen across the desk in his consulting room.

'A patient of yours, Doctor, a Mrs Susan Mary Port,' said Detective Inspector Sloan, his notebook at the ready, 'of Pear Tree Cottage, Church Lane, Bishop's Marbourne.'

'Ah, yes. Died yesterday,' said the doctor promptly. 'I had already arranged for her to be admitted to hospital in Berebury as an emergency because she had taken a turn for the worse, but in the event she died suddenly at home after a fall and before the ambulance could get her there. Naturally, in those circumstances I wasn't prepared to issue a death certificate.'

'Why not?' asked Detective Constable Crosby naively. 'She was dead, wasn't she?'

'Because, Constable,' explained Dr Browne patiently, 'I couldn't certify the cause of death. The fact of death certainly, the mode of death possibly, but not the cause, and I therefore immediately advised the coroner to that effect.'

Sloan made a mental note that that meant the coroner's officer, PC York, would have been involved, it being his responsibility to carry out the coroner's orders as to the removal of the body. He would have a word with him back at the police station later.

The doctor was still talking. 'As far as I was concerned, her problems started off as what at first sight appeared to be a straightforward case of food poisoning. Vomiting, diarrhoea, abdominal pain and so forth.'

'The usual,' put in Detective Constable Crosby, who had once dined unwisely on mussels and lived – just – to regret it.

'Quite so,' said Dr Browne, peering at the two policemen over the top of his glasses. 'She lived alone so there was no one else involved with the same symptoms. I was waiting to see if she was an index patient, but she wasn't.'

Detective Inspector Sloan asked what one of those was.

'An index patient is the first person in an outbreak to have a particular disease, Inspector. And if there had been others out there at Bishop's Marbourne with the same symptoms at the same time, it would probably have clinched the diagnosis then.'

'But it didn't?' suggested Sloan, something about the outbreak of the plague at Eyam coming into his mind. That had come, if he remembered rightly, from a bale of cloth from the south. As a holiday destination for children, he'd thought at the time that the plague village had left a lot to be desired. He'd wanted to go on the Big Dipper in Blackpool instead.

'No.' The doctor was still talking. 'There were no other similar cases. In any case, Mrs Port then went on to develop some other signs and symptoms that didn't quite fit that diagnosis. They only appeared a little later, as it happens, which didn't make it any easier.' He pulled a medical record towards him. 'Bradycardia, for a start.'

'And what would that be, Doctor?' Speaking in tongues was how Sloan thought of the usage of medical terms by doctors to lay people. He saw it as a display of power and never liked it.

The general practitioner translated the term for him. 'Very slow heartbeat. That was one of the reasons why I wasn't too worried about her – to begin with, that is. Her blood pressure was rather on the low side, too. Again, nothing really to worry about at that stage. I prescribed something for her digestive symptoms and thought she'd recover quite soon. I did tell her to come back and see me if she didn't, because you can't be too careful these days.'

Detective Inspector Sloan agreed heartily with this sentiment. Banking establishments might have compliance officers, but the police had the even more powerful combination of the press and public ganging up to make quite sure they didn't overstep the imaginary line of what they expected of the force. And always in the background was Her Majesty's Inspector of Constabulary. He wasn't sure how doctors coped – probably, like everyone else, by writing everything down.

'And then?' he asked.

'And then Mrs Port telephoned me to say that she had had another attack and was now having great trouble sleeping. She told me she hadn't slept a wink for three days.' The doctor paused. 'A lot of people say that, of course, and don't really mean it. They usually doze off and forget by morning that they've done so.'

Sloan nodded in agreement. 'Almost a manner of speech, you might say, Doctor. Not sleeping a wink.'

'In the event it transpired that she did mean it, which was a quite unusual symptom in itself. I prescribed her a sedative but then, after giving it a fair go, she told me that it wasn't working at all.' He paused. 'There would have been problems in increasing the dose . . .'

'Problems?' queried Sloan.

Dr Browne leant back in his chair. 'My old professor used to say that the correct dose of any drug was enough to produce the effect you desired. It seemed to me that enough to deal with her state of sleeplessness would have killed her and that wouldn't have done at all.'

Sloan nodded. The phrase 'Death, and his brother Sleep' floated into his mind and was gone again.

Dr Browne was still talking. 'She told me she was getting

worse and said she had now got a bad place on her leg. She just couldn't sleep at all and was getting absolutely worn out.'

'Well I never,' said Crosby, visibly bored.

'Then,' went on Dr Browne, 'yesterday I had this urgent call from a neighbour saying the woman had suddenly gone berserk. Her exact message was that Mrs Port had completely lost her marbles. So I went straight out to Bishop's Marbourne but by the time I got there she was in a really bad state. She was having a full-blown psychotic episode.'

'Away with the fairies?' suggested Crosby.

'Completely out of her mind,' said the doctor tersely. 'If she hadn't been a respectable late-middle-aged woman with no history of drug taking I would have said she had been full to the gills with illegal substances – lysergic acid, most probably, or perhaps heroin, since she was hallucinating and really high. Apparently, she had had this impulse to jump from a great height – she had been climbing up the cat-slide roof at the back of her cottage when Mrs Dyson found her and sent for me.'

Detective Inspector Sloan turned over a page in his notebook. 'Very worrying,' he said.

'Especially,' said Browne dryly, 'as the first duty of the doctor is to remove the danger from the patient or in this case remove the patient from the danger.'

'And then, Doctor?'

'While Mrs Dyson tried to talk her down I rang the hospital. I arranged for an ambulance to take her in as soon as possible. The minute she put a foot back on solid ground – she slid down off the roof in the end, landing on an ankle and breaking it, which could have been what we call a distracting injury – I pumped a dose of powerful sedative into her gluteus maximus muscle.'

Sloan didn't need a translation of that for all that it was a medical term. 'Glutes' was the one he would have used himself.

'Without her by-your-leave?' asked Crosby indignantly. Nobody had asked him about whether he had wanted childhood injections and he still nursed resentments in the matter.

'As Shakespeare put it, "Dangerous diseases demand dangerous remedies",' said Dr Browne. 'I thought that would quieten her down long enough for the ambulance people to get her into Berebury Hospital and that then I could come back here to tackle a full waiting room.'

'But she didn't get there,' said Sloan.

Dr Browne shook his head. 'In the event she died just before they'd loaded her in the ambulance to get going.' He straightened his shoulders and pushed the patient's record away. 'We'll know all the answers soon enough, Inspector. The pathologist is doing the post-mortem first thing tomorrow morning. The outcome of that will make the practice's next M and M meeting a lot simpler, too.'

'M and M?' asked Sloan.

'Morbidity and Mortality Conference. All the doctors in our practice here have a quarterly meeting to discuss the outcome of problem cases, to see whether we've missed something, made a mistake or could just have done better for our patients. Or, more often, I am happy to say, agree we couldn't have done anything more for them.'

It was the Independent Police Complaints Commission that did that for the force but Sloan did not say so. He had not met them yet and he didn't want to.

Dr Browne added in a matter-of-fact tone, 'Sometimes people say that breast-beating helps, but I don't think anything at all could have been done for Mrs Port. She was beyond aid.'

Miss Florence Fennel placed a folder on Simon Puckle's desk before announcing the two policemen. 'The Mayton file, Mr Puckle.'

He thanked her before punctiliously rising to greet the newcomers.

'You wrote to the police yesterday, sir,' began Detective Inspector Sloan, 'about the late Mrs Susan Port of Bishop's Marbourne.'

'Indeed, I did,' agreed Simon Puckle. 'I felt that I should advise the police that I was somewhat concerned about her death – that is, about her sudden death.'

'"Somewhat concerned"?' It seemed a curious choice of phrase to Sloan, although you never knew with the nuances of the law. But then 'Let's be having you' was an expression usually understood only by police and villains.

'You see, Inspector, I was not aware that she was other than in good health when I last saw her.'

'And when exactly would that have been, sir?'

Simon Puckle glanced down at a note. 'About two months ago.'

'And you had no reason to believe that she had been suffering from anything before or since?'

'Not then or now,' said the solicitor vigorously. 'If she had been, she certainly didn't mention it when I saw her then.'

'I see, sir. And might I enquire exactly what your interest in the circumstances of her death is?'

'I really wanted to be reassured that it was from natural causes, Inspector.'

'And why would that have been, sir?'

Simon Puckle tapped the file on his desk. 'Mrs Port was one of half a dozen legatees due to inherit a share in a considerable inheritance from an old trust set up by her great-great-great-grandfather.'

'Going back a bit, isn't it?' muttered Detective Constable Crosby.

The solicitor said, 'Not by trust standards. They can go back generations.'

'Ah, now I understand, sir.' Detective Inspector Sloan got the picture without difficulty. In his view, where there was big money about there were usually big worries as well. The corollary that where there was big money about there were usually solicitors, too, he did not admit to his conscious mind at this moment.

'Where there's a will there's a relative,' muttered Detective Constable Crosby.

'And would you therefore happen to know, sir,' went on Sloan, ignoring this, 'of any person or persons who might be expected to benefit from her death?'

'Oh, yes,' said Puckle promptly. 'To be exact there are five of them known to me. That is, not including their eventual dependants, of course. There may be others, naturally, but the late Mrs Port's own legatees, who I'm afraid are not known to me, don't come into it as her claim on the trust lapses with her death, she being childless. The benefit of her death to those other five dependants is somewhat – shall I say – tangential?'

'Like I said,' muttered Crosby, sotto voce, 'where there's a will there's a relative.'

'I take it that there is a will in Mrs Port's case?' said Sloan. Again, he found the word 'somewhat' difficult to quantify.

'I'm afraid I couldn't say, Inspector,' replied Simon Puckle unexpectedly. 'The late Mrs Port was not a client of this firm.'

'I take it, then, that you have other professional reasons for your enquiry about Mrs Port's death?' Detective Inspector Sloan hadn't thought he needed to spell this out.

'Yes, indeed. My own specific interest is as the current trustee of the estate of the late Algernon Mayton,' explained Simon Puckle, lightly tapping the file on his desk again. 'As I said, he was Mrs Port's great-great-great-grandfather. He had made a fortune out of selling a useless nostrum to the credulous Victorian masses.'

'Nice work if you can get it,' remarked Crosby from the sidelines.

'Yes, indeed, Constable,' agreed the solicitor, adding wryly, 'Most of us have to work a little harder.'

'This product . . .' began Sloan, who wasn't quite sure what a nostrum was.

'It was called "Mayton's Marvellous Mixture" and consisted largely of water coloured with cochineal and sprinkled with pepper. The advertising, though, was impressive.'

'That would have been, I take it, sir, before there were any legal restrictions in the matter?' Some situations had benefited from regulation – the Advertising Standards Authority was one of those institutions that had helped bring this about. Sloan himself warmed to whoever it was who was trying to corral the more exotic ambitions of the banking industry.

'Yes, indeed, Inspector. In those days you could make any spurious claims you liked for the properties of what you sold in the way of patent medicines.' He paused. 'In fact, I'm not sure that Mayton's Marvellous Mixture had even been patented.'

'It was profitable, though, I take it?'

'Immensely. To which inheritance,' the solicitor continued, 'has to be added the interest on the capital over many years . . . very many years – compound interest, naturally.'

'So there have been no disbursements,' deduced Detective Inspector Sloan. The important difference between compound and simple interest was still a dim memory from his school-days. So was something his mother used to quote from Charles Dickens about it. Some character in *Bleak House* used to call compound interest 'the old pagan's god', and if there was anyone who knew about money, it was Charles Dickens.

'None, Inspector. That was on the express instructions of the testator,' said Simon Puckle, 'except, naturally, the firm's fees for establishing the trust and for its administration of the estate over very many years.'

'Naturally,' said Sloan in a tone that he trusted was entirely devoid of irony.

'Naturally,' echoed Crosby quietly, with quite a different emphasis.

The solicitor expanded on the trust. 'There were, of course, good reasons why Algernon Mayton left his estate to his great-great-great-grandchildren rather than to his more immediate heirs. Good reasons.'

'Gone to the dogs, had they?' suggested Crosby, his interest engaged at last. 'His heirs, I mean.'

'Not as far as I know,' began Puckle.

'Taken to the bottle, then?' Crosby persisted. 'Or the gee-gees?'

'I understand that they were as sober as was usual at the time,' said Puckle a little stiffly. 'And not, as far I know, gamblers.'

'So why, then?' asked Sloan, firmly wresting the line of questioning from Crosby.

'There were greater risks in those days to an estate than now,' temporised the solicitor, skating lightly over the depredations of the twentieth-century's inheritance tax. 'Even though it was a long while before Lloyd George came to power.'

'In spite of that, cutting the immediate descendants off without a shilling does seem a bit hard,' said Sloan.

'Not without a shilling,' said the solicitor. 'They were adequately provided for.'

'Risks of what, then?' intruded Crosby insouciantly.

'Risks from his daughters' future husbands,' said Puckle elliptically. 'Old Algernon Mayton died in 1868. If he had left his money to his three daughters at that time, any men they married could spend their wives' inheritance from their father exactly how they wished.'

There was a pause while Detective Constable Crosby absorbed the enormity of this state of affairs. 'And without their say-so?'

Simon Puckle nodded. 'I'm afraid that was the case.'

'That's not fair,' said Crosby indignantly.

'Life isn't,' murmured the solicitor.

Detective Inspector Sloan, old enough to have learnt this too, nodded in agreement.

'Until, that is, the passing of the Married Women's Property Acts in 1870, 1882 and 1893,' resumed Puckle. 'But, of course, the testator was dead by then.' He gave a little smile. 'As Shakespeare nearly put it so well: "He should have died hereafter".'

'And Algernon Mayton had a lot to leave, you said,' concluded Sloan, sticking to the point.

'Indeed, a great deal,' said the solicitor, 'and he didn't want his future sons-in-law making hay with it.'

'So,' asked Sloan, policeman that he was, 'who exactly benefits from Mrs Port's death now?'

'As to that, Inspector, I couldn't say. It will depend on her own testamentary depositions but I can tell you that her personal estate will get nothing from the Mayton Trust now that she has died. As she had no living descendants, her rights in it are extinguished by her death before its distribution. Under the terms of the trust these automatically revert to the remaining survivors . . .'

'Thought of everything, old Algernon, didn't he?' said Crosby, who was getting restive.

'In that sense, of course, the five of them do benefit marginally from her death,' continued Simon Puckle. 'That would be by the division of an extra sixth share of the Mayton Trust among them.'

'And who knew this?' asked Detective Inspector Sloan, himself cutting to a chase that had hardly begun. There would be those who could quantify the division of a sixth of something among five people but he wasn't one of them.

'Only three of the legatees for certain – two men and a woman. They all heard Mrs Port announce to everyone that she had no siblings or descendants. Another man arrived later and thus didn't hear it said and there is also one man we haven't been able to trace so far. Therefore I am not in a position to know if either of those other two knew that. Mrs Port mentioned it before Tom Culshaw arrived at the meeting – he had been held up on his way to Berebury that morning – and before the trouble began.'

FOUR

'Trouble?' echoed Superintendent Leeyes back at the police station, rising at the word like a trout to a mayfly. 'Tell me, what sort of trouble, Sloan? And be quick about it. I'm in a hurry.'

'Apparently the fifth person to arrive at Puckle's office that day was the brother of a man already there and they were at daggers drawn. I understand that the two brothers had gone to law over the ownership of the family firm – a big bakery. You may have heard of them, sir. They make Culshaw's cakes.'

'Everyone's heard of Culshaw's cakes,' grunted Leeyes. 'They eat them all the time.'

'Very true,' agreed Sloan. 'Well, it seems that Clive Culshaw won the case and his brother, Tom – his elder brother – got chucked out of the firm on his ear.'

'And no doubt resented it.' Superintendent Leeyes giving it as his considered opinion that there was a lot to be said for primogeniture.

'Sir?'

'Everything going to the eldest son of the eldest son without question,' said Superintendent Leeyes. 'Saves a lot of argument about who owns what. It keeps it all in the family, too, and in one place.'

'I'm sure, sir,' said Sloan, hoping that the superintendent wouldn't say this to Woman Police Sergeant Perkins, who held strong views on any male – eldest or not – taking all.

'And I assume that this Tom Culshaw still isn't happy?' divined Leeyes without too much difficulty.

'Far from it, sir. According to Simon Puckle, at the time of the meeting they – Clive and Tom Culshaw – made it pretty clear that they hated each other's guts.'

'How does this affect this big inheritance that the solicitor is telling us about?'

'That I couldn't say, sir.' One thing that could be said for Superintendent Leeyes was his capacity for sticking to the trail. Especially if it was a money one.

'And what has all this got to do with that dead woman out at Bishop's Marbourne that Simon Puckle is going on about?'

Sloan said that remained to be seen as it was too soon to say and that he and Crosby would be attending the post-mortem on Susan Port the next morning and would report back.

'Do that,' said Leeyes, reaching for his hat. 'And if the pathologist doesn't find anything to worry about then we can all stop worrying too. That can include that solicitor fellow, Puckle. Now I've got to go to another meeting of the town's Rough Sleeper Forum and I'm late already.'

'I'm sure there are more of them about in doorways these days than there used to be,' said Sloan, thankful that those who slept on the streets weren't his problem.

'Probably because we're too soft on them in Berebury,' said Leeyes, clamping his hat firmly on his head. 'And the Vagrancy Act's no good these days. It's not any use even trying to prosecute them for anything less than aggravated begging, and as they don't have any money, the fine doesn't hurt them.'

Sloan decided against saying that the law was an ass. They both knew that. After all, they were policemen.

'The mayor thinks they give the town a bad image and now the council wants it cleared of them.' Leeyes sniffed. 'That's naturally without saying where we should put them instead and under what statute. That forum of the council's doesn't even know the difference between rough sleepers, begging and street drinking.'

'No, sir,' said Sloan, anxious to get on, too.

'And to cap it all we've had a complaint from that do-gooder who runs Latchless – you know, that charity for the homeless down by the Postern Gate here in Berebury.'

'We do know him, sir,' sighed Sloan. 'Only too well – he's always speaking up for them at the station. Name of John Holness. His heart's in the right place, I'm not so sure about his head.'

'It seems that the Berebury supermarket in the high street was getting so fed up with those layabouts sleeping rough every night in that covered delivery lobby of theirs at the back of the shop that they've fitted some sonic device there that keeps the homeless awake all night.'

Sloan nodded. 'I understand from the wildlife people, sir, that they use something like that to keep minke whales safely away from offshore turbine workers.'

'It makes 'em feel pretty ill, too, I can tell you, man and beast,' said the superintendent with some satisfaction. He wasn't into animal welfare, either. 'Dizzy for starters. Gives them headaches, too. And some of them have been insisting they've got some hearing loss. It's meant to keep them feeling so out of sorts that they won't use that shelter of the supermarket's there overnight.'

'Which is presumably what the store wants,' concluded Sloan without difficulty.

'And now that man Holness from Latchless wants to know if what the supermarket's done is legal.'

'Offences against the person?' suggested Sloan off the top of his head.

'That's for the courts to decide,' said Leeyes airily. 'Not for us. We're policemen, not politicians. And as for getting them to accept advice on alcohol dependency and employment opportunities . . .'

'Not usually welcome,' agreed Sloan.

'Just wasting your breath,' said the superintendent, making for the door, 'if you ask me.'

*   *   *

The word 'trouble' had never once crossed Tom Culshaw's lips
when he told his wife about his visit to Simon Puckle's office.

On the contrary.

'It was beautiful,' he crowed joyously, rubbing his hands
together. 'Absolutely beautiful. You should have been there,
darling.'

'Not if I had to look at your brother, I shouldn't,' said Sophie
Culshaw spiritedly. 'I never want to set eyes on that man ever
again.'

Her husband wasn't listening. 'You should have seen Clive's
face when I walked through the door and he realised that I
was part of the action, too,' he chortled, 'although I would
have thought he could have worked it out for himself. You
see, there was a bit of a hold-up on the road this side of
Calleford . . .'

She sighed. 'Tom, I told you that you wouldn't be there in
time.'

'And so I got there a bit late, didn't I. Besides I had to drop
off that old carburettor for the classic car on the way. It works
a treat now.' Tom and Sophie Culshaw ran a little boutique
business called Gordian Knots Cut. Their oft-repeated credo
– and advertising – was that every problem had a solution.
'And the solicitor had started without me.' He grinned again.
'I bet Clive thought he was going to get away with all the
money this time, too.'

'Not again,' she groaned. 'Tom, we can't possibly go through
all that again.'

'No, no, it's not like that, darling. Not at all. I promise you.
It was all about this old boy, Algernon Mayton, who seems
to have left shedloads of dosh to his extended family. In fact,'
went on Tom cheerfully, 'it's even better than that.'

Sophie looked at him expectantly. 'Tell me.'

'Because I got there a bit late, I took Clive by surprise. By
then they'd all got down to the nitty-gritty of an old trust this
ancestor of ours had set up.'

'I've never heard of him.'

'Me neither. Seems as if he was a bit of a charlatan.'

'So that's where your brother gets it from, is it?' she said
acidly.

'This money . . .'

'What money, exactly?' asked his wife. She found that when her husband's feet did happen to touch the ground it was akin to anchoring a hot air balloon to keep them there.

'What this Algernon left behind when he died. It's got to be divided between six of us.'

'How much?' Sophie prided herself on having her own feet on the ground. One of the pair of them had to.

'The solicitor fellow wouldn't say. You know what they're like, darling.'

'Only too well, and there's one thing I will say, Tom, and that is no matter what happens, we're not going to law over this.'

'Not this time and never again, darling, I promise you.' He essayed a smile. 'At least this time we won't have to try to claim primogeniture.'

'Much good that did us last time.'

'Don't remind me.'

'And what about the last will and testament of this ancestor of yours? Is it as watertight as your mother's will was?'

He frowned. 'The thing is that it's not a will at all but a trust deed, which it seems is a bit different. At least, that's what this Simon Puckle said.' He sat down beside her and put his arm round her. 'Wait until you hear this, though, Sophie. You see this legacy comes down through Dad . . .'

'But your father died years ago.' She sighed again. 'That was the whole trouble.'

'I know, but according to the terms of this old Mayton Trust, it's descendants of Dad's generation that collect the dibs and so Clive and I only get half each of what everyone else there gets.' He grinned again. 'You should have seen Clive's face when he realised that he was only going get half of what he'd thought he would because of me. And half of what everyone else is getting, too. It was lovely.'

'It means you only get half, too, though,' she pointed out. 'Although I agree half a loaf is better than no bread.'

'It's miles better than the nothing I got last time,' he said.

'True.' She stretched languorously on the sofa. 'And half of what, do you think? We could do with some new carpets.'

'The solicitor wouldn't say. Not until a missing man is found.'

She was unsurprised. 'Solicitors are always cagey. You should know that by now, if anyone does.' She pummelled a cushion into a more comfortable position. 'What missing man, anyway?'

'Someone called Daniel Elland.' Tom Culshaw wrinkled his nose. 'I've never heard of him but then I didn't know any of the others there either, even though we were told we were all related one way and another to each other there and to the missing man.'

'Except Clive,' she said. 'You knew you were related to your dear younger brother all right, worse luck.'

'Except Clive,' he agreed. 'And I get my half whether he likes it not.'

'He won't like it,' she said, 'but, my love, it still means that you only get half, too.'

'But without any aggro this time. The solicitor said we could all have our share of the dibs as soon as this fellow Elland is found and our bona fides are established. After that it should be plain sailing.'

'I'm sure I hope so,' sighed Sophie Culshaw, 'but I'll only believe it when I see it.'

Her husband refused to be deflated. 'This time we'll be all right, you'll see.'

'Time will tell,' she said. 'At least the money comes through your father and so your mother hadn't had anything to do with it.'

He looked downcast as he always did when his mother's name was mentioned. 'That's something to be thankful for, anyway,' he muttered.

'And did you tell this Simon Puckle that your mother cut us out of her will and left the business and everything else to Clive?'

'Except for a hundred pounds,' he pointed out.

'That was just a legal device to show it was quite deliberate and that she hadn't forgotten us.'

'A bit less of the "us", please. It wasn't anything to do with you, darling. You know that. Mother died before we got married.

It was all to do with me,' he said miserably. 'She never loved me. Ever. That was the whole trouble. And I've never known why.'

FIVE

Christopher Dennis Sloan, devoted husband and father, always tried to make a point of not still being a policeman, let alone a detective inspector, as soon as he crossed the threshold of his own home. Unlike many men, he usually went even further in consciously refraining from bringing his work home with him, although he was the first to admit that switching his mind into off-duty mode could sometimes be difficult. Instead, he symbolically tried to shed the burdens of office when after supper he took his shoes off and rested his stockinged feet on the fender in front of the fire.

Usually as soon as he did so, a cup of coffee would appear at his elbow.

So it was this evening.

As he took it from his wife, Margaret, he knew where his duty lay. If he was able to talk about his particular day at the office, so to speak, this was always the moment for it. That she would understand if he couldn't went without saying.

Some of his work, of course, was highly confidential, the Official Secrets Act as ever looming in the background, some of it too gruesome to be described to anyone other than a fellow officer, and some just routine work in progress and rather dull. Even so, he felt that sometimes domestic harmony should be preserved by supplying the odd titbit of gossip. And every now and then something cropped up that he did feel could be talked about without breaking confidences or upsetting his wife's sensibilities by introducing murder and mayhem into the home.

'I had quite an interesting day today,' he began. This was

the signal that there was something that could be shared in front of the domestic hearth.

Margaret Sloan took up her own cup and saucer and sat down beside him. 'Go on.'

'Nothing may come of it, of course.'

'That happens,' she said, loyal police wife that she was.

'I was with Simon Puckle, the solicitor.'

She sipped her coffee. 'Tell me more.'

'Apparently, there was this very rich old boy who'd made a mint of money out of some quack medicine a long time ago.'

'A cure-all,' nodded Margaret Sloan. 'Very popular, they were, with the credulous in those days.'

'Loads of credulous people about, then and now,' said Sloan feelingly. He had had to deal with plenty of victims of scams in his own day, too. More abashed than injured, most of them. 'Anyway, this man, name of Algernon Mayton, didn't have any sons to inherit the business or his fortune . . .'

'Poor man,' said Margaret Sloan, her gaze drifting subconsciously towards the undeniably masculine toy fort in the corner of the sitting room. It was well past the bedtime of its owner.

'Poor man in more ways than one, apparently,' said her husband. 'You see, he only had daughters, three of them . . .'

'Even so, he was a lucky man . . .' she said, raising her eyebrows in enquiry.

'Ah, but in those days – his day, that is – the daughters' husbands automatically got their hands on all of whatever the daughters inherited.'

Margaret Sloan stiffened. 'That's not right,' she said militantly. 'You meant they didn't have any say at all in what happened to what they inherited?'

'None. Not then. Or so Simon Puckle told me.' He wriggled his toes against the fender. 'So their father – Algernon Mayton – didn't leave his daughters more than they needed in their lifetimes.'

'Hoping that they themselves had sons, I suppose?'

'Yes, I'm sure, but I'm afraid that they didn't.' Sloan set his cup down. 'And it gets even more complicated. One of his granddaughters only had a girl, called Horatia, but the other had a girl and a boy, Clementina and Arthur.'

She frowned. 'They would have been his great-grandchildren, I suppose?'

'That's right.'

'Let me guess. He didn't leave them his money either?'

'Dead right, he didn't. And it must have been mounting up by then.'

Margaret Sloan said, 'He was keeping the money in the family with a vengeance, wasn't he?' She reached out a hand for his cup. 'More coffee?'

'Thank you.'

'And putting off the day in his mind,' she said reflectively, 'when a woman wouldn't be married for her money but just for herself.'

'So, hoping for the best,' said Sloan, nodding, 'he left his fortune tied up in trust for the grandchildren of the said Horatia, Clementina and Arthur and their issue.'

She wrinkled her nose. 'Could he do that?'

'According to Simon Puckle there was a precedent. A Sir William Rowley apparently did just that in the eighteenth century.'

'And a precedent makes it right, does it?' she asked ironically, having her own views on the ways of the law.

'I know precedents aren't quite the same things as Holy Writ for lawyers, but pretty nearly.' Sloan yawned. 'In the event, old Mayton needn't have bothered.'

'They had sons?'

'No. The first Married Women's Property Act was passed in 1870 and that changed things. It gave a woman full control of her own property, and high time, too.'

'Oh, I know all about that,' said Margaret Sloan unexpectedly. 'Soames Forsyte was very upset about those new laws when they came in.'

'Who?'

'Soames Forsyte. Timothy Forsyte might have been the most cautious man in England, but his brother Soames really minded about money. It meant a lot – too much, actually – to him. And those Acts of Parliament meant he couldn't get his hands on his wife's money.'

Seeing his blank expression, she went on, 'Don't you remember, Chris? You gave me the boxed set of *The Forsyte Saga* one Christmas.' She scooped up his coffee cup and said with some complacency, ruffling his hair as she passed him, 'So seeing that I wasn't married for my money, dear, it must have been for something else, mustn't it?'

It was even later that evening when the Accident and Emergency Department at the Berebury District General Hospital got really busy. Sister Samantha Peters had straightened her tunic, stowed her handbag in her locker, checked her watch and, like the rest of the night shift, reported for duty at eight o'clock as usual. Her opposite number, coming off the day shift, had performed the handover.

'Not a great day, Samantha,' she said to her, stifling a yawn. 'The cardiac infarct in Bay One isn't doing at all well. He'll need an eye keeping on him – his family are on their way. The motorcyclist in Bay Two is waiting to go to theatre and there's an old lady with a fractured neck of femur needing an orthopaedic bed. See if you can talk the ward into taking her off our hands soonest. We need the cubicle.'

'Will do,' promised Samantha Peters.

The other nurse sighed. 'We've started to get the alchies in early tonight.'

'It's raining,' said Samantha simply.

'That explains it,' she nodded, not having had time on her own shift to look out of the window herself. 'They're making a row and disturbing everyone else as usual. Oh, and we've had an attempted suicide.' She gave a thin smile. 'We've washed out her stomach and now she wishes that she hadn't done it or hadn't been saved. Either one or the other would have done, she says.'

But the flow of patients didn't really swell until more drunks and other casualties were brought in after midnight.

Battered, bruised and in some cases quite belligerent, they represented both a nuisance and a nightmare to the staff. The nuisance was in clearing up their vomit, stitching their wounds and preventing them doing violence to staff and other patients alike. That, as young Dr Dilys Chomel, the duty doctor, was wont to say, was the easy bit. So, she insisted, was dealing with the heart attack, the injured motorist, the fractured hip and even with the overdose.

The difficult part, she was also wont to say, was making quite sure that the slurred speech, unfocussed eyes and unsteady gait presented by some of those in the Accident and Emergency Department represented an overindulgence in alcohol or drugs not a subdural haemorrhage following a fall or a blow to the head. A missed head injury – often fatal – would be a serious blot on the medical career of the young African woman doctor's career and well she knew it.

By the time Dr Chomel got round to seeing the drunks and the other casualties in the department, Samantha Peters had persuaded most of them to lie on the floor on crash mats before they fell down and, in the case of two of them, to stop them fighting. Swiftly relieving one of the pair of the wine bottle with which he was trying to hit his neighbour, Samantha said firmly, 'That will do, Mr Smith, if that's what you're called.'

'He stole my drink,' hiccupped the man, dancing about like a whirling Dervish, his arms and legs all over the place. 'I'm going to kill him.'

'No, you're not,' she said briskly.

The man's face screwed up into crying mode, tears starting to well out from rheumy, bloodshot eyes. 'He took my drink away.'

'No, he didn't. I did. We don't allow alcohol in the department.'

The man, struggling to keep on his feet, declared with great dignity, 'Then I'm going somewhere where they do.'

'Not until we've stitched that cut on your head, you aren't,' she said. 'And the one on your friend's face,' she added, turning to the next man. 'He's got quite a nasty laceration on his forehead, thanks to you.'

'He's no friend of mine,' said Mr Smith, trying to give the man beside him a kick and very nearly falling over in the attempt. 'I've never seen him in my life before.'

'So why did you hit him?' she asked.

'Because he was there,' said the drunken man ineluctably.

'Like Everest, I suppose.'

'I feel sick,' announced his friend, to whom the allusion had meant nothing either.

'There's an emesis bowl beside you.'

He wasn't sick. A minute later he had collapsed onto the crash mat and was deeply asleep, breathing noisily.

Samantha Peters turned to the next patient, a man perched on a chair, one foot sticking forward a little, a blood-soaked pad on his forehead. 'And why are you here, Mr . . . er,' she glanced down at a list and frowned. 'Mr Pickford? You?' she said.

'Martin, please.' He grinned. 'After all, we are related.'

'Much too distantly to count,' she said. 'Besides, with you in the state you're in. I wouldn't want to broadcast the fact.'

'I've injured my eye, that's all, Samantha. Some fellow's elbow got in the way of it. It's all the blood that makes it look worse than it is.'

'I'm Sister Peters when I'm on the ward and don't you forget it.'

'Sorry, Sister,' he said, hanging his head with every sign of penitence.

'And what about that limp?'

'I got that at my first away match. The other team were animals.'

'You men are all the same.'

'And I'm not drunk, by the way.'

'Oh, yes?'

'Strictly speaking, someone else injured my eye. Not me. Their scrum half, I think it was, but I couldn't be sure, not having had much sight in it afterwards.'

'Are you talking about being the victim of an assault?' she said primly.

He grinned up at her. 'Only in a manner of speaking.'

'If you have been, we'll have to record it properly.'

'The ref's already done that on the field. My eye didn't hurt at first, but it does now. Like hell, actually, so I thought I'd better come in otherwise I wouldn't get any sleep tonight.'

'The effect of alcohol beginning to wear off, I suppose,' she said, markedly unsympathetic.

'I'm not drunk,' he repeated.

'At this rate,' she said dispassionately, waving a file in front of him, 'looking at your record here, you'll be dead long before you collect any of the Mayton money. Accident prone isn't in it.'

'That's rugby for you. Besides, money isn't everything.' He winced as he touched the bandage over his eye. 'Or so I've always been told.'

'And rugby is, I suppose?'

'I've got to be well enough for our next trial match, Samantha, so do what you can for me,' he pleaded. 'I'm up for the county team and I don't want to miss any games.'

'Sister Peters, if you don't mind.' She gave him a considering look. 'And while money may not be everything, young man, I can tell you it helps.'

'Don't care.'

'Neither do I,' she said in a sudden burst of anger. 'All the more for the rest of us, if you ask me, should anything happen to you. Now, we'd better get you cleaned up. And then I'll ask Dr Chomel to take a look at your eye.'

SIX

'What do you mean, Sloan, the solicitors say they can't find a man?' Back at the police station in Berebury first thing the next morning, Superintendent Leeyes sounded sceptical. 'People can't just disappear these days.'

'According to what Simon Puckle told us, sir, this man has,' said Sloan. 'The solicitors have tried all the usual ways of finding someone – by advertising and so forth – and put a firm of professional enquiry agents on to it with no joy either, except that they discovered that he was made bankrupt quite some time ago.'

'Ah.' Bankruptcy ranked high in the superintendent's personal Newgate calendar. He said, 'He would have been allowed to keep his car. He could have gone anywhere, then.'

'He didn't have one,' said Sloan. 'We checked with the vehicle registration people. Not under his own name, anyway.'

'And the tools of his trade. He could keep them after bankruptcy.'

'He ran a business,' said Sloan. He couldn't think offhand what those tools would have been. The Midas touch, a lack of scruple and a willingness to do his rivals down were all that came immediately to mind. Then perhaps he, a policeman, might be prejudiced as he usually only met the criminal ones.

'Mind you, Sloan, even if he does come into this Mayton money, his creditors will have a prior claim on it. The preferential ones – the ones that have the first go at it – I imagine will be the Inland Revenue. Crown debt always takes precedence. 'I understand it's different in the United States.'

'Quite so, sir,' said Sloan, murmuring under his breath, 'No Crown.'

'So,' carried on Leeyes, 'presumably after that there was nowhere for him to go but downhill.'

'Well, he was a bit old to start again, sir.'

'Start again was what all those monks turned out by Henry VIII had to do after he shut all the monasteries down,' said the superintendent, whose recondite areas of knowledge were a source of constant wonder at the police station. 'The ones who couldn't or wouldn't go away were known as sturdy beggars.'

'Really, sir?'

'And you're actually telling me that even though there's a mountain of money waiting for this missing person when he's found, you still can't put your hand on him?' He sounded sceptical.

'So I am given to understand, sir.' He coughed. 'Of course, they don't know quite how much yet. The recipients, I mean.'

'I should hope not, otherwise they'd be breaking Simon Puckle's door down.'

'Quite so, sir.' He paused and then said, 'And it would appear that the other four present in his office when they were told about the legacy hadn't known anything about the inheritance at all until then, either. Or anything about the other people who were there come to that, except Clive Culshaw, who obviously knew about his brother but didn't mention the fact.'

'A bit odd, that,' said Leeyes.

'Yes, indeed,' agreed Sloan. 'And those two who weren't there presumably didn't know anything beforehand either.'

'Two?'

'The brother was late.'

Superintendent Leeyes ignored this and unerringly put his finger on what mattered. 'You say one of those who was there at that meeting was Mrs Susan Port, the deceased.'

'So I understand, sir.' Sloan looked at his watch. 'I'm sorry, sir, I must go. We're due at the hospital for her post-mortem any minute now.'

'Which, I take, is what's got Simon Puckle worried?'

'He is the sole administrator of the Mayton Trust,' said Sloan with apparent inconsequence. 'And he tells me that none of the estate can be distributed until all of the beneficiaries are found. It's this man called Daniel Elland who's missing and causing the hold-up in the settlement.'

'Do we know him?' asked Leeyes.

'The Police National Computer doesn't,' said Sloan cogently.

'So, he's not in prison either.'

'First thing we checked, sir.'

'He could have died.'

'They've searched the death registers.'

'And he could have changed his name – there's no law against that – or just be living under an alias.'

'Yes, sir. Either. Or both.'

'First catch your hare, of course,' said Leeyes.

'Sorry, sir, I don't quite . . .'

'You catch your hare,' said Leeyes elliptically, 'before you start to make hare pie.'

'Really, sir?'

The superintendent asked, 'How old is this Daniel Elland supposed to be?'

'Sixtyish, sir, by now. Nothing's been heard from him since he was divorced ten years ago. We got his old address from the solicitors, but he was chucked out by his wife at the time. Seems she took him for half of everything.'

The Married Women's Property Acts passed through
Detective Inspector Sloan's mind as he pondered on the rights
and wrongs of this. He thought of Soames Forsyte, too – it
didn't sound as if the equal division of the marital assets after
a divorce would have suited him either. He would have to
check on that with his wife, this evening. Perhaps the law
could only get some things half right. 'She's still there, sir, in
their old home,' he said. 'Elland's wife, I mean. She's married
again, though.'

'Sounds to me as if she's sitting pretty,' grunted Leeyes.
'Some women are good at housekeeping. I mean at keeping
houses after a divorce,' he explained as if Sloan hadn't understood him.

'She swears she hasn't heard from him since the divorce
and made it quite clear to us that she didn't want to either.'

'And where, pray, does this big money come from? They
didn't have lotteries and sweepstakes then, surely?' Leeyes
paused. 'Though now I come to think of it, there was once a
racket called the Numbers' Game. You took big money from
lots of little punters, gave a very small modicum of it back to
the lucky winners and kept the rest.'

'The fortune came from something phony but very
successful called Mayton's Marvellous Mixture, sir.' They
had had big wagers, though, in the old days, thought Sloan,
with the fate of an entire estate determined by the turn of a
playing card. Men had fought duels for high financial
stakes too then, as well as their honour. They must have
needed the excitement if there didn't happen to be a war on
at the time; today's equivalent of extreme sports, perhaps.
Or boy-racing. Or even old-boy-racing, a real thorn in Traffic
Division's flesh – men only now able to afford the sports car
of their adolescent dreams but beyond handling its fancy
acceleration.

'I knew it would be phony if it was that big,' said the
superintendent cynically. 'Honest money doesn't grow on
trees.'

'It was guaranteed to be a miracle cure and sold as such.'

'Just what I said. Phony.'

'Yes, sir.'

Leeyes tapped Simon Puckle's letter. 'There were six legatees and now there are five. That right?'

'Yes, sir.'

'So, Sloan, just make very sure that you keep it that way.'

Dr Hector Smithson Dabbe, Consultant Pathologist at the Berebury District Hospital Trust, hastened to welcome Sloan and Crosby to the mortuary. 'Come along in, gentlemen,' he said genially. 'I understand that you may have an interest in the cause of death of Susan Mary Port here.' He indicated what looked just like an unclothed shop window mannequin lying on the steel table.

'That all depends on what you have to tell us, Doctor,' said Sloan cautiously. 'It's much too soon to say otherwise.' That there was a crime scene to examine only applied if there had been a crime and he didn't even know that yet.

'Then, Inspector, to quote Mr Asquith, we'll just have to "wait and see", won't we?' said the pathologist, who appeared to be in a jovial mood.

'Your opinion, Doctor, would be a great help,' said Sloan.

'That's as may be,' responded Dr Dabbe philosophically. 'The post-mortem laboratory is a place where science and law meet, so sometimes I set people's minds at rest and sometimes I don't.'

'Quite so,' said Sloan.

'And sometimes I upset the apple cart, too,' said Dr Dabbe. He grinned. 'And more often than not I upset the insurance companies as well.' He did not sound too upset about this. 'And some families,' he added mischievously.

'I can believe that,' muttered Detective Constable Crosby, already beginning to edge his way towards the further wall of the mortuary. He didn't like attending post-mortem examinations.

'All I can tell you at this stage,' said the pathologist, 'is that it's not often Angus Browne can't say what someone's died from.' The pathologist gave a wolfish grin. 'So at least this isn't an open-and-shut case.'

Detective Constable Crosby visibly winced at the similarity with a post-mortem.

The pathologist nodded in his direction. 'Your trouble I expect, young man, is that you didn't have a gerbil or, better still, a hamster as a pet when you were a child.'

The constable looked bewildered. 'No, Doctor, I didn't.'

'Pity,' the pathologist said elliptically. 'Hamsters and gerbils have short lifespans – they die quite soon, you see, which is a very good thing. It gets children used to death.'

For a moment Sloan toyed with the idea of saying that it was young policemen, newly on duty, not children, who had to get used to death and its ten thousand doors, but he decided against it.

'And dissection gets everyone used to it,' said the pathologist. 'Just as the sainted surgeon William Hunter said, "Anatomy is the basis of surgery, it informs the head, guides the hand, and familiarises the heart to a kind of necessary inhumanity".'

Detective Inspector Sloan nodded. A necessary inhumanity came into some police work, too. The arrest of a man that left his wife and children homeless and destitute as a consequence was one of the instances that never sat well on his conscience.

Dr Dabbe was still talking. 'The history of the deceased's last illness is a bit confusing, gentlemen, to say the least, which is why Angus Browne wasn't prepared to sign a death certificate. A good man, Browne.'

Detective Inspector Sloan nodded. The general practitioner had a reputation as a canny Scot of a notably careful disposition.

'Are we ready, Burns?' Dr Dabbe asked his taciturn assistant. Burns nodded and the pathologist, already gowned and now masked, pulled an overhead microphone down over the steel post-mortem table, adjusted it to the level of his mouth and began his report. 'Body of a well-nourished female, identified by a next-door neighbour, Mrs Doris Dyson, as Susan Mary Port, age given as . . .' He looked round for Burns. 'Age given as what, Burns?'

'Sixty-six, Doctor,' said the mortuary attendant.

'Sixty-six,' the pathologist said into microphone. 'On macroscopic examination the body appears a little but not seriously jaundiced. It is also very dehydrated, consistent with the history

of much vomiting and diarrhoea.' Dr Dabbe peered system-
atically all over the body on the examination table. 'Some
recent bruising of the right trochanter and a fracture in the right
talocrural region . . .' He turned away from the microphone
and said, 'That's an ankle to policemen.'

'She is said to have slid down on to the ground from a low
roof,' volunteered Sloan, not rising to the translation.

'That would explain it, Inspector.' He raised his voice to a
hortatory tone and resumed speaking into the microphone. 'No
signs of any other external injuries visible . . . Ah, hang on,
there's an old appendectomy scar in the right iliac fossa, if
you call that an injury – more of a surgical assault if you ask
me, if not even wounding with intent – near where what we
used to say was McBurney's point, only they don't call it that
any more. Strictly Latin names now, more's the pity. You knew
where you were with McBurney.'

'Nothing stays the same,' said Sloan sententiously. There
had been many changes in the police force since he was a
constable, too – only some of them for the better.

'And a healed Colles fracture of the left wrist. Hullo, hullo,'
said the pathologist alertly, examining the arm further, 'what
have we here?' He was bending over the body now, peering
at the tips of the subject's fingers. 'A little bit of gangrene in
both hands. Now what's that doing on the deceased, I wonder?'

Since Sloan had no answer to this, he kept silent while
the pathologist moved swiftly down the table to stare at the
deceased's feet. 'And in the toes. Now that is interesting, Sloan.
Very interesting.' He straightened up. 'Let's have a look at her
back, Burns.'

His assistant moved forward and turned the body over.

'There's many a good pathologist caught out by not looking
at the deceased's back, Inspector.'

'I'm sure, Doctor.' The police equivalent was failing to look
everywhere – but everywhere – for fingerprints at a crime
scene. And these days, DNA, too.

'Gangrene,' murmured the pathologist absently. 'I haven't
seen gangrene like this in a month of Sundays. Not common
nowadays.'

Detective Inspector Sloan had never seen it at all ever before and wished he hadn't now. Crosby had moved himself out of the line of vision to a spot where he couldn't see anything of the body.

'And I wonder what gangrene's doing here on her digits, now?' mused Dr Dabbe.

'That I couldn't say,' said Sloan.

Detective Constable Crosby might not have had the body of the deceased in direct view but nevertheless he winced visibly as he heard the pathologist starting to open the subject's brain.

Sloan decided that this organ must have passed muster, until the pathologist said that there was some congestion there. 'Now the thorax, Burns.'

'Yes, Doctor.' His assistant moved forward.

'Congestion of all internal organs,' reported the pathologist a few minutes later. 'Burns, there's quite a lot for the path lab here, bearing in mind that food poisoning is suspected.' He turned to Sloan and remarked, 'The Radio Doctor described that sort of pathologist as a man who sits on one stool and examines others.'

'Really, Doctor?' murmured Sloan as Burns advanced obediently with a variety of little bottles and collected and labelled specimens wherever the doctor pointed.

'Gastrointestinal tract shows distinct inflammation.' The doctor peered at Sloan over the top of his mask. 'Browne did say that he suspected food poisoning, didn't he?'

'At first,' temporised Sloan.

'There's quite some degeneration of the internal layers of the smaller arterioles, too, and there are thrombus formations all over the place. Interesting, Inspector, all very interesting.'

'Yes, Doctor, I'm sure.' He cleared his throat and asked, 'But what does it all mean?'

The pathologist tugged his mask off. 'I can't tell the coroner exactly what killed this woman. Not yet, that is. Not until I hear back from the laboratory about those specimens and do a little more research but . . .'

'But?'

'I can tell you one thing, Inspector, something you do need to know. In my opinion, whatever it was this woman died from, the immediate cause was the ingestion of a noxious substance of some sort.'

'Not natural causes, then,' said Detective Inspector Sloan, opening his notebook and turning over to a new page.

SEVEN

'Ah, Sloan, come in.' Superintendent Leeyes laid his hat upside down on the top of the filing cabinet in the corner of his office and tossed his gloves into it. Then he flopped down into a chair at his desk and waved an arm at Sloan to sit down as well. 'They told me that you wanted to see me as soon as I got back this morning. So?'

'Yes, sir,' began Sloan. 'It's about the post-mortem examination on Susan Mary Port.'

'The mayor's a real old windbag,' grumbled Leeyes, pushing a pile of papers on his desk to one side.

'Yes, sir, so I've heard,' said Sloan, tugging his notebook out of his pocket and opening it out.

'And as for the town clerk, or the chief executive as he likes to be called these days,' snorted the superintendent sarcastically, 'all he wants is his precious town cleared of anyone sleeping rough in it. He kept on talking about reclaiming the streets as if it was some sort of a mantra.'

Sloan decided against saying that it had been a famous slogan somewhere once.

'The mayor insists that the corporation underground car park be properly policed, too,' snorted Leeyes. 'I'm not surprised that the homeless are sleeping down there since it's the warmest place in town to spend the night in if you're sleeping rough in winter. They will congregate there as well as behind the Berebury supermarket – you know, near St Peter's Church in Water Lane.'

'Yes, sir, now I've just come back from the—'

'As if we've got the men and the time to do any such thing, Sloan.'

'No, sir, of course not.' Sloan opened his notebook at the new page, gave a preliminary cough and began again. 'As instructed, sir, I duly attended the post-mortem conducted by Dr H. S. Dabbe this morning on Susan Mary Port.'

'But what has really upset our worthy councillors, Sloan,' continued the superintendent, still mentally in the mayor's parlour, 'are the couple of alkies living on the roundabout on the West Polsby road. They need to get on with evicting them.'

'Living?' echoed Sloan, in spite of himself.

'They've pitched a tent on the grass and insist they're quite happy staying there, thank you very much. They've even had the nerve to say that they've quite got used to the traffic noise by now and they don't have any difficult neighbours either.'

'I should hope not, sir.' The detective inspector could see that the site would be very handy for the supermarkets and their shelves of cheap drinks but kept his own counsel on the matter. 'It was Mrs Port's sudden death at Bishop's Marbourne, sir, if you remember,' he said, 'that so interested Simon Puckle.'

'I told them,' said Leeyes, ignoring this, 'that Highways should get a warrant for trespass. After all, it's their round-about. A court order should do the trick, all right.'

'Quite so, sir.' The County Highways surveyor was an old enemy of Superintendent Leeyes. His unsporting response to all requests and suggestions from the superintendent could best be described as 'extended bureaucratic'.

'And you won't believe what that man, Holness, from the homeless charity wants now. I ask you, a shooting gallery.' He sniffed. 'We had to explain to the mayor that it meant somewhere quiet and private to shoot drugs not stuffed toys. The mayor wasn't happy.'

'No, sir, I'm sure.' Sloan plodded on, 'Dr Dabbe has found that the deceased had died as the consequence of ingesting a noxious substance.'

'If the pathologist means poison why doesn't he say so?' demanded Leeyes truculently, his full attention engaged at last.

Sloan knitted his eyebrows. 'Perhaps, sir,' he suggested, 'it's because the word "poisoning" automatically implies an illegal action.'

'And ingestion doesn't?'

'It can do but it doesn't have to. The deceased could have swallowed a noxious substance by accident. We don't know yet.' He wanted to say that you needed malice aforethought for the other sort of poisoning, but the superintendent had no time for the antiquarian language of the past.

'The food that you eat,' said Leeyes sententiously, 'can also be poisonous if you eat too much of it.'

'Quite so, sir,' said Sloan, averting his eyes from his superior officer's incipient paunch. 'In fact, as it happens that was exactly the point the pathologist made. Dr Dabbe would only say that his post-mortem findings were suggestive of ergot poisoning – I think that was because of the gangrene.'

'That's a first,' observed the superintendent.

'Not exactly, sir,' said Sloan. He chose his words with care, since contradicting his superior never went down well. 'Dr Dabbe said there was a famous outbreak in France in 1951.' Actually, any mention of the French didn't go down well either, since Superintendent Leeyes was inclined to blame them for everything that had gone wrong since the Norman Invasion. He hurried on before Napoleon's name cropped up. 'He said that ergot poisoning used to be known as St Anthony's Fire.'

'And from where might I ask, Sloan, would anyone get ergot that wasn't in France?'

Sloan explained what he'd learnt, then looked down at his notebook. 'Of course, we don't actually know yet if it was from rye or, if so, how it got into the deceased's system – or even if it actually did.'

'Splitting hairs,' pronounced Leeyes flatly. 'Just like lawyers do.'

'It could have just been bad luck, sir, like eating the wrong end of a sausage.'

'It's more likely that the pathologist doesn't really know himself exactly which poison,' said Leeyes uncharitably, 'and isn't saying so.'

Detective Inspector Sloan saw fit to ignore this since he intended to talk to the police laboratory himself as soon as he could. Instead he swept on. 'I've been back to Simon Puckle and he says he's quite sure that the deceased didn't have any immediate family. Her husband had predeceased her many years ago and there had been no children. Apparently, his firm – Puckles, that is – had gone into her antecedents quite carefully in the course of planning to wind up this Mayton Trust.'

'Then you'll just have to do all the groundwork yourself, Sloan, won't you? And if you ask me, Sloan, you should follow the money. First principle of policing. And don't forget that cash cows, even potential ones, are an endangered species. So get out there and check on the other legatees before anything happens to them, too.'

'Yes, sir, of course, sir.' He cleared his throat and went on, 'Simon Puckle says as far as he had been able to establish, Mrs Port was a retired civil servant with an impeccable record.'

'I've met some of them in my day,' said Leeyes. 'Dangerous people.'

'Civil servants?'

'No, Sloan, people with impeccable records. They need watching.'

'Sir?'

'It's not natural, is it? Think Dennis Nilsen.'

'Yes, sir.' Sloan smoothed down the page in his notebook and said, 'We're going to need access to the deceased's house next. Now that I know it's possibly a case of poisoning, however brought about, I'm arranging for scenes of crime to give it a good going-over soonest while forensics get on with the lab work. Then I'll just check that all those other people who saw her at the solicitors don't know anything more about her than Simon Puckle thought.'

'Let's hope nobody's been in the house first and tidied it up,' said Leeyes pessimistically.

'PC York will know,' said Sloan. It would have been Ted York who, as coroner's officer, would have arranged for Mrs Port's body to be conveyed to the mortuary. 'Bound to.'

PC Edward York, when consulted on the matter, agreed that he had indeed locked up the house at Bishop's Marbourne after supervising the removal of Mrs Port's body to the mortuary.

'And, Seedy, I checked with the neighbour that there weren't any animals to be taken care of.'

'The dog had been rehomed,' said Sloan absently. 'Anything out of the ordinary about the house, Ted?' he asked. 'No signs of disorder, panic and so forth? Or intruders?'

'It was all a little bit untidy, like you'd find when someone's been ill for a while, but that's all. I did give it a bit of a going-over since food poisoning had been mentioned, but I didn't find anything out of the ordinary in the kitchen before I locked up. I looked in her medicine cabinet in the bathroom and there was nothing there except a bottle of tablets from the hospital labelled "Take two every four hours for pain" and the usual home remedies – for indigestion, mostly. I've seen worse in my time, I can tell you.'

'I'll bet you have. Tell me, did you look for the name and address of any next of kin?'

'I sure did. It was in her bureau, all written out nicely, her having been a civil servant and all that.'

'Find anything?'

'You're going to like this, Seedy.'

'Go on.'

'A godson called Terry Galloway domiciled in Australia, who,' he grimaced, 'is said from his postcard to her to be presently backpacking his way across Europe to England.'

'Mobile phone?'

'Not responding to calls.'

'Him or it?'

'It,' said the coroner's officer pithily. 'He must be out of range of any mast. Looks as if he was last heard from in that postcard from India. I found that in her bureau, too.'

'And I daresay that wasn't sent yesterday,' said Sloan with some experience of holiday postcards arriving long after the traveller's return.

'Over a month ago, Seedy.'

'You can travel a long way in a month, Ted.'

'Sure, you can. But – wait for it, Seedy – there was the address of the deceased's own solicitors, a small family firm in south London, in the bureau, too.'

'That's a help.'

'And they've got her will.' He grinned. 'Guess what?'

'Don't say everything goes to her godson?'

'Got it in one, Seedy. Only son of her oldest and dearest friend, it says in the will.'

'Therefore,' said Detective Inspector Sloan, the cogs of his mind working slowly and surely, 'it would naturally be very interesting to know if the deceased had told her godson about the potential inheritance before he left Australia for England.'

'It would indeed,' said the coroner's officer.

'And if she had done so,' went on Sloan, still choosing his words with care, 'it would also be very interesting to know whether he had left for England immediately after learning that fact.'

'It would. Very,' agreed York. 'Of course, on the other hand, there's always a chance that the godson doesn't know yet that she'd come into a basketful of readies or perhaps even that she's dead.'

'Well, I for one very much hope that he doesn't,' said Sloan, snapping his notebook shut. 'For obvious reasons.' He got up to go. 'I'll ask the neighbour to keep an eye open for a visitor, although she always does, anyway.'

'Tell our local man out there to look out for a stranger,' added the other policeman.

'That too,' said Sloan, taking his leave.

EIGHT

I t was Tom Culshaw who picked up the telephone at his home outside Calleford. 'Gordian Knots Cut,' he said.

'Good,' said a man's voice. 'You're just the chap I need to talk to.'

'And how may we be of assistance to you, sir? No problem too big or too small for us to tackle,' carried on Tom Culshaw fluently, although he was now old enough and wise enough to know that this was not always strictly true. 'We solve them, anyway.'

'It's small. By the way, this is Martin Pickford speaking.'

'Who?'

'You know, you met me in that lawyer fellow's office when he was going on about the good old *araucaria araucana*.'

'About the what?' Tom Culshaw asked.

'The monkey puzzle tree.'

'What monkey puzzle tree? I don't remember anything being said about a monkey puzzle tree then.'

'All right, all right. The family tree, then – same thing, seeing as we're all descended from monkeys and in our case it's all a bit of a puzzle anyway. You were one of the Mayton crowd there, weren't you?'

'So I was,' said Tom Culshaw warily. 'I remember you now. What about it?'

'I'm afraid you'll also remember that I was a bit hungover at the time,' said Pickford.

'It was quite early in the morning.' Tom Culshaw had been on a business course, which had included learning how to project sympathy to potential clients whatever your private opinion of them. Censure was only allowed if customers didn't pay their bills. 'So what can I do for you? Or is this all a joke?'

'I only want a chap delayed from getting somewhere in time, that's all.'

'We don't do anything illegal,' said Tom Culshaw stiffly.

'No, no, it's just that I need him held up for a while. Diverted, you might say. For a couple of hours at the outside.'

'And we don't do anything physical, either,' said Tom Culshaw.

'Perish the thought, old chap,' said Pickford. 'All I need is for him to be a little bit late in getting to a meeting.' He paused and added meaningfully, 'Like you were when you arrived at the solicitors' that day.'

'That was because of heavy traffic between Calleford and Berebury,' said Tom Culshaw.

'Could happen to anyone, heavy traffic,' mused Pickford thoughtfully.

'I think I get your drift,' said the other man.

'So can punctures,' went on Martin Pickford. 'Happen to anyone, I mean. A flat tyre can hold you up no end. Look here, this isn't anything sinister. You could truthfully say it's a sporting matter rather than a joke.'

'A bet? Look here, Pickford, I'm not getting involved in anything crooked.'

'Certainly not. This is only to do with a game.'

'And that makes it all right, does it?' Tom Culshaw was a painter manqué, not a sportsman.

'No, old chap, it doesn't but it makes it much more fun. I'm sure you're game for that.'

'Supposing – just supposing – we were to take the job on, how long would you need this man delaying for?' Tom Culshaw stopped, halted by a sudden thought. 'If it is a man, that is.'

'Oh, it's a man all right,' said Pickford airily. 'That's the whole trouble.'

'I see – so it's a case of all being fair in love and war, is it?' said the other man.

'Not quite and not war, I promise you,' said Pickford.

'And what is this man like? He's not a nasty piece of work, I hope.'

'Certainly not. He's a helluva good fellow. Everybody likes him. That's part of the trouble.'

'And how will I know what he looks like?'

'I'll send you a photograph of him in rugby kit. Without a mouthguard or headband, of course. He's actually quite good-looking, if a bit on the beefy side. That's part of the trouble, too.'

'How long do you need him delayed for?' asked Culshaw, now suspecting, as the other man had hoped, that there was a love rival involved.

'A couple of hours would be perfect.'

'And his name – I'll have to have that – if we take it on, that is.'

'Jim Stopford, otherwise known,' replied Martin Pickford with sudden savagery, 'as Twinkletoes.'

'And where, may I ask, isn't he to get to?'

'Oh, he can get there all right but not until after nine o'clock.'

'Where?' asked Tom Culshaw, this time more sharply.

'The Bellingham Hotel in Berebury high street. Do you know it?'

'Oh, yes,' said Tom Culshaw, 'I know it all right and I also know that we can't just barge in there. It's not that sort of place.'

'I don't want you to. I want him held up before he gets there
– and I don't mean what you think I mean by that. This isn't
a game of cops and robbers.'

'I should hope not.' Tom Culshaw took a deep breath. 'And
when, may I also ask, isn't this Jim Stopford to get there until
after nine o'clock?'

'This coming Thursday evening.'

'And where will you be while all this carry-on is happening?'

'Me? Oh, I shall be at the Bellingham myself,' said Pickford
lightly, 'but with him safely out of the way.'

'Oh, you will, will you? And in the restaurant, I suppose?'

'Look here, Culshaw, I can assure you it's all quite above
board.' That he hadn't given the man a straight answer to his
question – and that there was quite a different board involved
– Martin Pickford had not seen fit to tell him.

'Where to, sir?' asked Detective Constable Crosby, crouching
ready for the off at the wheel of the police car.

'Calleford,' said Sloan. 'The main hospital there.' He
glanced down at a note. 'To see a Dr Helston at their Poisons
Unit.'

'With nee-naws?' suggested the constable hopefully.

'A siren is not necessary,' said Sloan repressively. 'Nor,
Crosby, is a blue light either, should you happen to have been
thinking of switching one on.'

'No, sir. Of course not, sir. It's only that it's a good fair
way over there and if you should have an appointment at the
hospital, then . . .' He gave Sloan a sideways glance and went
on slyly, 'It does help when it comes to parking.'

What proved even more difficult than finding a parking
space was finding the whereabouts of Dr Helston in the vast
teaching hospital at Calleford. While Sloan could take or leave
anonymous backdoor visits to mortuaries for the purpose of
attending post-mortems, he was rather less sanguine about
entering major hospitals by the front door. The receptionist at
the desk there didn't help.

'The Poisons Unit?' she said. 'It's not signposted because
you're not supposed to go there.'

Detective Constable Crosby asked why not.

'Because if someone thinks they may have been poisoned, they want them in Accident and Emergency straightaway.' She looked appraisingly at Sloan. 'And if you've taken something you shouldn't have done then you must go there immediately.' She fixed him with her eyes. 'Like now.'

Detective Inspector Sloan said in an austere tone that he hadn't taken anything that he shouldn't have done but that he did have an appointment at the Poisons Unit and wanted to know how to get there. 'Like now.'

The receptionist, obviously a last-ditcher by nature, said, 'They don't usually have visitors in that department.'

'They do now,' said Detective Constable Crosby as Sloan started to feel in his pocket for his warrant card.

'I'm afraid that it's a bit tricky to explain how to find it,' said the receptionist, still keen on having the last word.

'Try me,' said Sloan tightly.

'For the Poisons Unit you'll have to follow the blue arrows on the floor to Haematology, then turn left, go past Neurophysiology and you'll find it on your right.'

'Thank you,' said Sloan.

'It should have been red arrows for the blood place, shouldn't it?' remarked Crosby to nobody in particular.

'The Poisons Unit door's not labelled,' said the receptionist, firing a Parthian shot in the direction of the departing policemen with grim satisfaction.

'It's worse than foot patrol,' grumbled Crosby as they eventually reached the door they were looking for.

'Not a dark night in winter in the rain, it isn't,' said Sloan, more experienced in the matter.

'All the same, I reckon finding Dr Livingstone would have been easier,' said Crosby, knocking on an unmarked door.

'We've got an appointment to see Dr Brooke Helston,' said Sloan to the young girl in a white coat who answered their knock.

'Police,' supplemented Crosby.

'That's me,' she said. 'I'm Brooke Helston, the chief chemist here. Come in.'

Following her into the unit, Sloan experienced a moment of melancholy. He was aware that doctors of whatever variety, like constables, were getting younger, but surely they shouldn't be as young or as pretty as this girl? He banished the thought immediately. It wasn't one of which Sergeant Polly Perkins would have approved.

'And how can I help you?' she asked, waving them towards high laboratory chairs. 'Sorry we haven't anything more comfortable to sit on, but we don't get many visitors here.'

'And I don't suppose they stay long when they do come,' said Crosby, looking round at an unpromising collection of bottles, retorts and balances and stationing himself, although he didn't know it, beside an electric centrifuge.

'We don't often get to see them in the first place,' she explained. 'We just get their history and their body fluids as a rule.' She smiled, revealing a row of perfect white teeth. 'It's usually enough.'

'We are investigating a death that in the opinion of Dr Dabbe, the pathologist at Berebury,' began Sloan formally, getting out his notebook, 'was the result of the ingestion of a poisonous substance. All the tissue samples that he took have gone to the police forensic laboratory but he suggested we talked to you, too.'

'The Sailor King,' sighed the girl, instantly coming over all dreamy-eyed. 'Hector Dabbe, I mean. He took me out in his Albacore last month. Round the headland beyond the Cunliffe Gap. It was a wonderful trip and I haven't forgotten it yet. Isn't he great?'

'The poison he suggested was ergot,' persisted Sloan, ignoring all mention of boats, the pathologist and the sea at the Cunliffe Gap.

'*Mal des ardents*,' said Dr Helston promptly. 'That's what they used to call ergot poisoning in France.'

'Beg pardon, miss?' He knew he shouldn't have called her 'miss', but it didn't seem right to address this little slip of a thing as a doctor of chemistry or of anything else.

To his relief the girl didn't seem to take it amiss. She said, 'St Anthony's Fire.'

'Who's St Anthony?' asked Crosby.

'What's St Anthony's Fire?' enquired Sloan, more to the point.

'St Anthony's Fire,' explained Dr Helston, 'was called after a French saint who is said to have caused those suffering from gangrenous erysipelas to recover. Only he didn't.'

'No?' said Sloan.

'They recovered from ergot poisoning because they moved away from the source of the poison.'

Sloan nodded. That would have saved many a victim of domestic violence too, let alone poisoning. Had they known they were being poisoned, of course, Madeleine Smith and arsenic coming to mind. They didn't always know, indigestion getting much of the blame to begin with. Domestic violence they did know about but weren't always willing to acknowledge.

Or act upon. That was the trouble.

'And not because the sufferers wore the tau cross, either,' she went on, unaware of his train of thought.

'You've lost me, miss,' said Sloan.

'An artefact in the shape of the Greek letter "T", thought to save the wearer from St Anthony's Fire.'

'But it didn't cure them either?' said Detective Constable Crosby, who had been paying more attention than usual.

She shook her head. 'Nope. They could still say *amens accedit* about anyone who was wearing it.'

'And what might that mean?' asked Sloan, who'd never liked hearing words he didn't understand. It sounded like Latin and it was Greek to him anyway.

'A rough translation is "He arrives out of his mind",' she said.

'That figures, anyway,' said Sloan, remembering what Dr Browne had told them about Mrs Port's behaviour.

'The doc said the deceased was absolutely bananas by the time he got there,' supplemented Crosby.

'They say we share a lot of our chromosomes with bananas,' remarked the chemist inconsequently.

'And what exactly is it? This St Anthony's Fire?' persisted Sloan.

'Well, for starters, it wasn't the gangrenous erysipelas they thought it was.'

That came as no surprise to Sloan. Medical cases had been misdiagnosed for centuries, the miasma theory being a case in point. 'No?'

'As you know, Inspector, it was poisoning from a mould on rye.'

Detective Inspector Sloan made a note. He would have to find where the rye came from in rural Calleshire.

And the mould.

And, more importantly, how it had got into the late Mrs Port's system.

And, more importantly still, exactly why.

Dr Helston was still talking. 'And so it wasn't a miracle at all. All the sufferers had to do to be cured was to stop eating rye bread with the mould in it.'

A working lifetime in the police force had caused Detective Inspector Sloan not to believe in miracles anyway.

'And in any case, as I said,' went on Dr Helston, 'it wasn't erysipelas that they were suffering from, either.' She looked across at the two policemen and shook her head. 'Sadly, it was gangrene, though.'

'So Dr Dabbe said.' Sloan couldn't bring himself to refer to the pathologist as 'Hector'. Instead he flipped through the pages of his notebook until he found the place. 'In both hands and feet of the deceased.'

'That figures,' she said. 'Ergot, ergotamine tartrate or ergonovine poisoning. Take your pick.'

'What's ergotamine tartrate?' Sloan asked.

'One of the therapeutic versions of ergot, Inspector. They use a product called ergometrine in hospital more these days when delivering babies.'

Detective Constable Crosby frowned, taking this on board. 'Doesn't that mean it does good, too?'

'It is often used at a certain stage in childbirth,' she said with scientific precision.

'A therapeutic preparation?' Detective Inspector Sloan made a note. That opened up a whole new ball game.

'Yes, indeed, Inspector. It's a derivative of ergot.' She brushed her hair away from her eyes like a child and grinned at them. 'So's LSD.'

Detective Constable Crosby sat up. 'You're talking acid?'

She beamed at him. 'I am, Constable. And trips. Ergot's where LSD comes from, too.'

'Well I never,' marvelled the constable. 'We know all about that back at the station.'

'This mould,' said Sloan, firmly sticking to what he needed to know.

'*Claviceps purpurea*,' she said promptly.

Sloan was still feeling a certain melancholy. It didn't seem right to him that a head as pretty as Dr Brooke Helston's should be full of learning of this sort. No doubt, though, that Woman Sergeant Perkins would take a different view. He made a note, at the same time revising his opinion of the pathologist. Dr Hector Dabbe obviously wasn't such a dry old stick as he seemed to be when giving evidence in court.

'The rye gets made into bread and there you have it,' Dr Helston said. She gave a little twinkle with the bluest pair of eyes that Sloan had seen in many a year. 'Ergo and then ergot, you might say.'

'Quite so, miss,' said Sloan, not really a player of word games. 'Thank you for all your help. Dr Dabbe was right to send us here.'

She looked wistful. 'He's promised to show me his jury-rigging next time we go for a sail.'

'Not his etchings, then,' said Detective Constable Crosby under his breath.

Detective Inspector Sloan, his hand on the door, hurried into speech. 'The only sort of jury-rigging we have anything to do with in the police, miss, are the attempted corruption of twelve good men and true.'

'And we don't like it,' added Crosby.

NINE

'Where to next, sir?' asked Crosby, after they had found their way back out of the hospital.

'Culshaw's Bakery,' said Sloan. 'Follow your nose to the east of Berebury. You can tell where they are a mile away.'

'Nice smell, though,' said Crosby, usually hungry.

'And then, Crosby, you can put out an alert at all ports and airports for a young man called Terry Galloway, arriving here from Australia via India. You can't be too careful in this game and we'll need to keep an eye on him once he gets here.'

In spite of him usually giving the impression of being the world's busiest man, Clive Culshaw made no bones about seeing the police as soon as they arrived at the bakery. Obviously very much a hands-on owner, the man was wearing a white coat and had a white cotton trilby-style hat on his head, all his workers being similarly attired. He was located by a secretary on the factory floor among a welter of vats, cooling trays and moving conveyor belts. An array of commercial-sized ovens covered one wall, exuding heat. Every few minutes a bell rang beside one of them and a worker advanced and lifted out trays of cakes and buns on a long board, whilst another minion loaded a batch of prepared cake tins into it.

'Come along in,' Culshaw said, leading the way back to his office. A model of a great big harvest loaf stood on the shelf behind his desk, depicting sheaves of corn spilling out of a plaited basket.

'Is that real bread?' asked Detective Constable Crosby, pointing to it.

'It can be,' said Culshaw. 'We call it our Ceres piece. Goddess of Plenty and all that. We sell a lot of them come September time for harvest festivals.'

'"We plough the fields and scatter the good seed on the land",' chanted Crosby, prompted by the memory.

Clive Culshaw eyed the constable carefully before turning back to Sloan and saying, 'Now what can I do for you two gentlemen?'

'We're just checking on people who might have known the late Susan Port,' said Sloan.

'The late who?' he said.

'Susan Port.'

Clive Culshaw shook his head. 'The name doesn't ring a bell. Does – did – she work here? I'll have to ask. I can't know everyone, you know. Not in a place this size.'

'It is big,' agreed Sloan, quite surprised himself at the scale of the Culshaw operation.

'Smells good, too,' said Crosby.

'All the bread will have gone out to the shops long ago,' said Culshaw. 'That's what smells so good, but there'll be plenty of cakes around if you're interested.' He opened the door and called out for coffee.

'You met Mrs Port a couple of months ago,' persisted Sloan.

'Did I?' Culshaw's face was politely blank.

'At the offices of Puckle, Puckle and Nunnery.'

His face cleared. 'Of course. I remember her now. Neat woman. Not young. What about her?'

'She's dead,' said Crosby, leaping up to hold the door open for a young woman carrying a tray.

'Sorry to hear that,' said the baker.

'Do you remember anything else about her, Mr Culshaw?' asked Sloan.

'Not particularly. I was in a hurry to get away and the solicitor fellow was havering a lot.'

'Havering?'

'Well, for one thing he wouldn't get to the point and tell us how much money he was talking about. I needed to know if the whole exercise was going to be worthwhile.' He waved a hand to indicate the factory. 'After all, I've got a pretty big business here already.'

'So I can see,' said Sloan.

'On the other hand,' Culshaw gave a tight little smile, 'nobody can usually say that a bit more money doesn't always come in handy.'

Detective Inspector Sloan, owner of just that part of his house that didn't belong to the mortgage company, could only agree with him. He reckoned that at the present time the kitchen, dining room and staircase were his by now. And perhaps half the hallway.

Clive Culshaw said in a worldly-wise tone that anything divided by six didn't usually amount to much.

'Five now,' said Crosby insouciantly.

'So, sir,' carried on Sloan swiftly, 'we're just checking up on the people who might have known her.'

Culshaw looked at him, eyebrows raised. 'Something wrong?' he asked shrewdly.

'She doesn't appear to have had any family we can contact, that's all.'

Clive Culshaw pushed his hat to the back on his head. 'I suppose that technically I might be said to be related to her – all of us there were – but so distantly I don't see how it could possibly count.'

'And that would therefore naturally apply to your brother, Tom, too, wouldn't it?' said Sloan.

The physical temperature of the whole baking operation at the Culshaw factory was definitely on the high side but, at the mention of his brother's name, an emotional *froideur* in the owner's office was immediately apparent.

'Naturally,' agreed Clive Culshaw stiffly.

'I gather,' said Sloan, 'that you are both descendants of Algernon Mayton?'

He nodded. 'Through my late father. That's the connection. Dad died when he was quite young, which I understand is why we figure in the trust and not him.' He waved a hand in the direction of the shop floor. 'So my mother was left with two small boys to bring up. She had to take over the firm after he died and it was she who built up the business to what it is today.'

'Today?'

'Well, to what it was when she died two or three years ago, of course,' he conceded. 'I've done my best ever since then, although it's hard work.'

'I'm sure,' murmured Sloan.

'She was a redoubtable woman,' the baker went on. 'She worked her fingers to the bone for us when we were boys. Mind you, she was a natural businesswoman through and through. Taught me everything I know about the trade. And kept up with modern trends, too. You know, fancy breads and that sort of thing.'

'What sort of fancy breads?' asked Sloan casually. Wholemeal was the product of choice in his own household.

'Sourdough, rye, ciabatta, focaccia – you name it, we make it.'

'And your brother, too? Is he in the firm?'

It was as if a cloud had descended again. 'Tom's got no head for business at all. Mother did her best and tried to teach him, of course, although they never got on,' muttered Culshaw, shaking his head. 'He failed at every single thing he touched and lost a lot of her money in the process.' He essayed a thin smile. 'She used to say that the only board he could understand was an ironing one and he wasn't too good with that either.'

'I see, sir.'

'All Tom ever wanted to do was paint.' He sniffed. 'Not that he's any good at that either. All that he does these days is tinker. That's why she left all the business to me.'

'All?' echoed Crosby, advancing to help the young secretary with her tray. 'Nice,' he said appreciatively. 'These cakes, I mean,' he added hastily as the girl looked up into his eyes and gave him a winning smile. 'Nice icing.'

'Mother said she wasn't having Tom ruin everything she'd ever worked for,' said Culshaw. 'And that was that.'

'So she didn't let him?' said Crosby.

'No,' he said brusquely. 'In fact, she made quite sure he couldn't even try. She tied everything up very tightly in her will, leaving everything to do with the business to me.' He waved a hand round his office. 'This is all my responsibility.'

Detective Inspector Sloan, son of a churchgoing mother, tried to recall the parable of the Prodigal Son. As he remembered it, this situation seemed to be the exact opposite.

Clive Culshaw was still talking. 'My brother had a go at upsetting her will, but it was absolutely cast iron from a legal standpoint. He lost his challenge even though the judge did say that hard cases made bad law. She always said he wasn't worth a bag of beans.'

'Quite so,' said Detective Inspector Sloan, duly making a note. They knew more about unhappy families in the police force than most people did and were more understanding than many.

'Nice,' said Crosby again, carefully selecting an iced cake with help from the young secretary.

'Presumably, Inspector, you'll be talking to all the others who were there at Puckles that day?' said Clive Culshaw.

'All in good time,' said Crosby quite unnecessarily.

'And what I will be doing,' said Detective Inspector Sloan to Detective Constable Crosby as they left the baker's premises, 'is checking on the finances of his firm. As a matter of routine. Don't ever underestimate the importance of routine, Crosby.'

TEN

'Have you ever played a card game called Happy Families, Crosby?' asked Detective Inspector Sloan. They had driven back into the town from Culshaw's Bakery and were now parked in the police station yard before taking to the road again.

'No, sir.'

'I don't think that the Culshaw family can ever have done either.' Policeman that he was, Sloan had automatically wondered what Clive Culshaw's brother, Tom, could have done to occasion being disinherited so determinedly by his own mother. The first thought that had crossed his mind was that since Tom was the elder child he might have had a different father from his brother – one that was perhaps unknown to him and resented by his mother. That might explain things. He would have to look into it.

He had put in another check on whether the man had form, too, as soon as they had got back to the police station: criminal form, that is. Unfortunately, transgressions in some families didn't always reach the police – or, often as not anyone else's – records. What families could sweep under the carpet in the way of secrets was something that always amazed him.

Oh, yes, resolved Sloan to himself, he would certainly await the check on what records there were before he saw Tom Culshaw. In his book, as in that of soldiers in war, time spent in reconnaissance was seldom wasted.

'Daniel Elland and his wife can't have played Happy Families either, Crosby, not from the sounds of it, anyway,' he added, going on to quote Baroness Orczy, '"We seek him here, we seek him there, we seek him everywhere . . . that damned elusive Pimpernel".'

'Beg pardon, sir?'

'Nothing, Crosby, nothing. Before your time, I'm sure – *The Scarlet Pimpernel.*'

'Yes, sir. Where to now, sir?' asked Crosby, playing with the gear lever. He had already placed the car in pole position on an imaginary starting line.

Sloan flipped through the pages of his notebook. 'We'll try Martin Pickford next.' He read out an address on the far side of the town. 'It's beyond the cattle market. And then we'll come back to the station again, just in case there's any message through from forensics, although,' he added pessimistically, 'on past form it's a bit early to expect anything from that quarter just yet.'

'I reckon from all accounts whenever we arrive we'll be a bit early for that man Pickford,' said Crosby. 'The solicitor thought so, anyway.'

It was too early for Martin Pickford.

Much too early.

The young man took his time to answer their knock and open the front door. He peered at Sloan and Crosby standing on the doorstep through bleary eyes, one distinctly bloodshot. 'I didn't do it,' he said, focussing his eyes with difficulty on Sloan's proffered warrant card.

'I didn't think you had, sir,' said Detective Inspector Sloan at his most formal.

'Whatever it was.' Pickford's face was bruised and his hair tousled. He looked, too, as if he'd gone to bed in his clothes.

'It was whatever it was you had had in mind that you'd done,' contributed Crosby.

'I am innocent,' declaimed Pickford histrionically. 'My mates took me home.' He frowned. 'At least, I think they did. Or did they take me to the hospital first? I can't quite remember. I didn't drive back here, anyway, if that's what you're on about, and I've been in bed with a wonky eye most of the time since I did get back home. I've only just got out of bed.'

'As it happens, it isn't what we've come about, sir,' said Sloan distantly. 'We're not Traffic.' The unhappy association between the police and the motorist in the minds of the public didn't always help in an investigation.

'I can't remember much else now, anyway,' said Pickford, 'whatever it was that you wanted to know.'

'Really, sir?'

'My mind's a blank,' he confessed, swaying slightly as he spoke. 'An absolute blank. Was it something that happened on Saturday night?' Looking slightly abashed, he gave them a cheeky grin. 'I'm afraid, for starters, I can't remember much about Saturday night.'

'I'm sorry to hear that, sir,' said Sloan. Amnesia, however temporary, however fictional, was no help to a working police officer who liked his interviewees to be able to do better than that. It also gave those being interviewed time to think about an alibi. If they needed one, that is. 'Why would that have been?'

'We won,' said Martin Pickford simply. 'Against a brutal side from Luston.'

'Sounds like a grudge match to me,' contributed Crosby.

'Won what?' asked Sloan, remembering that there were always those who considered sport was war without weapons.

'Our match, of course.' Pickford pointed to his bloodshot eye. 'One of them got me just there, though, with an elbow. They're a rough lot, over at Luston, I can tell you.' He felt the orbital area round his bad eye tentatively and winced as he did so. 'We celebrated at the Bellingham and I've just got their bill. That's enough to give a fellow a headache even if he hadn't got one in the first place. Which, I may say, I have in spades.'

Detective Inspector Sloan made a mental note to check what had been going on at Berebury's popular hotel last Saturday night, whilst Crosby muttered something under his breath about playing for the sympathy vote. 'I would like you to cast your mind back a bit further than last Saturday night, sir, if you wouldn't mind,' he said.

'You'd better come in,' sighed the young man, 'and then I can sit down. I feel better sitting down.'

The two policemen followed Martin Pickford into what was very obviously a bachelor pad. The computer that sat in the middle of the only table was surrounded by used coffee mugs. A plate with some cold burnt toast on it nestled dangerously near the keyboard, while a pair of studded sports boots covered in mud was parked just to one side of the fireplace. Since his own wife, Margaret, would never even have let him inside the door wearing anything as dirty as that, let alone get near the fire, Sloan deduced that if there was a woman in Pickford's life she wasn't around the house very much.

Or was as undomesticated as he was.

Pickford slumped down into a chair and sunk his sore head between his hands. 'That's better. Now, what's this all about, Inspector?'

'Can you cast your mind back to your visit to a solicitor's office?'

'Which one?' He gave a wry grin. 'I've been to quite a few of them in my time.'

'Really, sir?'

'Mostly those of them who specialise in defence cases. Motoring ones. Funny that, when you consider that that's where I play on the rugby field.'

'And where would that be, sir?'

'Fullback, Inspector.'

'I see, sir. Defence.' In Sloan's book that would make him a muddied oaf rather than a flannelled fool. It could also account for the black eye and bruises and the slight limp in his left leg. 'The meeting we're interested in took place in the offices of Puckle, Puckle and Nunnery a couple of months ago.'

'Oh, that? I can remember that – most of it, anyway.' Martin Pickford eased his leg into a more comfortable position. 'Go on.'

'There was a woman there called Mrs Port.'

He nodded, evidently found that doing so hurt and sunk his head between his hands again. 'About my father's age? Grey-haired? Looked all right to me but a bit severe, if you know what I mean. What's up?'

'She's died,' said Crosby before Sloan could speak.

'It happens when you get on,' said the young man with all the assurance of youth.

'From something she ate,' said Crosby.

'Ah, that's different.'

'Very,' said Sloan. 'Had you by any chance ever seen her before?'

Martin Pickford started to shake his head, and wincing, thought better of that, too. He said instead, 'Not that I'd noticed.'

Sloan wasn't surprised at that. His own mother always insisted that all grey-haired women were invisible. 'Or any of the others there that day?'

'Only the nurse one. Samantha Peters. I'd come across her in the hospital once or twice when I'd gone there on a Saturday night with an injury. I only thought afterwards that I recognised her, although I didn't know her name or anything else about her until then. You see, I hadn't seen her out of uniform before, so I wasn't sure it was her. Not the sort of thing you ask in the Accident and Emergency Department, and anyway, they make darn sure that you can't read their name badges at the hospital. They turn them the wrong way round if they can.'

'Quite so,' said Detective Inspector Sloan, only too well aware that there were some policemen who, rightly or wrongly, removed the numbers from their uniforms when attending major disturbances. Rightly should they have feared dangerous repercussions; wrongly if they had planned on behaving less than well by the strict standards set in the comfort of their offices by some faraway watch committee.

'Not fair, that,' said Pickford.

'No, sir.'

'Nowadays, Inspector, when we're on the field we have numbers on our shirts so that the ref can spot who's done what.'

'I thought all refs were blind,' remarked Detective Constable Crosby to nobody in particular.

Pickford turned his head towards him, found that that hurt too and turned it back again. 'Not quite all of them, mate. But, in my experience, some of them do practise what you might call selective blindness.'

'Well I never . . .' began Crosby sarcastically.

'They're like you lot,' insisted Pickford. 'They catch some

lawbreakers and not others. They only book the ones they have a mind to – those whose faces don't fit.'

Detective Inspector Sloan firmly wrested the transactional initiative away from this heresy. 'Have you seen any of the others who were at that meeting since then?'

'Only Samantha Peters. Put her in uniform and she's a real tartar, I can tell you. What is it that writer fellow said about being dressed in brief authority?'

'That I couldn't say, I'm sure, sir,' said Sloan. He himself was of a generation that considered a policeman's helmet an inviolable symbol of the law rather than the rest of his uniform. Attacks on it represented to him attacks on authority and were not to be tolerated. 'But you've seen none of the others since?'

'Nope.'

'And I take it that the name Daniel Elland means nothing to you?'

'Never heard of him, Inspector.'

'Quite so, sir,' said Sloan, rising to leave. 'But should you ever come across him, we'd like to know.'

'Believe you me, Inspector, so would everyone else who was at the solicitors that day,' Pickford said heartily. 'We can't get our hands on the dibs until we do.'

Back in the police station yard, Sloan unhitched his seat belt and pushed the car door open. Writing up his notes and visiting the canteen both seemed entirely proper procedures at this stage of the day. As he began to clamber out of the vehicle, he became aware that on the other hand Detective Constable Crosby was making no move at all.

On the contrary, in fact.

The constable remained in his seat showing no signs of getting out of the car for so long that Sloan himself paused and looked back at him. 'Coming?' he asked.

The constable unhitched his own seat belt with conspicuous slowness. 'The custody sergeant said I had to report to him as soon as I got back, sir.'

'And what have you done now, Crosby?'

'Mucked up an arrest good and proper,' said Crosby gloomily. 'And what makes it worse was that they said it would be an easy one for a beginner.'

'How come?' Personally, Christopher Dennis Sloan, a detective inspector now but once a rookie constable himself, hadn't found making an arrest too difficult even then – once the suspect was handcuffed, that is. Until that moment, of course, all the options were open. 'Up for grabs' might be a better way of putting it, since not everyone went quietly.

'You know Larky Nolson's eldest lad, sir? The one they call the Varmint?'

'Who doesn't?' asked Sloan rhetorically. 'He couldn't lie straight in bed.'

'His boy's a right chip off the old block if ever there was one, sir.'

'I can well believe it.' Larky Nolson might only be a petty thief but his list of convictions was of epic length. 'What's he been up to now?'

'He nicked a couple of frozen chickens from the superstore down by the railway.'

'Following in his father's footsteps, then.'

'Not half – I mean, in a way, half is part of the trouble.'

'Explain yourself, Crosby.'

'Well, sir, it was like this. Larky's boy took these two chickens – caught red-handed, he was. There was no doubt about it. In fact, he admitted it straightaway.'

'So what was the problem?' asked Sloan, intrigued.

'The chickens were on sale, two for the price of one, and so I booked him for nicking two.'

'Which he had done,' said Sloan.

'But Larky's son argued that as what he'd stolen was only worth half of two, he should only be booked for nicking one.'

'And the value of the stolen goods comes into the charge, of course,' said Sloan thoughtfully. 'So?'

'So I said I thought he had a point and only booked him for stealing one.'

'And the custody sergeant blew his top?'

'How did you guess, sir?'

ELEVEN

'Any progress to report, Sloan?' asked Superintendent Leeyes, guaranteed to wrong-foot any subordinate with ease.

'Not yet, sir.' This, Sloan would have been the first to admit, was a tendentious reply, implying as it did that there would in fact be some progress to report at some stage. He wasn't even sure if there ever would be anything to report in this case – it was all a bit too nebulous for him, save only for the presumption of ergot poisoning. There had still been nothing back from forensics.

'Seen everybody in the loop now, have you?' Leeyes growled.

'Except the nurse – Samantha Peters. She's been on night duty this week and we've got to be a bit careful exactly when we get to talk to her and Tom Culshaw.'

'In my experience,' pronounced the superintendent loftily, 'you always have to be careful talking to anyone on night duty. It upsets their equilibrium.'

'And then there's the missing man, sir. Obviously I haven't spoken to him yet.'

'There's a flying formation called that,' remarked Leeyes inconsequently. 'When the squadron's lost someone – like you appear to have done, Sloan.'

In the interests of his pension, Detective Inspector Sloan, married man and father, forbore to retort that he hadn't lost Daniel Elland. He just hadn't found him, which was quite different. All he knew about the man so far was that his descent from Algernon Mayton was through his father and had passed Simon Puckle's scrutiny. Instead he said that he was planning to get out to Ornum, the village where Samantha Peters lived, by six o'clock that evening.

When apprised of this, Detective Constable Crosby sounded aggrieved. 'Six o'clock, sir. That's a funny old time.'

'It was the one that her ward manager at the hospital suggested would be best,' said Sloan. 'She says Samantha Peters will have just got up about then.'

'Funny old time for toast and marmalade, too,' sniffed Crosby.

'Let me tell you, Crosby,' said Sloan feelingly, 'that there's nothing at all funny about night duty. It plays hell with your sleep pattern and upsets your digestion for days.'

Samantha Peters, though, when the police arrived at her cottage in the village of Ornum, exhibited no sign of disturbed sleep.

Or surprise at their visit.

'Police?' she said, ushering them into chairs. 'Who about this time?'

'Mrs Susan Port.'

'She's not a patient. At least, not now. She was at one time, I know.' She stared at them blankly. 'If you mean that Susan Port.'

'I do,' said Sloan soberly.

'What about her?'

'She's died,' said Sloan.

'Good Lord, Inspector! What on earth happened? She was all right when I last saw her.'

'Would that have been that day at the solicitors, Miss Peters?'

'No, no,' she said, shaking her head. 'I've seen her several times since then, usually in Berebury. We've met up for a cup of coffee at the Bellingham when she's been in town and I've been off duty, and I've been out to Bishop's Marbourne for a cup of tea two or three times. As she said after that meeting at the solicitors, it was rather silly our not getting to know each other better since we must be related, however distantly. And, like me, she didn't have any really near relatives, either. So, please tell me, what happened?'

'We're not exactly sure, Miss Peters,' replied Sloan, choosing his words with care.

'We don't know,' interrupted Crosby before he could go on. When Sloan glared at him he muttered, 'Same thing,' under his breath.

'And was she pleased at the prospect of a large inheritance?' asked Sloan.

Samantha Peters considered this. 'I should say quietly pleased but not excited,' she said after a moment's thought. 'She told me that whatever it amounted to, she wouldn't want to change her lifestyle all that much at her age. She liked the way she was living – she said it suited her.'

'And you, miss?'

Samantha Peters gave a light laugh. 'I think we all liked the idea of a legacy at first, but when I thought about it later on, I realised that I quite enjoyed my job at the hospital. Besides, I've found over the years that working with the badly injured and dying gives you a different perspective on life. Money isn't as important in the long run as you might think then.'

Detective Inspector Sloan had established his own priorities while first married and still a constable. 'Go on,' he said.

'So, Inspector, I decided that what I would do when – if, that is – I came into that sort of money was to travel, big time. Mind you, that solicitor was so cagey none of us had any idea at all how much money was involved.'

'You can't usually get any info out of doctors either,' contributed Crosby feelingly. 'You can never tell whether they're not saying something because they don't know or because they know but they don't want you to.'

'There are tricks in every trade,' she responded lightly. 'Doctors don't know everything, anyway, even if they want you to think that they do. The young ones, especially.'

Detective Inspector Sloan, older and wiser, had long ago decided that policemen didn't have to explain anything at all – until they got to court, that is. What information they had gathered they were entitled to keep to themselves.

And usually did.

It was different when cases came to trial, when everything had to – should, in theory – come out. He said now, 'These meetings at the Bellingham, miss – what did Mrs Port talk about then?'

Samantha Peters frowned. 'Her new lifestyle, mostly – she hadn't ever lived out in the country before and she was still finding out about it.' She waved a hand to encompass her own cottage and its rural surroundings. 'The country isn't anything new in my case, of course. Me, I've lived in this village all my life and my mother and grandparents before me, but Susan'd been a townee, long-time. Had had to be because of her work, of course.'

'But she had no family, you said?'

'She'd got a godson somewhere she was very fond of, but no one closer than that.'

'Did he visit her?'

'Oh, no. He lived a long way away – Australia or New Zealand, I think. I don't remember which. She did spend a fair bit of time in her kitchen, I do know that – she was very proud of her bread-making, you see. She said she'd never had time to cook properly before when she was working – she'd been a civil servant in one of the departments. And gardening, she liked that, too.' She looked across at Sloan and said, 'I'm sorry she's died, even though I didn't know her really well. I shall miss our little chats.'

'Yes, miss, I'm sure.'

Samantha Peters hesitated. 'You didn't say what it was that had happened, Inspector.'

'We don't exactly know, miss. Not yet.'

'I see.' She obviously did see because she nodded and then sat up very straight and said, 'I should like to go to the funeral.'

'All in good time,' said Crosby quite unnecessarily.

Unlike that of his brother, Tom, Clive Culshaw's return to his own home the next evening had not occasioned any mirth whatsoever. And even if he should have happened to feel mirthful there was no one there with whom to share the feeling.

Or share anything else. This was evidenced by a note on the kitchen table in his wife's handwriting, which read: *Supper in the oven. Back by 11 p.m.*

Even though bakers are in the nature of things usually early to bed, as perforce they are also early to rise, Clive Culshaw did not head for his bedroom after he had eaten his solitary reheated supper. And it wasn't because he was waiting for his wife to return from her bridge club. It was because he was still poring over the last week's sales figures at the bakery.

There was no occasion for mirth lurking in them – quite the contrary, in fact.

There was nothing amusing either in the long list of the moneys owing to his suppliers, some payments already considerably overdue. Or in the latest letter from the bank, which hovered somewhere about the middle of a scale that stretched from the unhelpful to the downright threatening. He brushed aside with his customary impatience a sales brochure from one trade supplier suggesting he sold artisanal bread as well as the famous Culshaw loaf.

'Baked only with their expensive new equipment, no doubt,' he muttered aloud to the empty kitchen.

His staff wouldn't have credited the change from Clive Culshaw's customary public persona as a busy captain of industry to a worried and rather subdued businessman. Gone was the impatient, testy owner chasing every minute, instead there was only a very worried man. Pushing aside the remains of the fish pie, he picked up a pencil and did a few calculations and then sat silent and still.

But not for too long.

Always given automatically to converting worry into action, he turned his mind somewhere where he thought salvation might lie. Actually, now he came to think it through, he realised that it was the only place from whence any help could come.

Finding Daniel Elland would be the answer to all his problems.

Just as Simon Puckle had said: 'Dead or alive.'

TWELVE

Detective Inspector Sloan was at his desk promptly the next morning, but it wasn't long before Crosby put his head round the door.

'About the case of Susan Mary Port, deceased, sir,' the constable began, entering the room waving a sheaf of papers in his hand.

Sloan looked up. 'I must remind you, Crosby, that so far we do not appear to have any case at all.'

'Yes, sir. I mean, no, sir.'

'What we have at this stage is only a professional opinion by a consultant pathologist and no more than that.' Sloan sat back in his chair. 'Indeed, she may well have been killed by – what was it Dr Dabbe told us? – by the ingestion of a noxious substance . . .'

'Ergot,' supplied Crosby.

'Ergot or one of its derivatives, but I must also remind you that she might have taken—'

'Or been given,' persisted Crosby gamely.

'Or she might have taken – that is, swallowed – the afore-mentioned noxious substance by accident or ignorance.'

'Yes, sir. Of course, sir.'

'On the other hand,' said Sloan, mellowing slightly, 'we must certainly take note of the fact that Culshaw's Bakery not only bakes loaves of rye bread, said to be one of the sources of the mould that produces ergot, but also sells rye flour for customers' home baking in its shops. And that baking bread was something the deceased used to do at home.'

'Yes, sir,' said Crosby. 'I remembered that that's what did for all those people in France.'

'But,' admitted Detective Inspector Sloan honestly, 'I'm hanged if I can think of any reason why killing Susan Port would help any of the other legatees in any significant manner. The godson's a different kettle of fish. That is, if he knows about the legacy, and we don't even know that.'

'Yet,' said Crosby optimistically.

'And all the rest of them at that meeting insisted that they hadn't known each other before they met that day at Puckle's office either. Except for the two brothers, of course. They knew each other with a vengeance.'

'Tweedledum and Tweedledee.'

'More like Cain and Abel, if you ask me,' said Sloan. 'Anyway, the other four of them . . .'

'Five,' said Crosby.

'True. I was forgetting the missing man for the moment.' He straightened up. 'In fact, that reminds me, I think we might pay a visit to the last known address of Daniel Elland sometime soon. It won't do any harm and might even do some good.' This was a precept learnt at his churchgoing mother's knee and related in her case to the value of prayer. Privately, Sloan thought it could also be applied to a number of actions, mostly by the medical profession.

Detective Constable Crosby plonked the handful of papers that he had brought with him on Sloan's desk. 'There hasn't been a squeak from anywhere about the deceased's godson, Terry Galloway, arriving, sir.' He tapped one of the reports. 'The immigration people said something unnecessary about looking for needles in haystacks when I asked if there was any record of anyone of that name coming into the country from Australia via India or anywhere nearer and was I having a laugh? And when I couldn't begin to tell them exactly when in the last month we thought he might have arrived, the bloke I was talking to got quite ratty.'

'Something every investigating officer has to get used to,' said Sloan bracingly. 'Nobody likes unanswerable questions.'

'And when I told them we didn't know his last known address or even if he was here already, let alone where exactly he might be staying in this country, they more or less told me to get lost.' He consulted his notebook. 'They did say that if it would be any help and if we were to follow their proper procedures – to the letter, they said – they could put him on their watch list.'

'They did, did they?' said Sloan, unimpressed.

The constable said that he thought that what they were implying was that the police ought to be able to do their own donkey work.

'Searching for a loose cannon before it's done any damage, Crosby,' said Sloan, 'is never easy. All the same, we should ask the next-door neighbour – Mrs Dyson, wasn't it? – to let us know if anyone at all appears asking for the deceased. She didn't mention anyone coming to see his godmother before the woman died, remember. And I think the deceased would have told her if he had, as they seemed very friendly.'

'He – her godson – could easily have turned up at her cottage, though, without anyone knowing. It's not that over-looked,' pointed out the constable.

'And then what?' asked Sloan.

'Put ergot into the flour.' Crosby frowned. 'Into anything, come to that.'

'Remember her next-door neighbour did tell us that she baked her own bread,' mused Sloan, making a note. 'Perhaps it would be just as well to see her again.'

'Suppose he's already been and gone, sir?'

'Then we shall be locking the stable door after the horse has bolted, won't we?' said Detective Inspector Sloan, ever the realist.

'Job done.' Tom Culshaw had walked in through his own front door early that morning, visibly tired and unshaven.

'So you're back at last, thank goodness,' said his wife, giving him a quick peck on the cheek and then making for the kitchen. 'You must be starving.'

'I am. We got there in good time, though, which was the main thing,' he said, slipping off his coat and following her into the kitchen.

'Thank goodness for that, too.' Sophie Culshaw had reached for the frying pan and was swiftly layering it with rashers of bacon.

He pulled up a chair and sat down at the table. 'The nurses had already begun stripping him down ready for the operation before I'd even got out of his room.'

'I believe every minute counts with kidney transplants,' she said, pricking some sausages before adding them to the frying pan.

'Another good job for Gordian Knots,' he said, yawning prodigiously. 'The poor fellow had tried everywhere to get someone to drive him to London the minute the call came. It was just his bad luck that it came at four o'clock in the morning and he couldn't get anyone else.'

'His good luck,' she pointed out.

'What? Oh, yes, of course.' He gave another yawn. 'He was frantic. He'd even thought of driving himself there and abandoning his car at the hospital, he was so desperate.'

Sophie paused from chopping up some tomatoes. 'I hear you did a good job over at Childe Benstead, too.'

'Oh, that was weeks ago.' He reached up for the mug of coffee she handed to him. 'I'd forgotten all about it.'

'Well, apparently whatever it was you did over there worked a treat, and the mother rang up this morning to say so. What was the problem?'

He grinned. 'It was the worst case of sibling rivalry that I've ever come across.'

'How come?' she asked, shovelling the tomatoes into the frying pan and deciding against mentioning anything about the fraught relationship between her husband and his brother. 'I thought it was just two young sisters not getting on.'

'It was. They had to share a bedroom, you see.'

'Tough.'

'That wasn't it. What they were doing was fighting a turf war.'

'Ah, the good old territorial imperative.'

'Apparently they spent all their time arguing about the other one straying into their half and borrowing their lipstick or whatever it is that matters to young girls these days. Their rows were driving their poor mother crazy.'

'I'm not surprised.' Sophie reached for some eggs and then asked, 'So what did you do?'

He grinned. 'Set up an invisible beam down the middle of the room, which rang out like the clappers if either of the little perishers strayed out of their own half. And I put some special tape down on the carpet like they do on the line on tennis courts and electrified it in case they tried to get under the ray. That's what did it, all right.'

'They'll laugh about it later on in life.'

'I doubt it,' said Tom Culshaw seriously. 'Sibling rivalry is a terrible thing.'

'You don't have to remind me,' said his wife tartly.

He sniffed. 'That bacon smells good.'

'It won't be long,' she said, answering the thought behind the statement. 'Well done, anyway. That's two good jobs for Gordian Knots.'

'I've got another one for Thursday,' he said slowly.

'That's good, too,' she said, deftly turning over the bacon and breaking two eggs into the sizzling frying pan. 'Aren't you pleased?'

'I'm not too sure that it is good,' he said.

'How come?'

'Getting a guy to hospital in a hurry in the middle of the night for emergency surgery and stopping two youngsters fighting was easy. I have a feeling that the next job isn't going to be. In fact, I'm beginning to wish I hadn't taken it on. I don't think I would have done if he hadn't been one of us.'

'What does that mean, may I ask?'

'If he wasn't one of the descendants of my sainted ancestor.'

'Sainted? Algernon Mayton?' She raised her eyebrows. 'You can't be serious. The man who made his fortune selling a fake remedy?'

'Him,' said Tom Culshaw. 'I'm beginning to wonder if bad genes can be inherited.'

She paused, the kitchen spatula in her hand poised over the sizzling frying pan. 'Even if it does,' she said loyally, 'it doesn't mean that everyone in the family inherits the bad ones.'

Only some of them, she added to herself, her hated brother-in-law in mind.

THIRTEEN

'Ah, Sloan, come in and tell me how you're getting on with that ergot business.'

'Not a lot to report as yet, sir,' said Detective Inspector Sloan. 'In fact, so far you might say we've only accomplished a fact-finding exercise. We've got two more potential legatees to interview, not counting the missing man, but Tom Culshaw's wife insists he's sound asleep just now, having been up all night.'

'In my experience, Sloan,' said the superintendent lugubriously, 'wives will usually say anything to protect their man. And if they won't, you need to know why. They're always notoriously unreliable in the matter of alibis and you should remember it.'

'Yes, sir.'

'And in spite, Sloan, of the prominence of that famous saying "Well begun is half done", you must also remember that it does not apply to a police investigation.'

'No, sir.'

'An investigation once begun should be completed.'

'Quite so, sir,' said Sloan, forbearing to mention the unclosed files that were the bane of every Criminal Investigation Department. 'Talking of wives, sir, I thought it wouldn't do any harm to interview the wife of Daniel Elland, the missing man. He's what you might call an "unknown factor".'

'And could be up to anything,' said Leeyes morosely.

Detective Constable Crosby was only too happy to drive Sloan to an expensive address on the outskirts of the town. 'The Lodge, Acacia Road, please, Crosby, and there is no need to floor it.'

'Of course not, sir.' The constable looked as injured as if he had never ever done any such thing in his life before.

'The lady concerned might not even be at home.'

'The lady, sir?'

'The former Mrs Daniel Elland, now Mrs Jaqueline Prothero.'

The lady was in but not particularly pleased to see two plain-clothes policemen at her door asking about her first husband. She was dressed in skinny trousers of a distinctive *pied-de-poule* patterned fabric complemented by a shirt of such simple cut that it must have been very expensive. Sloan caught a glimpse of flawless manicuring as she gestured to the two policemen to enter.

'So what's Daniel been up to now?' she asked.

'You don't see him, then, madam?' said Sloan.

'Not on your life, Inspector,' she responded immediately. 'We had a clean settlement, drawn up by my solicitors. Daniel didn't have a solicitor then, being bankrupt. Whatever he's done, I can assure you that he's got no call on me and I've never seen him from that day to this.'

'He lived here, too?' enquired Detective Constable Crosby, staring round the remarkably well-appointed sitting room with interest.

'Oh, yes. We were together, once upon a time,' she said, adding complacently, 'but I got to keep the house. He'd put it in my name anyway when things started to go pear-shaped with his business. To be on the safe side, he said.' She gave an unpleasant little laugh. 'I'm told it's often done when a business is at risk.'

'So I understand, madam. It's usually considered very prudent in those circumstances,' observed Sloan, drawing a veil over the fact that it hadn't been in this case – for her husband, that is.

'It meant that there was no room for argument when Berebury Sound Ltd went broke, possession being nine-tenths of the law.' She curled her lip. 'Sound it wasn't. Not no way.'

'Quite so,' murmured Sloan, that sort of law being a civil matter. 'Tell me, what made your husband go bankrupt?'

She waved an arm dismissively. 'One of his customers – an important one – owed him a lot of money and couldn't pay his bill. Some other quite big people were very late settling theirs and then one of his creditors turned nasty.'

'As they do,' contributed Crosby, who had once been chased for the late payment of his rent by a strong-minded landlady.

Jaqueline Prothero's lip curled. 'It was after that when Daniel told me that we'd have to downsize big time until he got back on his feet. That was when his firm – I told you that it was called Berebury Sound, didn't I? – folded. I told him no way, José. Catch me living in some nasty little two-up two-down place down by the river.'

'Then what?' enquired Crosby with genuine interest.

'That's when I threw him out,' she replied with chilling simplicity. 'And that's when he started really drinking.'

'Took to the bottle, did he?' said Crosby.

'I'll say,' she said. 'And his mother having died not long before, he'd got nowhere to go, either.'

Somewhere at the back of his mind Sloan remembered something Shakespeare had written about troubles coming not in single spies but in battalions. Daniel Elland would seem to have had them in spades.

'The Aston Martin having to be sold was the last straw,' she said, a look of pure malice coming into her face. 'They didn't want him as captain of the golf club after that, either.'

Sloan remembered reading somewhere, too, that it only took three things to go wrong to lead to any man's downfall. Daniel Elland would seem to have had plenty to choose from.

'So, is Daniel still being a drunken no-good boyo?' she asked.

'I couldn't say, madam,' he said.

'Then why are you here?'

'We're interested in the present whereabouts of your former husband. And,' he gave a little cough, 'if we may, we would like to have something with his fingerprints on . . .'

'He's not dead, is he?' she said swiftly.

'Not as far as we are aware, madam.'

'I suppose there'll be something around with them on. Try the tools in the garden shed. He liked doing the garden. We have someone to do it now, of course.'

'So, if we might examine them to see if Mr Elland's prints are still extant . . .'

'My ex is how I think of him, which I may say is not often now.' She sat back in her chair. 'The night I threw him out onto the doorstep I locked the door behind him and said I never wanted to see him again.' She smiled thinly. 'It was raining, if I remember rightly.'

Detective Constable Crosby stared at her, about to burst into outraged speech. Sloan beat him to it – but with greater subtlety. 'You're quite sure, madam, that he has no further financial call upon you?'

'Quite sure, Inspector,' she said firmly. 'Or me on him, not that that's likely. Jake – that's the man I married afterwards – made certain of that. And so did my solicitor.' She let her gaze drift round the well-appointed room. 'Jake's got money, you see, serious money and he didn't want Daniel or his creditors getting their thieving hands on it.'

'In that case, madam,' said Detective Inspector Sloan with the utmost civility, 'we won't be troubling you any further.' He rose to leave. 'We were hoping to find Daniel Elland because it would seem that he has come into money. Rather a lot of it.'

*   *   *

In spite of his reservations about the assignment, Tom Culshaw did not delay in setting out for the home of Jim Stopford in the far-off village of Capstan Purlieu. Even though it was broad daylight when he explored the terrain, it hadn't been easy to spot the farmhouse where the man lived. It was deep in the remote countryside, houses few and far between. Much too few, anyway, to make any sort of surveillance simple, each passing car all too noticeable by anyone peering out at the road.

Spurred on in his mind by the motto of his firm Gordian Knots, Tom drove past Stopford's farmhouse without slowing down, as if he was going somewhere else. Nevertheless, he took note of any number of farm buildings and the three vehicles standing in the yard. He decided without difficulty that the mud-spattered Audi 6 belonged to Jim Stopford. At a guess it was about five years old, while the Land Rover beside it was younger. At the back of the yard was a little runabout truck loaded with sacks of feed, clear evidence of its role on the farm.

He soon realised that it had been a mistake to carry on up the valley. The road got narrower and narrower, a signpost pointing over the hill ahead to a little settlement several miles away.

The only place he could turn his car was outside the last house on the road, where he caught sight of someone staring out of a window at him as he did so. He sped back the way he had come, taking care again not to slow down in front of Jim Stopford's farm as he passed it.

All that the reconnaissance had convinced him of was that there was nothing to be gained by attempting to disable the man's car at his home. Not with two other vehicles within easy reach in an emergency.

His preliminary survey of the car park of the Bellingham Hotel was equally unpromising. It was well lit, much overlooked and had a steady stream of traffic coming and going in and out of it. He toyed briefly with the idea of casing the joint from the inside by having a drink at the bar but decided against being seen and perhaps recognised there, either before or after Thursday.

Something, he reluctantly realised, would have to be done to delay Jim Stopford after he left the farm at Capstan Purlieu but, if at all possible, before he reached the Bellingham. Answer, for the time being anyway, came there none.

Tom Culshaw turned and drove home thinking deeply.

He didn't have long in which to cogitate on the problem. Waiting in his sitting room was his wife, Sophie, clearly on tenterhooks, and with her two policemen.

'Oh, Tom, there you are at last,' she burst out as he came in. 'I've been so worried in case anything had happened to you. These gentlemen won't say why they've come, you see. Only that they're here on police business.'

Tom Culshaw, not particularly fazed by this, turned apologetically to Detective Inspector Sloan. 'I'm afraid I did push it a bit the other night, Inspector, but there was nothing on the road and it was very urgent. The man was frantic to get to the hospital.'

'It's not about that, sir,' said Sloan, sighing inwardly. Surely infringers of the speed limits were not what the great upholders of the law Henry Fielding and Sir Robert Peel had had in mind when they created their police force. Even the Bow Street Runners had only run.

'No?' Tom Culshaw remained polite and attentive.

'We're making enquiries into the recent sudden death of Mrs Susan Mary Port,' said Sloan.

'You remember, darling, you told me she was one of the other legatees,' supplied Sophie quickly.

His brow cleared. 'So she was. Sorry, she's died, though. What happened?'

Sloan said that they were not at liberty to say but enquiries were proceeding.

'Where do I come in, then?' asked Culshaw.

'You probably don't,' said Sloan. 'On the other hand, we do need to know if you've seen her since that meeting at the solicitors.'

He shook his head. 'Not that I know of.'

'Or before?'

Culshaw shook his head again, waving a hand round his house and garden. 'As you can see, we live a good way from

Berebury – nearer Calleford, actually – so I'm not likely to have bumped into her, anyway.'

Crosby sat up. 'And she'd never been a client of Gordian Knots?'

Sloan gave another sigh. This time it was at Crosby's naivety in revealing that the police had already checked the man out. He would have to have a word with him later, when he would try to explain to the rookie constable that the role of the police was to acquire information, not dispense it, although he doubted whether Crosby would take the fact on board.

Crosby, for a wonder, still looked interested in the man. 'So what exactly does this outfit of yours do, then?'

'Jobs that other people can't,' Culshaw said briefly.

'Or won't,' added Sophie loyally.

'Thinking outside the box?' said Crosby.

'You could call it that,' said Culshaw. 'I prefer to describe it as thinking laterally.' He sat back and relaxed. He'd just had a great idea for keeping Jim Stopford away from the Bellingham on Thursday evening. He only hoped that Martin Pickford was being truthful when he said that there was no funny business involved. There would sure be trouble if there was.

FOURTEEN

The station sergeant looked up as Detective Sloan and Constable Crosby came back through the door of the police station. 'Ah, Inspector,' he said. 'The SOCO is waiting to see you. I suggested he went to the canteen, seeing as I didn't know how long you'd be.'

'Thanks, Bill, good idea,' said Sloan. 'I could do with a bite myself, anyway.'

Crosby started to follow the inspector.

'Not you, young man,' said the station sergeant sternly. 'I want a word with you. Now.'

'Yes, Sergeant.' Crosby halted, downcast.

Detective Inspector Sloan left him to his fate and made for

the canteen. The SOCO was already well into a plate of the canteen's renowned all-day breakfast.

'Good stuff, Inspector, all this,' he said, waving a fork with half a sausage impaled on the end of it about in the air.

'Too right,' said Sloan, taking the seat opposite the SOCO and starting to tackle his own sausage. 'So how did you get on over at Bishop's Marbourne?'

'There was nothing much of interest that our team could find, Inspector. We took the remains of a loaf and a bag of that heavy flour for baking it away with us, like you said, and got it off to forensics for analysis. Otherwise there wasn't a lot to find out, short of a strip search.'

Sloan raised an eyebrow. 'Strip search?'

'You know, Inspector,' he said, taking a bite of his sausage. 'We didn't split open the cushions or go through the books for microfiches.'

Sloan nodded. 'I take it,' he said, mindful of a word often used by Dr Dabbe, 'that the official word for your examination of the premises then would be "superficial"?'

'If you like,' said SOCO, finishing off the sausage and giving his attention to the bacon. 'Not fingertip, if you take my meaning,' he conceded.

'But fingerprint, I hope?'

The SOCO nodded his head. 'Oh, yes, even though I understood that there was not much call for that since I was told she died out of doors. We found a lot of one set everywhere and odd sets of someone else's in the kitchen and bathroom. We can always go back if you want us to.'

'No need,' agreed Sloan. 'Anything else at all?'

'Everything seemed OK to me. A few home remedies in the bathroom cupboard and a bottle of painkiller tablets from the hospital.' He frowned. 'They had their name on them – the tablets, I mean – and hers, too. I didn't make a note but I'm having them checked.'

'Good man.'

'Oh, and a lot of jars that looked like honey. I took one away to check.'

'If it looks like honey and tastes like honey and smells like honey, then it probably is honey.'

'Actually, Inspector, now I come to think of it, it was labelled honey.'

'Doesn't have to be,' Sloan, ever the detective, reminded him.

The SOCO looked reproachful. 'You having me on?'

'Just pointing something out, that's all. Things aren't always what they seem.' Sloan speared a fried tomato and asked, 'Did she have a computer? You can never tell with those, either.'

'Computer, yes. And what we did notice was what she was doing with it. It was still on the screen.'

'Tell me.'

'Family history. She'd obviously been working on someone's family tree. There was a lot of paper about with death certificates and the like pinned to it. And there was this thing like half a roll of wallpaper with lots of names scribbled on it all over her dining-room table.'

Suddenly alert, Sloan asked if she had dated her work.

'Come again, Inspector?'

'I'd very much like to know when she started work on this family history,' said Sloan, tugging his notebook out of his pocket. 'Such as whether it was begun before or after a certain meeting at Puckles, the solicitors, a few weeks ago.'

The SOCO wrinkled his brow. 'To be honest, I never thought to look.'

Sloan changed the subject. 'Never mind, I can always check with Puckles. She could have got a lot of guff from them. Anything else?'

'Nothing to speak of. The cottage all looked pretty normal to me. We had a bite at the village pub afterwards and chatted up the natives, who were talkative enough. They said the deceased seemed a harmless old biddy.'

'So did Madame de Brinvilliers,' said Sloan.

'Who?'

'A French mass poisoner,' said Sloan.

'And there was this nosey old bag next door who kept a pretty sharp lookout on us while we were there. She made out that the deceased's solicitor in London had asked her to keep an eye on the place for him seeing he's not local. She's got a key and forwards the post and that sort of thing.'

'All right if she's all right,' said Sloan with a wisdom born of long experience. 'I can't honestly say yet that it's a true crime scene, though, but thanks all the same for what you've done so far.'

The detective constable who slunk into the canteen a few moments later bore no relation to the demon driver of 'F' Division of the Calleshire County Constabulary. Clearly crestfallen, he dealt the canteen chair a savage blow as he swung it into place at the table. He plonked himself on the chair, scowling.

'And what have you done?' enquired Sloan.

'Brought disgrace on the force,' Crosby muttered miserably.

'How come?' asked Sloan with interest.

'I attacked a child verbally with abusive language unbecoming to a member of the police force. Furthermore, I raised my hand to him as if I was going to attack him and threatened to knock his block off.'

'Tell me more,' said Sloan, demolishing a fried egg with enthusiasm.

'You know Larky Nolson's boy, sir?'

The SOCO leant forward. 'Is that the one they call the Varmint?'

'Him,' said Crosby richly.

'Even if you were severely provoked,' said Sloan, conscious that he was supposed to be a mentor to the young, 'you shouldn't rise to it.'

'Provoked!' echoed Crosby bitterly. 'I'll say I was provoked and made to look a fool into the bargain, too. He said he had come in for charging.'

'Not like him,' observed Sloan. 'Quite out of character, in fact. We usually have to winkle him out from under his bed before we can charge him.'

'I didn't know that, did I, sir? I thought he was admitting to something when he said that.'

'So?'

'So I got out a charge sheet and started to write it up like everyone says it should be done and called the station sergeant up to tell him what I was doing.'

'And?'

'The little blighter whipped out his mobile phone and charger and said would we plug it in for him and he'd be back for it later.'

The SOCO burst out laughing although Sloan heroically kept a straight face.

'That's when I said something I shouldn't have, sir, and raised my fist to him. I didn't actually hit him, sir, but it was a near thing.'

'And the station sergeant isn't happy?' said Sloan.

'Not with me or him. He said I'd brought the force into disrepute. And that he's as sure as eggs is eggs that Larky'll be round in the morning with an official complaint and what did I propose doing about it.'

As was her wont, Miss Florence Fennel presented herself in her employer's office at ten o'clock precisely on the Thursday morning. She took with her, as always, a folder in which reposed the day's post, neatly docketed, and her own notebook. Whilst more modern methods of communication existed they hadn't yet penetrated the stately premises of Puckle, Puckle and Nunnery, Solicitors and Notaries Public. Already on Simon Puckle's desk was a typed list of his appointments for the day but this routine meeting with his personal secretary always had its own priority.

'And while you were in court yesterday, Mr Puckle,' she began, 'there were a number of messages for you.'

'Go ahead.'

Miss Fennel enumerated these, finishing with the information that Detective Inspector Sloan had requested a note of the exact extent of the family histories of the prospective legatees that he had had explored.

'Tell him,' he said, pointing to her notebook and poised pen, 'that we have copies here of the death certificates of all their parents and their own birth certificates of all of the potential beneficiaries. And that he is welcome to inspect them, if he so wishes. They are, after all, documents already in the public domain.'

'Certainly, Mr Puckle.'

'Oh, and those of their offspring, where applicable.'

Many a younger secretary might have responded with a laconic 'Will do'. Miss Florence Fennel belonged to an older school. 'Certainly, Mr Puckle. I'll attend to it at once.'

Which she proceeded to do.

FIFTEEN

'Well, Sloan?' barked Superintendent Leeyes. 'Are you getting anywhere with that dead woman out at Bishop's Marbourne yet?'

The morning meeting of principal and subordinate at the police station in Berebury was rather less formal than the similar one at the solicitors: but equally to the point.

'In some respects, sir,' said the detective inspector warily. 'For a start, I've been taking a look at last year's accounts for Culshaw's Bakery.'

'Piece of cake?' said Leeyes, baring his teeth to show he was making a joke.

Sloan acknowledged this with a politic smile, bearing in mind that he had his pension to think of. 'On the contrary, in fact, sir. He's sailing pretty close to the wind. It would appear as if the firm's been running at a loss for a good year or two now. He's getting a lot of opposition from the multiples.'

Leeyes drummed his fingers on his desk. 'So the man could do with the money?'

'Looks like it. I'm not an accountant, but Fixby and Fixby are and they set it all out very clearly in his last set of accounts for Companies House.' Sloan offered the folder to the superintendent, who promptly waved it away, so he carried on. 'The place is mortgaged to the hilt and while it would seem he's keeping his creditors at bay just now, they're not getting any fewer. And there's a history in that family that needs looking into. Sibling rivalry, big time.'

'A touch of the Cain and Abel, you think?' The superintendent sat back in his chair and reasoned aloud. 'If one of them killed the other there would be gain for the survivor, all right.'

Detective Inspector Sloan forbore to remind him that, if caught, the survivor couldn't benefit from killing his brother, profiting from murder not being allowed by ancient statute.

Leeyes ploughed on. 'If either of them were to come to grief, the survivor of the pair would get twice as much as they would have done from this old trust, I'll give you that, because he'd come into all the deceased brother's share.'

'True, sir. Very true.' Christopher Dennis Sloan, proud father of a son, resolved that should he and his wife have another baby, sibling rivalry would not be allowed.

'But all the same, the economic enemies are at the bakery gate, then?' said Leeyes, whose early reading had been of the G. A. Henty and Kipling school.

'Head just above the water, sir,' said Sloan, as good at mixing a metaphor as the next man. 'I should imagine that a big cash injection would come in very handy.' Not being an accountant, he wasn't sure how you circled the wagons for financial protection.

'Not in itself a reason to suspect him of anything,' said the superintendent, whose usual credo was that a man needing money badly was automatically a prime suspect in any case of wrongdoing that came his way.

'Certainly not, sir,' said Sloan robustly. 'Besides, the death of one childless beneficiary already has only increased the sum available to the survivors by a sixth. A sixth of what exactly, of course, we don't know.'

Leeyes grunted. 'Something divided by five instead of six doesn't usually amount to a hill of beans.'

'I reckon it would have to be a very big sum indeed to start with to get Culshaw's bakery out of trouble,' said Sloan. He wasn't a money man but even he could see that from the number of brackets indicating a loss on the balance sheet.

The superintendent leant back in his chair and gave it as his considered opinion that it wouldn't be all that long then before Clive Culshaw joined the down-and-outs on Berebury's streets. 'Which the mayor won't like,' he said. 'Or the natives there already.'

'No, sir. Or uniform, either, come to that.' Thankfully, it

wasn't up to his Criminal Investigation Department to sort out
the human detritus littering the streets of Berebury.

'They've got better things to do than make arrests under
the Vagrancy Act, which doesn't usually get you anywhere,
seeing that the offenders never have any money for fines,'
growled Leeyes. 'So what next, Sloan?'

'Something or nothing, sir. I don't know which yet. A bit
of Mayton family history, anyway. The SOCO found something
interesting in the deceased's cottage.'

'Makes a change,' grunted Leeyes. 'SOCO finding anything
interesting, I mean, beyond fingerprints and DNA.'

'Quite so, sir,' He coughed. 'It would appear that the
deceased had started to research her own family history –
the Mayton connection, that is.'

'Since when?'

'That we don't know yet, sir.'

'And?'

'We don't know why or what either, but it needs looking
into seeing as it could be tied up with this inheritance
business. I'm going out there as soon as I've heard from
Puckles to pick up her computer and take a look at what she
was doing with the family tree.'

'No stone unturned, eh?' said Leeyes, sounding unusually
jovial. 'You'll take Crosby with you, won't you? I'd rather he
was out of my hair. By the way, you're in court tomorrow
morning, aren't you?'

'Yes, sir. The Faunus and Melliflora case.'

'Make sure Crosby doesn't crash the car today, then. And
Sloan . . .'

'Sir?'

'If you win tomorrow, no grandstanding outside the court
afterwards, please, if you don't mind, whatever the public
relations people say. And no apologising if you don't win. I
don't like it either way.'

'Certainly not, sir,' said Sloan, who didn't either.

There was a neatly typed note from Miss Fennel awaiting
Sloan's return to his own desk. It stated that the firm had done
an exhaustive search of the birth and death registers and had
thus established from these the bona fides of all of those whom

they considered eligible beneficiaries under the terms of the Mayton Trust. Puckle, Puckle and Nunnery, the note stated, had no reason to suppose that all of the potential recipients of the trust money whom they had listed were other than legitimate claimants.

Or that there were any others.

Detective Inspector Sloan slipped the paper into his pocket and summoned Crosby. 'Bishop's Marbourne, please,' he said. 'And without undue haste, Crosby. I have to give evidence in another case tomorrow morning and would like to still be in one piece to do so.'

Mrs Doris Dyson welcomed the two policemen over the garden fence as they drove up to Pear Tree Cottage. 'I like to keep an eye on who's coming and going,' she said, dangling a set of keys. 'Want to have another look round, do you?'

Detective Inspector Sloan, who had in fact got another set of keys from Ted York, the coroner's officer, thanked her and let her lead the way in. 'I come in to see to the post and that sort of thing most days,' said the neighbour. 'There's been another postcard from the son of that old friend of hers. Can't rightly say where it's come from, though.'

Sloan peered at a blurred postmark and a picture of a snow-covered mountain and was very little the wiser himself. 'Could be Kashmir,' he decided, placing it carefully in his notebook, 'or Uzbekistan.'

'There was some other post,' she said, 'but they looked like bills and I've sent them on to her solicitor for him to pay, like he said to do.'

'Quite right,' said Sloan, who wished he could do the same with those that reached him.

'Come to have a look for anything in particular, have you?' she asked. 'I'll leave the windows open while you're here, Officer. Things start to smell musty if you leave a house shut up for too long.'

'We just want to have a general look around,' said Sloan vaguely. 'Oh, and to collect Mrs Port's computer while we're here.'

'I can't be doing with them things,' said Doris Dyson. 'But poor Sue, now she was never off hers.'

'They call them silver surfers,' offered Crosby. 'Oldies who use them a lot. Nothing better to do, I suppose,' he added with the insouciance of the young.

'She said she'd worked with them in her old job, so she knew all about them,' said Doris Dyson, leading the way into the cottage's dining room. 'Me, I wouldn't know what do with one. Nasty things that know too much about you.'

'If you let them,' agreed Sloan. The deceased's computer sat on the edge of the dining-room table. He carefully saved what was on it, then shut it down, unplugged it and put it to one side to take away with them. The rest of the table was taken up, just as the coroner's officer had said, with what looked like the underside of a roll of wallpaper. On this were numerous scribbles under a set of names, starting at the top of a pyramid with the name of Algernon Culver Mayton at its apex.

Detective Inspector Sloan rolled this up, pointing out to Crosby the names of the six beneficiaries of the Mayton Trust, which ran along the base of the pyramid. 'Just as in the case of the Culshaw Bakery accounts, Crosby, I suspect it's the bottom line that matters.'

It was at exactly a quarter to seven on the Thursday evening when Jim Stopford's mobile telephone rang. He was just on his way to his car and stopped in the farmyard to answer it.

A voice said that he was ringing from the reception desk at the Bellingham Hotel in Berebury. 'I'm very sorry to say, sir, that we're experiencing a considerable power outage here. I'm afraid that the electricians have told us that it will take some time to restore the power, so we've had to cancel all this evening's bookings and I'm told that you were one of those expected.'

'I am – I mean, I was.'

'However, sir,' went on the voice, 'I'm happy to say that the Almstone Towers Hotel has agreed to take all our customers this evening.'

'It's big enough,' conceded Stopford. 'But a bit posh for rugby players.'

'Indeed, sir. I take it you know how to get there?'

'Sure, but it's a fair way from Capstan Purlieu so I'd better get cracking.' Stopford switched the phone off and made for his car. Almstone village was well off his usual route so he knew he would have to step on it if he was going to make it for half past seven. He managed the journey with minutes to spare, drawing up with a screech of brakes in front the hotel's impressive green awning lined with bay trees.

As he did so a uniformed figure emerged out of the shadows of the entrance and said, 'From the Bellingham, sir?'

'That's right,' said Stopford, opening the car door. 'For the Berebury Rugby Club meeting.'

Trevor Skewis, trainee assistant manager at the Almstone Towers luxury hotel, and conscious of the very considerable tip presently residing in his back pocket, went into his well-rehearsed spiel. 'I'm terribly sorry, sir, but we've had to send your party over to the City Arms at Calleford tonight. We're having a big conference here at the Almstone Towers ourselves and couldn't accommodate any extra bookings.'

'Calleford? Good Lord, that's miles away.'

'I do apologise, sir. In the ordinary way we'd have been happy to help the Bellingham out. I may say the others in your party left some time ago.'

Jim Stopford didn't bother to reply. Instead he revved up his engine, did a quick U-turn and was soon gone while Trevor Skewis faded back into the shadows of the entrance to the Almstone Towers portico, patting his back pocket in a very satisfied way indeed as he did so.

Jim Stopford had a very different reception at the City Arms in Calleford when he finally skidded to a halt in their car park and hurried inside. The receptionist made it abundantly clear that she had never heard of the electricity outage at the Bellingham in Berebury or the conference at the Almstone Towers Hotel.

Or, indeed, the Berebury Rugby Club.

SIXTEEN

C live Culshaw decided that he would begin his quest for the missing Daniel Elland at that evening's monthly meeting of the Berebury Chamber of Trade while his wife was safely occupied at her bridge club. He could most easily canvass its members there. After the speaker had said his piece the businessmen congregated round the bar for their usual drinks and gossip. 'Anyone know what became of Daniel Elland?' he asked the man standing next to him at the bar as casually as he could.

'Went to the wall,' answered the man, unaware that it was an ancient way of describing those too old and frail to stand through a church service.

'I heard he got caught out by a very big outfit over Luston way that went broke owing him zillions,' said a man on his other side, overhearing them. He himself ran a furniture store on the high street and gave credit to no one.

'Big mistake to put all your eggs in one basket,' contributed another man sententiously. A successful optician, he'd never taken a financial risk in his working life.

'There's many a man walking the Embankment because he didn't pull trumps,' said Clive Culshaw elliptically. It was a well-known bridge expression he'd picked up from his wife over the years.

'Big customers are always dangerous,' opined someone else. He was an ironmonger whose clientele seldom bought more than one item at a time. 'They get above themselves.'

'Sure thing,' agreed Culshaw, most of whose customers were quite small, too. Actually, he could have wished some of them were a bit bigger and as usual he anathematised all diet gurus in his mind in passing.

'I heard Elland lost everything,' said the first man.

'Game over,' contributed the owner of a shop that sold computer ones, who was doing very nicely, thank you.

'Could happen to anyone,' murmured someone nearby more sympathetically as a corporate shudder passed through the group.

'True,' said Culshaw with real feeling. Those accounts from Fixby and Fixby had really frightened him. But not half as much as the thought of what his late mother would have said. 'Another drink, anyone?'

'Don't mind if I do,' said his neighbour, setting down his empty glass on the bar. 'Elland was damned unlucky if you ask me. Decent chap. Just as well there were no children.'

'It seems Berebury Sound Ltd wasn't sound after all,' said the wag of the group.

'I heard he'd taken to the bottle,' said a passing trader. 'Don't blame him if he did. Nothing else left. I'll have another gin and tonic if it's all right with you, Culshaw.'

'Probably living in the stews of Berebury,' added the wag, who had no idea what or where stews were. 'No room at the inn, anyway. Or anywhere else, come to that.'

'Some of those dropouts down by the Postern Gate in Water Lane tried kipping under cover at the back of my supermarket,' said its owner. He took a sip of his drink. 'I soon put a stop to that.'

'What's a postern gate?' asked a newcomer to the town. He was hoping to do well in selling saddlery to the horse riders roundabout.

The man next to him grinned. 'You should know that in your line. It's a medieval gate only big enough for a man, not a horse.'

'Elland? I heard he'd dropped out of circulation like a stone after being made bankrupt,' contributed their chairman, a banker, inching his way to the crowded bar. He was always careful never to say anything directly attributable to himself. Or his bank. Elland hadn't been his customer; time was, though, when he wished he had been, his business once having been so successful.

'Don't blame him dropping out,' said someone else. 'I'd have done the same myself in his place. Never heard what became of him after that – went to the dogs, I expect. By the way, Culshaw, I heard your brother did a good job for an old friend of mine the other day. He's a real lateral thinker, isn't he? Quite ingenious.'

'He doesn't seem to mind what he takes on these days,' said Clive Culshaw amiably enough but who always hated any mention of his brother. 'Jobs that other people can't or won't do, certainly,' he gave a light laugh, 'but business tycoon he surely isn't.'

'Likes a challenge, I expect,' said the chairman, passing on.

Clive Culshaw came away from the meeting aware that he was no nearer finding his quarry in the streets of Berebury or anywhere else. It didn't help that he had no idea at all – distant relative or not – of what the man even looked like or what name he might be using now. Probably not his own. He didn't even know if the Mayton family shared any facial characteristics.

Or if they did, what they were. In any case, as far as he was concerned family likeness was not a good thing.

Sister Samantha Peters regarded the two dishevelled and injured men in front of her in the Accident and Emergency Department of Berebury Hospital later that evening and then looked at her watch. It was nearly midnight. 'It's too late in the day for you two to have been playing rugby,' she concluded. 'Besides, it's dark now.'

'We weren't,' muttered Martin Pickford. He sounded as if he had a broken nose.

'Have the pair of you taken up boxing instead, then?' the nurse asked drily. 'Or Sumo wrestling, perhaps?' she suggested.

'Sort of,' mumbled Jim Stopford. He too had a missing tooth now. He pointed at his adversary. 'He was playing a much nastier game than rugby, I can tell you, Sister.'

'I noticed that you two came in the same ambulance. Does it,' she enquired icily, 'by any chance mean that your injuries are connected?'

'Got it in one, Sister,' lisped Jim Stopford, who was having difficulty in speaking between rapidly swelling lips.

'Connected in a way, Samantha,' admitted Martin Pickford. 'He hit me first.'

She turned on him. 'I've told you before now that when you're here you call me Sister.'

'Yes, Sister.' He hung his head penitently. 'Sorry, Sister.'

'And there was I,' she marvelled, 'thinking that Thursday was a quiet evening and that I'd take Friday as my night off this week instead because that's usually very busy.'

'His fault, not mine,' muttered Jim Stopford. 'He started it.'

Martin Pickford flushed. 'I didn't say it was your fault. I said I was blaming you.'

'I like that,' spluttered Jim Stopford. 'Splitting hairs.'

'Even so, Sister, he didn't need to go for me like he did.'

'I did need to,' growled Stopford. 'You rotten, deceitful bastard, you. Of all the dirty, low-down tricks to play on a fellow player . . .'

'How did you know it was me, anyway?' the other man responded.

'Because nobody else had any interest at all in keeping me away from the selection board for the county team, that's why, you cunning toad,' he hissed.

'It worked, though, didn't it?' smirked Pickford. 'I'm in the team and you aren't. The selection committee put you down as a "No Show".'

'I'll tell them what you did and get you banned from the game, if it's the last thing I do.'

'Too late, mate. They've offered me a trial place in Saturday's match against that crack side that calls themselves the "Calleshire Wanderers". I'll be playing for our side this week.'

'Not if I've got anything to do with it, you won't,' snarled Jim Stopford indistinctly. No lightweight, he started to move aggressively towards the other man, his right fist clenched.

'That will do,' pronounced Sister Samantha Peters, in a tone of voice honed by centuries of a nursing tradition founded by Florence Nightingale in the Crimea. It carried an authority that could have given points to a company sergeant major. 'Or I will call security and they – whether you like it or not – will call the police, who will undoubtedly charge you with assault. Both of you,' she added, taking in the injuries to each of them.

'He started it,' insisted Pickford.

'That's rich coming from you,' said Stopford scornfully, 'after what you'd done. You . . . you . . .' At this point words failed him and he subsided rather suddenly on to a chair.

'There was I, Samantha . . . Sister, sitting quietly in the bar at the Bellingham Hotel . . .'

'Which hadn't had a power cut at all,' muttered Stopford indignantly.

Pickford carried on, undeterred. 'Sitting in the bar, chilling out with a peaceful pint with some other players, when this lunatic comes rushing in and starts knocking me about.'

'Peaceful be damned,' snapped Stopford. 'He was sitting there gloating. I'm the better player – he shouldn't have been there at all. It's me who should have been in the county team and he should have been in here with all those deadbeats over there.' He waved a hand in the direction of a couple of unshaven men walking unsteadily into the unit. One of them had string round his jacket, the other sported an overcoat worthy of a fashion museum.

The sight of them spurred Martin Pickford into speech with an idea. 'I say, Sister, you haven't ever had that man Daniel Elland in here, have you? Much the worse for wear and all that?'

'I have no idea and wouldn't tell you if I had,' she said tartly. 'Mostly when those types come in they either refuse to give us their names at all or use false ones. Jack the Ripper's quite common, but patient confidentiality still holds.'

'Afraid of the police, I suppose,' murmured Stopford, temporarily forgetting his own troubles.

'Police? You're joking. This lot couldn't care less about the police.' Sister Peters gave an ironic smile. 'No, what they're frightened of are social services who want to make sure that they have a bath.'

'I can see why. They stink.'

'And they don't like do-gooders who want them to come off the drink, either,' she added.

'Fat chance of that,' said Pickford. 'Now, about my nose . . .'

But Sister Peters wasn't listening. She'd gone for a wound trolley.

*   *   *

It was the middle of the afternoon the next day when Detective Inspector Sloan got back from attending the Crown Court in the county town of Calleford. He had duly been sworn in and in due course given his evidence in the Faunus and Melliflora case. He'd spotted the two defendants exchanging glances in the dock as he did so and then saw the older one of them sending a note to their defence counsel.

That gentleman rose to his feet and swept his gown round him in a theatrical gesture that would have done credit to a thespian, which perhaps after all was what the barrister was at heart. His clients, he announced after a brief consultation with them, had decided to change their pleas to guilty, but would have a great deal to offer in the way of mitigation.

The judge, old and unsurprised, adjourned the case for sentencing later and Sloan got away without being cross-examined. And much sooner than he had thought he would. A guilty plea didn't provoke the public interest of a ding-dong court battle, especially without the savour of sentencing. This was something he always considered ghoulish, and he thus was also able to leave the Crown Court at Calleford without having to make a statement about the case to the press. He made his way back to the police station and checked in the wallet of papers that he had taken with him. He then joined his friend, Inspector Harpe of Traffic Division, for a bite of lunch in the canteen.

'Mitigation? That lot?' said Harpe. 'That's rich, that is.'

'They'll think of something,' said Sloan realistically. 'Or their brief will.'

'True. By the way, Seedy, you might have a word with that young constable of yours . . .'

'He's not mine,' protested Sloan with some vigour.

'Well, whoever he is, you can tell him from me that he shouldn't be practising doughnuts in our car park after the super's gone home.'

The unexpected release from the Faunus and Melliflora case had left Sloan oddly deflated, but it gave him his first chance to study the Mayton family tree on which Susan Port had been working on her computer so assiduously. He went back to his

desk to take a good look at it and at the same time study the
message from Simon Puckle. Whilst the solicitor had simply
stated that he had had the lineal descent from Algernon
Mayton of all six beneficiaries checked out beyond doubt, the
late Susan Port had gone into greater detail, especially with
her own family tree. And beside the name of Tom Culshaw
she had put a small question mark.

'I can't explain it, Margaret,' he said later that evening to
his wife, 'unless she had somehow found out that he wasn't
his father's child in spite of his birth certificate saying that he
was.' The two of them were sitting companionably together,
drinking coffee at their fireside. 'That would put the cat among
the pigeons with a vengeance, because it would put him out
of the running for Algernon's money. The old boy sounds to
have been pretty strait-laced.'

'Except in the little matter of duping the public with his
product,' she pointed out.

Detective Inspector Sloan, world-weary policeman, said that
was different.

'Though you did say, Chris, that the two brothers seemed
to be permanently at loggerheads.'

He shook his head. 'Brothers can be like that.'

'Are there any family characteristics shared by the pair that
would help?' Unspoken was a decision still to be made by the
Sloans whether or not to have a sibling for their small son.

Sloan thought about this. 'They're about the same height.
I wouldn't know about the colour of their eyes – I'd have to
look at them both again. They have roughly the same sort of
physique – that's something that usually runs in families – but
then they do share a mother. That seems certain enough.'

'All the same, Susan Port must have had a reason for
querying something,' argued Margaret Sloan. 'She doesn't
sound to have been silly.'

'She wasn't. She had the details of the birth certificates of
all the legatees on her computer and the marriage certificates
of those of them whose inheritance comes through their
mothers.'

Margaret Sloan's head came up at that. In her own way she
was as much a feminist as Woman Sergeant Perkins.

'To account for the different surnames,' said her husband hastily. 'Martin Pickford, for instance. His father doesn't come in to it.'

'More coffee?' she asked.

'Why not,' he said, passing her his cup. 'As I don't seem to be getting anywhere with the case.'

'Don't forget what Izaak Walton wrote, Chris,' she said, picking up her own cup, too. 'You've often said to remember what he said about the good angler.'

'A good angler isn't always a good detective, my love.'

'Oh, yes, he is,' she retorted. 'I haven't forgotten what he thought, even if you have.'

'What was that?' asked Sloan, who had indeed forgotten.

'He said the good angler not only brings an enquiring, searching and observing wit, but he must bring a large measure of hope and patience to the art.'

'So he did,' conceded Sloan. He hadn't realised his wife took his work so seriously. He admitted now that he'd got plenty of patience but not a lot of hope in the matter of the death of Susan Mary Port.

'Tomorrow is a new day and something might come up,' she said, yawning.

What did come up first thing the next morning was a frantic telephone call to the police station from an agitated woman who insisted on only speaking to Detective Inspector Sloan.

'It's Doris Dyson,' she gasped down the line, 'from Bishop's Marbourne. I've just gone in next door to see to the post and there's a dead man lying on the garden path.'

SEVENTEEN

At very much the same time Martin Pickford was knocking on the door of the home of Tom Culshaw. This also doubled as the offices of his firm, Gordian Knots Cut. Tom answered the knock himself. 'Good Lord, Pickford, what on earth's happened to you?'

'Nothing. I'm fine. It all went a treat.'

Tom Culshaw grinned. 'Did the best man win, then?'

'I'll say he did,' Pickford managed to utter between swollen lips. He had an incipient black eye, too.

'Ah, well I suppose all's fair in love and war.' Culshaw stood aside. 'You'd better come in.'

'You should see the other fellow,' mumbled Pickford, whom it obviously hurt to speak.

'Some husbands can be like that,' said Tom Culshaw, the nature of whose work had taught him a lot.

'It wasn't a husband.'

'Your rival in love, then.'

'Sort of,' said Pickford. 'But as I was over near you for the match at Calleford this afternoon I thought I'd look in and settle up.'

Tom Culshaw looked blank. 'Match?'

'At the county ground at Calleford. I'm on trial for their first fifteen today.'

Tom Culshaw's brow cleared. 'Ah, rugby. Of course, it's a Saturday.' He stared at the other man's face again. 'I see, these injuries are all from the game, are they?'

'Not quite all, old man, but most of them are, one way and another. Now, what do I owe Gordian Knots for all their good works?'

'Seeing as you're family,' said the other man slowly, 'I don't think I should charge you.' What he didn't say was that if there was any comeback from anybody's injuries he didn't want to be involved. Not that he himself had done anything other than follow a client's instructions but he still wasn't at all sure what Martin Pickford had been up to.

'That's what we rugby players call a nice try, Culshaw, but I'm not having any of that. I can pay my own way.' Martin Pickford opened his bad eye briefly, the better to take in the modest surroundings of Tom Culshaw's home. 'By the way, why haven't you started looking for Daniel Elland yourself?'

'The missing man?'

'Yes. Then we could all get our share of the dosh. Gordian Knots ought to be able to find him even if nobody else can. After all, you do specialise in doing odd jobs. You said so.'

'That's a thought,' agreed the other man. 'I'll have to think about it. I don't know that I'll get very far if nobody else has, though.'

'You did very well with me,' said Martin Pickford warmly. 'Better than I ever expected.'

'I'll think about it,' Tom Culshaw repeated.

The man out at Bishop's Marbourne wasn't dead. He was, though, giving a very good appearance of being so.

The first thing Detective Inspector Sloan did when he realised this was to reach for his mobile phone and send for an ambulance. The man was lying, flat out, face down, on the doorstep of Pear Tree Cottage, a nasty bruise still welling up on the back of his head. He spoke to him, but the man was quite unresponsive.

Mrs Doris Dyson was standing beside the prone figure, arms folded akimbo in front of her, as if to ward off further attack. 'Found him this morning, I did, Inspector, when I come across to see to the post like always, not that there was any. Must've been lying out here all night, but hubby and me always go to the Red Lion Friday nights for a game of cribbage.'

'Do you know who he is?' asked Sloan, stooping to feel the man's clammy hand and hoping that the ambulance wouldn't take too long to get there.

'Never seen him in my life before,' she said. 'He could be anyone. He's not from round here, that's for sure.'

Detective Constable Crosby came round the corner of the cottage at that moment and said, 'Break-in at the back, sir. Kitchen window forced.' He peered down doubtfully at the recumbent figure lying athwart the front doorstep. 'I don't like the look of him, sir.'

'Nor do I, Crosby,' said Sloan. 'And hit from behind, too, which means he might not know who by.'

'That's if he ever wakes up,' said Crosby, slowly taking in the victim's injuries. 'Not that that looks to me all that likely just now.'

'Notice anything else, Crosby?' asked Sloan, belatedly remembering his official role as tutor of jejune constables.

'He could have been here all night, sir. It would have

been cold lying out on these flags. His clothes are a bit damp, too.'

'Dew,' pronounced Mrs Dyson with the authority of an old countrywoman. 'Always plenty of dew mornings this time of year.'

'Quite so,' murmured Sloan. 'What we don't know is whether someone was lying in wait for him or if he surprised someone.'

'Who?' demanded Mrs Dyson. 'That's what I'd like to know.'

'That we don't know, either,' said Sloan.

'And why?' put in Crosby.

'Exactly,' said Sloan. While he said he didn't know that either, he chalked up that Crosby was at least thinking. And thinking aloud, to boot, as well as asking the right questions. Asking the right questions was what made a good detective. He lifted his own head like a pointer, hoping that what he could hear in the far distance was a siren wailing, heralding the approach of the ambulance. Victim or assailant, the injured always belonged first to the medical profession, then and only then, to the police force.

'Quite sunburnt, isn't he, sir, for now?' said Crosby.

'True,' said Sloan. Perhaps the constable might make a detective after all. He made a note to ring his old friend, Ted York, the coroner's officer. That policeman knew something, although not a lot, about a certain young man said to be travelling to England to see his mother's old friend, Susan Port. What neither he, Chris Sloan, nor Ted York knew, though, was what, if anything, the young man in question had known about his potential future inheritance.

It might matter. If it was him, that is.

Prompted by this thought and conscious of the need for speed, Sloan swiftly and carefully felt through such pockets as he could reach without disturbing the injured man. There was certainly no wallet in his back pocket now. Someone, presumably his assailant, had been there before him. And that someone had presumably also removed any luggage if the man had had any since there was none visible.

The mechanical caterwauling grew louder, and it was not long before the ambulance fetched up outside the front of Pear

Tree Cottage, blue lights flashing. Two uniformed men spilt out of it and made their way up the front path at speed.

'Nasty-looking head injury,' said Sloan briefly. 'Unknown male. Looks like a hospital job to me.'

The leader nodded and immediately produced two blocks to secure the man's head and a pen torch, which he managed to shine in the man's eyes, his mate opening up a blood pressure instrument the while. Sloan watched the two paramedics go through their routine without interrupting them. Eventually the senior man straightened up and announced that they were dealing with a casualty who was at four on the Glasgow Coma Scale.

'Is that good or bad?' Sloan asked.

'Not good,' said the ambulance man, emulating the ambivalent understatement ingrained in all the medical professions. 'We need to get him to hospital ASAP.'

But it was only when the leading man promised that they would be careful not to destroy a crime scene that Sloan realised that police and ambulancemen were of the same mind. He took out his notebook and instructed Crosby to take photographs of the man's face and position on the ground. He watched as the two paramedics fixed the man's head further still with two more blocks to steady it and load the unconscious casualty on to their stretcher with an almost maternal tenderness. 'Then, Crosby, we'll be going inside the house,' Sloan said.

What Detective Constable Crosby said as he focussed his camera on the face of the unconscious man was 'Say "cheese".'

EIGHTEEN

'So what's going on out at Bishop's Marbourne, then, Sloan?' demanded Superintendent Leeyes, who was sitting in the comfort of his own office. He was always there at the police station on Saturday mornings since Sunday ones were sacrosanct to the golf course and nothing – but nothing – was allowed to become between him and his standing on the first tee there, addressing the ball with his driver.

'I don't really know, sir,' admitted Sloan who, given the choice, would have preferred to have been standing in his own garden, lightly autumn-pruning his roses. 'The man found outside Pear Tree Cottage is still just about alive but that's all. I'm putting a team on bed watch as soon as the victim's taken to the ward, to be on the safe side. He hasn't started to come round yet and the hospital can't – or won't – tell me if he's ever going to.'

'Cagey blokes, doctors,' said Leeyes, who never allowed for any member of the medical profession being female.

'They won't commit themselves to anything at all yet, sir,' agreed Sloan. 'We've been over everything the man was wearing and there's not much in the way of clues there as to who he is, except he had on stout shoes that weren't made in England. He might have been living rough, but we can't be sure at this stage. He was muscular enough.'

The superintendent's head came up with a jerk. 'I'm fed up with men with no fixed addresses littering up the town. Anything else?'

'He's not undernourished and there are no signs of drug use on his person.'

'I suppose that's something these days, Sloan.'

'He could have done with a haircut as well, sir.'

In Superintendent Leeyes' view all young men could do with a haircut. He grunted. 'I suppose we should be thankful that he hasn't been mainlining.'

'Yes, sir.' He hesitated. 'PC York and I wonder if he could be the deceased's godson.'

'Come to see what he can collect?'

'We don't know that either, sir, but it's a thought.'

'If he's been travelling round the world, then what about his luggage? Any clues there?'

'If he had anything with him, including his wallet, it wasn't there when we arrived. No means of identification at all.'

'And there'd been a break-in there, you say?'

'At the back.'

'Anything missing?'

'We can't say yet, sir,' Sloan said. 'At first glance nothing looks to have been disturbed, but scenes of crime are on their way back there now. There's no luggage in sight at all, either. Whoever clobbered him would seem to have made off with it, that's if he ever had any with him in the first place. He could have left it in a hotel somewhere. We're checking to see if he's booked in anywhere local and left his luggage there.'

'This computer, Sloan, that you seem to have got hold of – without a warrant, if I may say so – what's on that?'

'Too soon to say, sir. It's being looked into further now, but it could have been the family history that someone might have been after – there's plenty of that in there. It's only a possibility but nothing else that I could see at first glance looks at all interesting. Simon Puckle, though, is quite sure everything is hunky-dory from his perspective.'

'Solicitors,' said Leeyes weightily, 'have different perspectives from normal men.' The superintendent riffled about among the papers on his desk, finally producing one and holding it up. 'Talking about the family history of the Maytons, there's a report here that one of them caused ructions at the Bellingham on Thursday night.'

Sloan looked up. 'Sir?'

Leeyes regarded the piece of paper in his hand. 'Martin Pickford – he's one of your Maytons, isn't he?'

Sloan nodded.

'He seems to have had an altercation with a man called Jim Stopford that got a bit out of hand. The manager threw them both out for using bad language. Can't have that in a respectable establishment like the Bellingham, Sloan. Not on my patch, anyway. I won't have it.'

'No, sir, certainly not.' Sloan frowned, searching his memory, and then it came back to him. There had been a memorable literature course once taken by the superintendent. It had been called 'Before the Bard' and had featured, among other early writers, the book *Pantagruel* by the author François Rabelais, a noted user of really ripe language. As he remembered, Leeyes had been preparing to charge the lecturer for his overenthusiastic quotations of Rabelais' robust humour on the grounds that by doing so the man was also committing an offence against public decency. Arguing that the author was both a monk and a doctor didn't get the lecturer off the hook as far as the superintendent was concerned and Leeyes had had to be removed from the class in a hurry, the lecturer muttering about true scholarship and academic freedom the while.

Sloan said hastily now, 'I can't for the life of me fathom why, sir, a fight in a bar on Thursday night involving Martin Pickford might have got anything to do with the Mayton money or the death of Susan Port.'

'Nor me, Sloan,' Superintendent Leeyes said soberly, 'but it looks as if it might be for the life of somebody else. Find out who.'

'A run in the country for you, Crosby,' said Sloan, walking into the station yard.

The constable, who had brought the car round, perked up immediately.

'We need to go to Capstan Purlieu – it's not Darkest Africa but it's still a long way out there.'

Crosby opened the car door with alacrity.

'But I am happy to say that time,' said Sloan, 'is not of the essence.'

'Come again, sir?'

'It means there's no hurry.'

'I get you, sir. And where exactly would we be heading for?'

'A farm called Hillside and a man called Jim Stopford.'

'The one who duffed someone up at the Bellingham on Thursday night?'

'None other.'

'Ah.' The detective constable settled down to the drive, soon leaving the town behind, and following one country road after another, eventually turned off a two-way one onto a single track. This did not suit his style of driving, neither did the constant warning to beware of sheep. He pulled into a passing place to let a tractor go by and into another when he had to give way to a farm lorry.

'I heard that this guy Stopford had just walked straight into the bar of the Bellingham and started hitting a man sitting there,' said Crosby presently, the farm lorry now well on its way. 'And that the other man gave back as good as he got.'

'Magistrates don't like aggression in any shape or form wherever it comes from. But that's not what this is all about,' said Sloan.

'No, sir?' Crosby spotted another tractor coming towards them and put his foot down on the accelerator to get the car into a position where it was the tractor that would have to back up the narrow road, not him. 'But sir, why are we going to see him and not leaving it to uniform? We don't usually do common assault.'

It was Sloan's mother who had inculcated in him the fact that everyone – but everyone, as William Thackeray had written – was snobbish about something. Crosby had unwittingly demonstrated just that.

'The other man in that fight was a Mayton legatee, Crosby, which is why we're going to see this man Stopford. And the late Susan Port was a Mayton legatee, too, and a man who visited her house is still lying unconscious in hospital – and there's another Mayton legatee somewhere unaccounted for. I want to talk to this man Stopford before seeing any other Maytons and before someone hits any more of them, too. There's something else besides . . .'

'Sir?'

'On Thursday evening, while Martin Pickford was sitting in the Bellingham bar, a stranger checked in to the hotel for four nights, giving his name as Terry Galloway, which is the name of Susan Port's godson who PC York says is usually domiciled in Australia. The hotel told me that he spent Thursday night there but went out on Friday leaving his luggage there and hasn't been back since.'

'The man out at Bishop's Marbourne?'

'Could be. Forensics are doing a DNA check as we speak.' Sloan wasn't entirely convinced about this, seeing it was a Saturday, but he didn't say so. 'Then they can match it with the luggage at the Bellingham.'

'Or not,' said Crosby.

'Or not,' agreed Sloan.

Jim Stopford was crossing the farmyard when the police

car arrived. 'I hope you're going to charge that man Pickford with assault and battery,' he said when he saw them.

'We need to know first how well you know him, sir.' Stranger danger usually meant something different, but it was still relevant.

'Know him?' howled Stopford. 'Of course I know him – too well, if you ask me. I've played rugby with him for years. We were both up for the county team and he engineered things so that I missed the selection meeting, rotten toad.'

'How?' asked Sloan. 'You told my officer on Thursday night that you'd been led halfway across the county. Pickford couldn't have done that while he was at the Bellingham all evening, which he certainly was.'

'I know that,' muttered Stopford. 'He must have had help from someone, somehow, but he won't let on who.'

'"Accomplice" is the word we use,' Detective Constable Crosby informed him.

'Partner in crime, more like,' growled Stopford.

'But you don't know who?'

'Or care,' snapped Stopford. 'I should have been playing in the county trials this afternoon, not him, and that's all I care about.' He glared at Sloan. 'Go ahead and charge me for assaulting him. I don't care about that either. It was worth it.'

Back in the police car after this interview, Crosby said, 'That was a wasted journey, sir, if ever there was one.'

'Not entirely, Crosby. Get going back now and then I want you to pull up by that field on the left. The third one down. Stop near the gate while I get out.'

'If you say so, sir.'

Detective Inspector Sloan climbed out of the police car and made his way into an almost bare field. Crosby watched as he stooped and scooped something up from the ground and dropped it into an evidence bag.

'Right, Crosby,' he said, back in the car. 'You can get moving again now.'

'Yes, sir.' The constable glanced down at the bag in Sloan's hand. 'Was there something there, sir?'

'A pocketful of rye, Crosby.' Detective Inspector Sloan waved a hand in the direction of the field. 'We'll leave the four and twenty blackbirds where they are. We don't need them.'

NINETEEN

By evening Sloan was back at his home in Berebury, a disappointed man. Sitting at his own fireside going over a case in his mind for the umpteenth time was in his view no way for a married man and father to be spending a family Saturday night.

'Bad day?' asked his wife, after he had sat silent, staring at the fire for too long.

'What? Oh, sorry. Yes.' He sat up straighter and said, 'We're not getting anywhere with the death of Susan Port. In fact, we seem to be going backwards. I had high hopes of ergot being found in either the loaves in her house or the flour she was using for baking, but it hasn't been.'

She nodded intelligently.

'Not only that,' said her husband. 'On top of it all there's now a badly injured man lying unconscious in hospital who may or may not have anything to do with the case.'

'The godson?'

He nodded. 'Terry Galloway, we're pretty sure. At least there's not a lot of doubt about that. We think he's the man who left his rucksack at the Bellingham when he checked in there on Thursday evening. Passport, letters from Mrs Port saying she was looking forward to seeing him, spare kit – the lot – all in his room. No, that's not quite true. He'd lodged his passport and money in the hotel safe.'

'Nobody's fool, then,' observed Margaret Sloan.

'It didn't do him any good. He's still hasn't come round, although the ward sister at the hospital did tell me that they thought he would be doing so pretty soon. Apparently, they can see signs of it after a head injury that a layman can't.'

'Everyone's a specialist these days,' she said.

'Sure, except policemen. We're just maids of all work.'

'Now, now,' she chided him.

'I've just come from the hospital, anyway, checking that the bed watch is set up there for the night.'

'You think he's still in danger?'

'I don't know what to think,' growled Sloan morosely. 'We can only surmise that it was the intruder who dotted him on the head.'

'It seems likely,' observed his wife.

'"Seems likely" isn't evidence,' he came back quickly.

Too quickly.

'Sorry, love. I'd forgotten I wasn't still at work.'

'You are,' she said drily.

'So we don't even know whether this man Galloway knew whether his godmother was already dead or if he knew that he was her sole beneficiary.' He paused. 'Actually, he still may be that, but he won't be getting any of the Mayton money, for sure. That's because she'd died—'

'Or been killed,' pointed out Margaret Sloan.

'Or been killed,' he said, accepting the amendment, 'before the trust could be wound up. There'll be nothing for him now from that quarter.'

'So that it still means that there's more money for the others?'

'Yes, it doesn't change anything else in that way,' he said.

'So why was he hit on the head?' Margaret Sloan frowned.

'The only reason that I can think of is that he saw someone at or in the house whom theoretically he might be able to recognise at some stage but who didn't want to be seen.'

'And what was anyone doing in the house anyway?'

'That we don't know either.' He sighed. 'If whoever it was had come looking for the computer, they were out of luck. That's sitting safely down at the station.' He shrugged his shoulders. 'And much good that'll do anyone, anyway. I've already told you that I've stared at it until I'm blue in the face. All the Mayton legatees look as if they've got cast-iron claims to the money. Simon Puckle had got all their descents from old Algernon laid out in just the same way – an unbroken line through whichever parent – father or mother – descended from him. We don't even know if it's relevant.'

'Difficult.' Margaret Sloan knitted her eyebrows together. 'Anything else in the computer that might come into it?'

'We've got the specialists looking at it now, but they always take their time. There was just the one thing that I told you about – the pencil question mark on the family tree after Tom Culshaw's name that Susan Port'd printed out from the computer.'

'But she didn't say why?'

He shook his head. 'Nope. Obviously, we'll be interviewing him soonest.'

'So what else beside the computer might the intruder have come to Mrs Port's cottage for?'

'Search me. It's just one more of the things we don't know.' He sighed again. 'I can't even say that I know what the death of Susan Port is all about. I wish I did.'

'Money,' said Margaret Sloan decisively, unconsciously echoing Superintendent Leeyes. 'Must be, if there's such a lot of it about.'

In the ordinary way Saturday evening was the best one of the week for Clive Culshaw. This was because it was the only night that he could stay up late and have a drink or two with impunity, Sunday morning not requiring him to be early at the bakery. It was the one evening, too, that by long convention his wife didn't head out to her bridge club. She usually made a point of staying in unless, that is, there was a really important match.

'It's against the Calleford Duplicate Club, dear,' she began tentatively, 'and I'd really like to play. The captain wants me to partner him. That's a real feather in my cap – he's such a good player.'

Clive Culshaw couldn't have been more magnanimous. 'You go, dear,' he said kindly, 'and have a good evening. Mind you and the captain win, now . . .'

She had barely left the house before he headed out himself. He made first for the Bellingham Hotel, parked his car in their car park and had a quick drink at the bar to validate its being

left there. Then he walked into the town, making for the east
and least salubrious quarter of it by the Postern Gate. It was
down by the river that the members of the congregation of St
Peter's Church there handed out soup to the down-and-outs
on cold nights. He soon found a man he decided was John
Holness, of his charity Latchless, presiding over a line of men
he himself mentally categorised as undesirables. John Holness
on the other hand, clearly saw them as human beings in need
of the help that he and his friends gave them.

Culshaw waited until there was a little lull in the queue for
hot soup and then went up to him and asked if indeed he was
the John Holness from Latchless.

'Yes, I am. Have you come to give us a hand? We're always
glad of any help.'

'Not exactly. I'm looking for someone.'

Holness's face hardened. 'Then I can't help you. It's strictly
a policy of "no names" for helper or helpless here.'

'It would be to his advantage.'

'They all say that and what they mean is that we'll take
him home, clean him up and get him off the drink and he'll
be all right for ever afterwards. What we've learnt at Latchless
is that it doesn't work like that.'

'Very much to his advantage,' persisted Culshaw.

'Not always, it isn't, mate. If a man chooses to live like
this, then who are we to stop him?'

'His family,' said Clive Culshaw.

'They,' declared Holness richly, 'are nearly always what
drove the man here in the first place. As far as I'm concerned,
you can stuff families.' He looked suspiciously at Culshaw.
'You family?'

'Only in a manner of speaking.'

'So like I said, it'll be to your advantage to find him, then,
will it? Not his.'

Culshaw changed the subject. 'All I want is a name and
whether or not you've seen the man.'

'Well, you won't get either info from me, mate, I can tell
you, whoever you are. Our help, unlike that of most people, is
unconditional. We are adjured to feed the hungry and that
is exactly what we're doing. I'm afraid we can't harbour the

harbourless, though – not here.' He suddenly moved quickly across the table and shouted to a man stuffing bread into his pocket. 'You, there! Two slices of bread a head. Not ten for tomorrow.'

'I heard you,' said a man with a grizzled beard, shuffling away. 'No need to shout.'

Culshaw quoted a line in the song 'One Meatball'. 'Except,' he added lightly, 'it looks to me as if they don't get the meatball here, either.'

'Hunger,' Holness said stiffly, 'is not a suitable subject for humour.'

'I suppose not. By the way, the man I'm looking for is called Daniel Elland.'

'Most men here don't use their real names, especially if the police should happen to want to talk to them, too.' Holness gave a half-smile. 'Mickey Mouse is quite popular, although we do get Bonnie and Clyde now and then if there's a woman about. Or Napoleon. That's very popular and doesn't need a psychologist to explain it.'

'But,' Culshaw went on as if Holness hadn't spoken, 'if you do hear the name mentioned, I'd very much like to know.' He fished a business card out of his pocket and handed it over to John Holness.

The man from Latchless took it in his hand and read his name out aloud. 'Clive Culshaw? You're the bloke that owns that big bakery the other side of the railway, aren't you?'

Culshaw nodded.

'We've often wondered what you do with your leftovers – bread and cakes you haven't sold and such like,' said Holness.

'There's a farmer out in the country who takes it for his pigs.'

'Really?' Holness leant back on his heels and regarded Culshaw for a long moment. 'There's an old adage about pigs being equal.'

'Is there?'

'Well, I don't think they are.'

'No?'

'No. What I think is that people should have first go at good food.'

Culshaw, a salesman at heart, automatically tried to do a deal. 'And if I were to steer it your way, would I get to know if anyone called Daniel Elland hangs out here?'

'You most certainly would not,' barked Holness. 'We respect a man's privacy even if you don't.'

As far as Clive Culshaw was concerned that left him with just the one option: finding the man himself. He drifted off into the shadows much as those taking their soup had done and considered what to do next. He went up to a man squatting in a doorway, his dog beside him.

'It isn't Daniel Elland, is it?' he began politely. As an approach he thought it was as good as any. The man's dog apparently didn't think so because it drew its lips back in a snarl that exposed quite a lot of teeth. Culshaw withdrew without getting any response from the man himself.

He next tried the same approach on a bearded man too firmly attached to the neck of a wine bottle to speak. The man's companion shouted something so offensive at him that Clive Culshaw decided that it was better not to have heard it. Catching sight of a little convenience store in the distance he changed his plan and went over to it.

The shopkeeper presiding over it was more useful when Culshaw explained his quest. 'You won't get much help finding your Daniel Elland from anyone living on the streets. They've mostly fallen out with anything that smacks of authority long ago. This man you're looking for – how old would he be?'

'Late fifties, I should say. Sixty, perhaps.'

'Then look for someone looking ten years older. You don't age well without a roof over your head.' The man behind the counter moved over to serve a single can of beer to a man smelling to high heaven. 'What does he look like, this guy you're looking for?' he asked when he slid back along the counter in front of Culshaw.

Clive Culshaw had to confess that he didn't know. 'It's a bit of a needle in a haystack job, I'm afraid,' he said. 'It's a long shot that he's round here at all.'

'The place where you would have been likely to find most of them congregating is in that shelter behind the Berebury supermarket because it's dry, but the firm have rigged up one of those sonic deterrents to keep them out and now they're kipping all over the place. Doorways, mostly.'

Culshaw thanked him and resumed his search, turning into a promising-looking alley hoping to find someone who would talk to him without being seen. He hadn't gone very far when he felt himself being grabbed from behind. A hoarse voice hissed into his ear, 'You looking for Daniel Elland?'

Clive Culshaw gave his head a jerk in assent and tried to turn his head to face whoever it was who was speaking to him but found himself too tightly pinioned to move. 'Yes,' he said.

'So are we,' said his attacker. 'And we want to talk to the clever sod before anyone else does. Get it?'

It was the last thing Clive Culshaw remembered hearing before being poleaxed and flung to the ground.

TWENTY

'Sloan,' bellowed Superintendent Leeyes down the internal telephone at the police station. 'My office. Now.'

Standing in front of his superior officer in a bad mood first thing on a Monday morning was not for the faint-hearted. Sloan wondered if yesterday's golf had gone badly. 'Sir?'

'We need to talk,' began Leeyes.

'Yes, sir.' It wasn't sympathy for a bad round of golf that was required, then. 'Of course, sir.'

'About Terry Galloway, the man with the head injury.'

'Bad news, I'm afraid, sir. It was reported to us by the constable on bed watch that he died during Saturday night. We're treating his death as murder now.'

'That's what I've just heard. What happened?'

'The man on bed watch – Simmonds – said that nothing happened at all until about three o'clock in the morning when the alarm on Galloway's monitor went off. Red lights flashing, bells ringing – that sort of thing. The medical people rushed in and did what they could, but they couldn't keep him going.

Apparently, they tried all the resuscitation tricks in the book, but his heart gave out in the end.'

'They say that's when sailors die,' grunted Leeyes. 'Three o'clock in the morning. Everything's at a low ebb then. They go out with the tide.'

'Quite so, sir.' It wasn't the exact moment when the man died that so interested Sloan, it was why.

'And what are you doing about it, Sloan, may I ask?'

'We've arranged a post-mortem with Dr Dabbe for this afternoon and taken a full report from Simmonds. He's adamant that no one came near the deceased during the night other than the nursing staff when the alarm went off.'

'And that he didn't go to sleep, I suppose,' said Leeyes.

'Yes, sir. Simmonds says he made a point of talking to the nurses whenever they turned up.'

'I'll bet,' said Leeyes cynically. 'This Mayton business – has it got anything to do with his death?'

'I wish I knew myself, sir. It seems tangential, but it may not be.'

'Did this man Galloway come for that computer that you abstracted from the house or did somebody else, I wonder?'

'I don't know, sir.'

'You must always consider every possibility, Sloan,' said Leeyes, sanctimonious as ever.

'He might have come from Australia for the money if he knew about it, sir. We don't even know whether or not he did.' Sloan spared a thought for a fellow police officer who even as they spoke was probably knocking on a door in Australia with bad news and at the same time trying to glean what helpful information he could from a distraught family. A policeman's lot was seldom a happy one wherever he worked.

'And you tell me that he might not have known he wasn't going to get any of the Mayton money if his godmother had already died before that peculiar trust was wound up,' snorted Leeyes.

'Yes, sir.'

'Too much not knowing all round for my liking, Sloan.'

'And mine, too, sir.' Sloan drew breath and put another

thought into words. 'It seems to me that rather a lot hangs on the missing man, Daniel Elland. The one that they can't find.'

'And can't get at the money until they do. That right, Sloan?' Superintendent Leeyes had an innate suspicion of all professions and expressed one of them now. 'Could that solicitor fellow have anything to gain by not finding him and therefore not winding up this trust?'

'That I couldn't possibly say, sir,' said Sloan, stiffening.

'The fees won't stop until Daniel Elland does turn up,' deduced Leeyes ineluctably. 'So go find the man, Sloan.'

'Lunch is ready, Tom,' called out Sophie Culshaw, plonking a little basket of bread rolls down on their kitchen table. There was no response to this, so she tried calling out more loudly this time. 'The soup's getting cold.'

That did the trick. Tom Culshaw appeared from the room which they kept for the affairs of Gordian Knots Cut. 'Ah,' he said, rubbing his hands, 'tomato. My favourite.'

'Busy week ahead?' she asked, ladling the soup into warmed bowls. She was always the one concerned about the future prospects of the firm. Tom never was.

'No actual work,' he admitted, 'but plenty to think about.'

'How's that, then?'

'I thought I might take on something that nobody else has managed to do.'

She sighed. 'Turn base metal into gold?'

'You know I like doing what nobody else can.'

'I do know,' she said wearily. 'You don't have to tell me, but we do have to eat.'

'Don't be like that, dear.'

'What is it this time? Perpetual motion?'

'Finding Daniel Elland.'

'The missing Mayton man?'

'Him,' said her husband, reaching for more bread. 'Not even the professional enquiry agents can trace him.'

'And you think you can succeed when no one else has done?' she said.

He grinned. 'You know I like tackling the impossible.'

'I do indeed.'

'Especially,' he said, 'if the professionals have tried and failed.'

'The other professionals, you mean,' she said loyally. 'Don't forget Gordian Knots are professionals, too.'

'I won't,' he promised.

'And who may I ask is going to pay you – us – for this work?'

He waved a hand and said airily, 'We'll get paid all right by all the other legatees, Clive included, if I find Daniel Elland, because we'll all get the Mayton money then.'

'And if you don't?'

'Is there any more soup? It's very good.'

'Don't change the subject.'

'As it happens, Gordian Knots hasn't got any other work on hand, anyway, so I might as well.'

'On the principle that the Devil finds work for idle hands?' she said, replenishing his bowl.

'It's as good as any other principle.'

'And might I ask exactly how Gordian Knots are going to succeed where everyone else has failed?'

He grinned again. 'It wouldn't be the first time.'

'True, but you would be looking for a man who may well have left the country or changed his name.'

'And for good measure without seeing a photograph of him, either,' he said in no wit put out, 'although I've had an idea about that. Did I tell you his wife burnt them all when she threw him out?'

'He sounds better off without her.'

'She practically threw me out, too, when I tried to talk to her. I think that bit in the marriage contract about in sickness and in health had passed her by. Standing by her man didn't seem to come into it.'

'You do realise, don't you, Tom, that this man Elland could be anywhere? Anywhere in the world, I mean.'

He nodded. 'Very true. That's what makes finding him such a challenge.'

'Oh, Tom,' she exclaimed in exasperation. 'You're incorrigible.'

'Remember, the solicitor told us the man had been made bankrupt.'

'At least they found out that much about him for their money,' she said.

'That was the easy bit. Bankruptcy is in the public domain – I think the details are actually published.'

'So?'

'So he couldn't have gone very far without any money for travel.'

'I suppose not,' she said doubtfully.

'I agree, though, that he must have been living on something for the last ten years.'

'The streets, I expect,' she said, pushing a platter of cheese in his direction. 'With a mattress of cardboard and newspaper for sheets.'

'I meant money for food.'

'Charity? Social Services?' she hazarded.

'They won't tell anyone anything,' said Tom. 'Besides, he hasn't committed any crime, unless it's busking.'

'Not as far as you know,' she said darkly.

'It would be a lot easier to find him if he had committed a crime. That's in the public domain, too.'

'So,' she said, 'where does Gordian Knots go from here?'

'Back to the drawing board,' he said cheerfully. 'Don't worry, I'm used to it. Oh, by the way, dear, Simon Puckle's secretary rang this morning.'

'Don't say he's found Daniel Elland?'

'No way, but she said Mr Puckle wants a meeting with all the legatees tomorrow.'

'Except Susan Port.'

She shivered. 'You will take care, won't you? There could be something funny going on.'

'No worries,' he said, adding to himself that he thought that there very well might be something very funny indeed going on.

'And Tom,' she reminded him, 'no fighting with Clive while you're there together, please.'

'I promise. I'll sit next to the nurse.'

'Or arguing with that Martin Pickford fellow, either. I think he could easily be up to no good.'

'If he is, I don't want to know and I've told him so. I

wouldn't let him pay me for that job I did for him just to be on the safe side.'

She sighed. 'Gordian Knots isn't a hobby business, you know.'

'Maybe not, my love, but at least I enjoy it. I don't go around with a long face these days like poor old Clive.'

'I don't like all this, Tom.' She shivered again. 'Do take care, won't you? Remember, this isn't an academic exercise. It's for real.'

TWENTY-ONE

'This is becoming a habit, Inspector.'

'Yes, Doctor.' Detective Inspector Sloan took up his stance in the mortuary while Dr Dabbe was flanked by his taciturn assistant, Burns. Detective Constable Crosby was in his usual position, too – that is, as far away from the scene of action as he could get.

'Have you got a crime wave starting up in your manor, then?' enquired Dr Hector Smithson Dabbe, regarding Sloan over the top of his face mask with raised eyebrows.

'I sincerely hope not, Doctor,' said Sloan. 'The doctors at Berebury Hospital told us straightaway that this man had a fractured skull, which wasn't exactly a surprise. But as well as the deceased – name of Terry Galloway – having all the appearance of being a victim of a non-accidental injury, we also have reason to believe that his death might be connected with that of Susan Port, his godmother.'

'Ah, the ergot lady,' said the pathologist. 'I remember.'

'That's right, Doctor. This man was found injured and unconscious on her doorstep out at Bishop's Marbourne on Saturday morning, which had been her home. We think he'd been there all night, the house being empty at the time.' Sloan wasn't quite sure yet about the house being empty then, it was just something else among many others that had still to be checked.

The pathologist bent over and examined the back of the

deceased's head and then his hands. 'He's got a fractured skull, all right, but whether that is the cause of death I can't tell you just yet. There's no sign of a subdural haemorrhage, anyway, and no bleeding from his ears or mouth.' He turned to his assistant. 'We'll need some photographs, please, Burns.'

'Yes, Doctor.' Burns reached for a large camera.

'And there's no sign either of the deceased having tried to defend himself, which is consistent with his having been hit from behind.'

'So he never knew what hit him,' concluded Crosby from the sidelines.

The pathologist turned back to the detective inspector. 'All I can say at this early stage, Sloan, is that this man's injuries are consistent with his having received a very considerable blow to the occiput.'

Crosby translated this at a distance. 'He was hit on the head with something heavy.'

'Obviously I can't tell you how it came about, Sloan, but it's a similar sort of injury as you can get from being hit by the boom of a yacht.'

Sloan thought he heard a faint 'Boom, boom' from Crosby's direction but decided to ignore it. He decided, too, against mentioning anything about yachts not being commonly found deep in the Calleshire countryside because he was aware that the pathologist's real interests lay in a certain Albacore lying in the marina at Kinnisport.

Or perhaps with a young lady scientist at Calleford Hospital?

'The weapon, whatever it was,' said Sloan instead, 'has not yet been found.' He would deal with Crosby later. 'Perhaps, Doctor, you could give us some indication of what it is likely to have been.'

'Blunt, anyway. And not too big.' The pathologist was still peering closely at the man's skull. 'We're talking iron bar or something of that order – poker, perhaps.' He motioned to his assistant. 'Some X-rays, too, Burns, please. And then we'll open the skull.'

Detective Inspector Sloan stood to one side as the pathologist proceeded with the rest of the post-mortem examination, motioning from time to time to Burns to take specimens of tissue and fluids from the cadaver. 'Especially the liver. Burns. It's enlarged and engorged and I don't know why.' He turned back to Sloan. 'Was he a big drinker, Inspector?'

'We don't know, Doctor. He had just arrived here from Australia.'

'There's no immediate sign anyway of his having been into drugs to account for the state of his liver. Several puncture marks from needles in the usual places – presumably from the attempts by the medical profession to keep him alive. He's not jaundiced, and he doesn't look as if he's been bleeding anywhere.' Dr Dabbe bent over the organ again. 'Question: what is life? Answer: it depends on the liver. And it really does, Sloan.'

'I'm sure, Doctor.'

Eventually Dr Dabbe straightened up, pulled off his mask and pointed to the body of Terry Galloway. 'Otherwise a relatively fit young man, quite muscular, pretty sunburnt and I would have said in very good condition before the fracture.'

'We think he'd been backpacking from Australia to England,' said Sloan.

The pathologist nodded. 'That fits. Whether the fracture – more of a little crack, really – was severe enough to be the cause of death, Sloan, is a different matter altogether. It's too soon to say at this stage. We'll have to wait for the lab results.'

'Actually, the doctors at the hospital saw some signs of his coming round during Saturday evening and were quite hopeful of his living, but then he seems to have taken a turn for the worse during the night.'

'Perhaps he took a turn for the nurse instead,' muttered Crosby, already bored.

Dr Dabbe looked up, his eyes bright. 'Ah, Sloan,' he said alertly. 'Now, that improvement's very interesting.'

'We found that interesting, too, doctor,' Sloan said. That was not strictly true, since Crosby did not appear to have found anything interesting about the case so far. 'In fact, we took the precaution of having a man on bed watch on Saturday night.'

'Anything happen?'

'Terry Galloway died. That's all.'

*   *   *

On this occasion Miss Florence Fennel allowed the visitors to bypass the waiting room at Puckle, Puckle and Nunnery's offices and showed all the Mayton legatees straight into Simon Puckle's room, explaining as she did so that the solicitor had been held up at the Magistrates' Court that morning.

Martin Pickford nodded his understanding. 'There's no arguing with our Hettie.'

'Who?' asked Clive Culshaw.

'The Chairman of the Bench, Miss Henrietta Meadows,' said Martin, settling his bad leg into a more comfortable position. 'Believe you me, she isn't good news.'

'I wouldn't know,' said Clive Culshaw distantly.

'Mr Puckle will be with you as soon as he can,' said Miss Fennel. 'Please make yourselves comfortable until he comes. Coffee is on its way.'

Making themselves comfortable included choosing where in the room to sit. Clive and Tom Culshaw made it quite clear that it wasn't going to be next to each other, while it soon became obvious that Martin Pickford didn't want any further encounter with Tom Culshaw after the job that Gordian Knots had done for him. That left Tom Culshaw pulling up a chair beside Samantha Peters. 'Any idea what this meeting's all about?' he asked her.

She shook her head. 'None. I hope it doesn't take too long anyway. I'm usually in bed by now. I work nights,' she reminded him. 'What about you? Do you work with your brother?'

'Not on your life.' He shuddered. 'My mother made very sure of that.'

The nurse looked interested. 'Tell me.'

'We never got on.'

She looked across the room where Martin Pickford was making heavy weather of talking to Clive Culshaw. 'Sibling rivalry?'

'It was her. My mother. She never got on with me,' he said dolefully. 'I would have done with her – I always tried – but she cut me out of the family firm from day one. And made doubly sure of it when she died, too.'

'Bad luck,' she said sympathetically.

'I was told that the doctors even had to take me away from

her when I was born in case she harmed me. Can you believe that of a new mother and her firstborn baby?'

'Oh, yes, I can. Quite easily, in fact,' the nurse responded unexpectedly. 'That means that she must have been suffering from severe post-natal depression at the time. Sometimes it can mean that the mother didn't bond with the baby.'

'She certainly didn't bond with me.' He sat up, intrigued. 'Tell me more.'

'I used to work in midwifery, you see, and came across a case there every now and then. It's quite difficult to treat and the baby can be in real danger.'

'She never even liked me,' he said.

The nurse patted his hand. 'That's a symptom of the condition. You shouldn't blame your mother.'

'I can't. She's dead,' he said bleakly.

'Or her memory, then.'

'I never did anything wrong and she always behaved as if I never did anything right.'

'You shouldn't blame yourself either,' added Samantha Peters. 'Not now or then. It was absolutely nothing to do with you. It's a clinical condition.'

'You can say that, but it always felt as if it was everything to do with me,' he said bitterly.

'It's to do with her pregnancy and sometimes a difficult delivery of the baby shaking up the hormones in a big way.'

'Someone did hint to me once that she'd had a bad time when I was on the way,' he admitted. 'I always assumed I got all the flack because of that.'

It was at that moment that Simon Puckle returned to his office, hot on the heels of the coffee. He got straight down to business. 'I felt that some further clarification was needed in relation to the Mayton Trust and that you should also be apprised of some recent events.'

'We're all ears,' said Martin Pickford easily, leaning back in his chair.

'As far as the trust is concerned,' said the solicitor, 'all of you must have been aware that following the death of Mrs Susan Port, there would be a percentage increase in your own inheritance.'

Clive Culshaw murmured under his breath that he could do simple arithmetic.

Simon Puckle ignored him. 'The capital sum will no longer have to be divided by six but by five.'

'When?' asked Clive Culshaw.

'In due course,' said Simon Puckle suavely, 'which originally meant when Daniel Elland was found.'

'You mean it doesn't now?' Clive Culshaw suddenly sat up very straight.

The solicitor said, 'Theoretically – and I do stress that I mean only theoretically – should some other legatee be known to have killed Mrs Port the capital would then be divided between the remaining four.' He coughed. 'In law as you may know a murderer may not benefit financially from the death of his or her victim.'

'Gets better and better, doesn't it?' said Martin Pickford cheerfully. 'If we go on at this rate I'll collar the lot.'

Tom Culshaw turned to Simon Puckle and said, 'Something's happened, then?'

'Two things,' responded the solicitor. 'Firstly, I am informed by the police that Mrs Port's godson turned up from Australia to see her. We think he went out to Bishop's Marbourne to visit her early on Friday evening and was assaulted outside her cottage. He was found on Saturday morning on her doorstep with serious head injuries.'

'How serious?' demanded Tom Culshaw at once.

'He died in the hospital during Saturday night,' said Puckle succinctly.

'That serious,' murmured Tom Culshaw.

Samantha Peters said softly, 'Poor man.'

'Not unnaturally,' went on the solicitor, 'the police are taking into consideration the possibility that there might be some connection between the two deaths.'

'I don't blame them,' shivered Samantha Peters.

'I must say that that's a bit worrying,' said Tom Culshaw. 'I don't like to think of something like that happening round here.'

Simon Puckle, experienced solicitor, said that that was a very common feeling after an incident too close to home for comfort. Detective Inspector Sloan, veteran policeman, would have been the first to agree with him that place, however familiar, did not confer immunity from iniquity. Or reduce the liability to road traffic accidents on your own patch. Both were common misconceptions that came as a surprise to victims.

'There is also another matter that I wish to bring to your attention,' went on Puckle fluently. 'As you are all aware, the sixth legatee, Daniel Elland, has not yet been traced.' He looked across at Clive Culshaw. 'Perhaps Mr Culshaw himself would like to tell us what happened to him?'

'Go on,' said Samantha Peters urgently. 'What else has happened? Tell us.'

'Get it out, man,' said Martin Pickford.

Tom Culshaw stared at his brother. 'Is someone gunning for you, too, now, Clive?'

Clive Culshaw looked round the room and began. 'I happened to be in the parish of St Peter's in Berebury – actually down by the Postern Gate – on Saturday evening—'

'You did, did you?' said his brother. 'Well I never did.'

'Got your sheriff's badge, have you?' asked Martin Pickford.

Culshaw stiffened. 'It had occurred to me that since this Daniel Elland is presumably without visible means of support, he might have joined the down-and-outs there, as it is the place where the homeless congregate. I thought Daniel Elland might be living rough there.'

'And?' asked Pickford.

'I think he might be.'

'Why?'

'Because someone hit me from behind when I mentioned his name.' He put a hand to the back of his head. 'I don't know who he was except that he was taller than me.'

Simon Puckle raised a hand. 'I can assure you all that our enquiry agents got no response when they asked his whereabouts among the – er – denizens of that locality.'

'Well, they wouldn't, would they?' said Martin Pickford. 'Companions in misfortune stick together.'

'Honour among thieves, more like,' suggested Clive Culshaw.

'But exactly what happened?' asked Samantha Peters

insistently. 'Did you find him? We get some very dubious characters from there at the hospital – very drunk, as a rule. But no one ever calling himself Daniel Elland. I checked our admissions register in the beginning just in case.'

The solicitor went on. 'As a result of this, the police have suggested that for the time being you all take reasonable precautions.'

'Against what?' demanded Tom Culshaw. 'Being hit on the head, too?'

'They advise against any of you going around the Postern Gate area and the riverbank at night and alone,' said Simon Puckle firmly. 'There appears to be rather more at stake in the distribution of the Mayton Trust than I had first thought.'

'That's one way of putting it,' said Martin Pickford.

Samantha Peters said that it did mean, though, didn't it, that Daniel Elland must be there?

'I understand, Miss Peters,' said the solicitor, 'that that is the police view, too, now. I am not, of course, privy to their plans in the matter, but I am sure they will be taking some appropriate action in due course.'

TWENTY-TWO

'Why me, sir?' wailed Crosby plaintively.

'It'll be a new policing experience for you,' said Detective Inspector Sloan. 'Do you good.'

'But, sir . . .'

'You're not bricking it, surely, are you?'

'No, sir,' he said hotly. 'Of course not.'

'All you have to do, Crosby, is to go over to the other end of town and buy some old clothes in one of the charity shops there. It doesn't matter if they don't fit you – in a way it might even be better if they didn't. More in keeping, you might say. And get yourself some bashed-about shoes. Policemen's shoes are a dead giveaway.'

'And then what?' asked Crosby mutinously.

'Scrounge a grubby sleeping bag from somewhere and stuff it with newspapers. Tabloids, mind you. Not broadsheets.'

'What for?'

'To help you keep something like warm, that's why. Then, after dark, creep into a doorway down there and try to get a good night's kip.'

'Fat chance.'

'All the better for keeping your ears open. Oh, and have a good backstory ready – lost your job, stepfather threw you out, just come out of prison and nowhere to go, wife trouble, drink, drugs. Take your pick.'

'I never—'

'I know you didn't, Crosby,' said Sloan patiently, 'but it won't be me sleeping in the next doorway. It'll be someone seeing what he can steal from you and someone suspicious of your being there in the first place.'

'I'll be cold.'

'And hungry, so have a good meal before you go there, and Crosby . . .'

'Sir?'

'Don't wash or shave for a bit.'

'Why can't I shave?'

'No money for razors, no hot water, and no soap and if you did once have a towel someone would have nicked it soon enough. Understood?'

'Yes, sir.'

'And Crosby . . .'

'Sir?'

'Mind how you go. That lot over there don't like the police all that much.'

'And what am I supposed to be doing down there, anyway?'

'Either finding Daniel Elland or better still finding out why someone else there wants him. It shouldn't be too difficult now we know where he is.'

'And how am I going to find him if I don't know what he looks like?'

'Use your ears and your imagination, man. And don't get injured yourself. That won't help anyone.'

'It won't help me, anyway,' muttered Crosby. 'That's for sure.'

'Remember Daniel Elland might be in danger himself. We know that there's someone else round there looking for him, too. That's as well as us and the solicitors.'

'But we still don't know why, sir,' he protested.

'No, but we know that the man's both a Mayton and may be in danger, which ticks all the right boxes for me at the moment. Besides, he's got a lot of money coming to him one day if nobody kills him first, and that might be a good enough reason, too, for some other person or persons unknown to have a go at him. It often is. Believe you me, Crosby, it often is.'

'Yes, sir.'

'Although technically we have no reason to suspect him of doing anything untoward, it would nevertheless be of interest to locate him. You have no need to take any action should you do so. You only have to report back. Understood?'

Superintendent Leeyes was not a happy man either. 'I don't like it, Sloan,' he said from the comfort of his own office. The detective inspector had duly reported that Constable Crosby had been dispatched to lie low among the rough sleepers by the railway in the east end of Berebury and keep his eyes and ears open, since they had reason to believe that Daniel Elland was there. 'But I suppose,' Leeyes sighed, 'that everyone else in the force except him looks like a real policeman and would be sussed out before you could say "knife".'

'He might get away with it, sir,' said Sloan, mentally crossing his fingers.

'Let's hope so, for his sake.' Leeyes tapped his desk. 'There're far too many loose ends in all this business for my liking and this missing man, Elland, is only one of them.'

There were far too many loose ends for Detective Inspector Sloan's liking as well.

Principal among them was still the death of a woman that turned out to have been a poisoning by ergot, in what form it was not known.

Or why.

That had been a couple of months after big money had come into the picture – its connection with her death not yet proven. Then, later still, had been the death of the man at the woman's cottage at Bishop's Marbourne – another loose end.

'There's this Terry Galloway, too, sir,' he reminded him, 'turning up on Susan Port's doorstep half-dead.'

'And then dying,' Leeyes pointed out acidly.

'It's that he died at all,' Sloan said to the superintendent, 'in spite of the fact that the doctors at the hospital thought he might live that worries me.' He himself wasn't at all happy about this. While he didn't confuse – as some patients, and indeed some doctors themselves did, too – members of the medical profession with God, he did respect their judgement. And if they had given it as their opinion that Terry Galloway was starting to regain consciousness – and not dying – then he probably had been.

'I'm having another interview with the man we put on bed watch at the hospital,' he said.

Leeyes nodded. 'Soon, I hope.'

'I can see that the assault on Terry Galloway might very well come into the picture, sir, but I can't see how or why yet. We're still awaiting the man's full post-mortem results, of course. Dr Dabbe was a bit cagey at the time – he said he didn't like something he found in the liver, but I don't know what – and he didn't want to say too much.'

'That means he doesn't know,' concluded Leeyes flatly.

'Or that he just wasn't going to say until he gets the lab results back.'

'Watching his back, that's what he's doing,' said Leeyes unsympathetically. 'No help to us.'

'No, sir.'

'Lateral thinking, Sloan,' pronounced Leeyes. 'That's what you need now. Very important, lateral thinking.'

'Yes, sir.'

'At this stage in an investigation you just have to think outside the box to get anywhere. Not that everyone appreciates it, I can tell you. Some people have absolutely no imagination whatsoever and won't listen to new theories.'

Sloan paused and searched his memory for a moment and then it came to him: 'The Causes of World War I'. That was it. A series of lectures attended by the superintendent – but not for very long. The usual events attributed to the start of that conflict – the Algeciras crisis, the Fashoda Incident and even German territorial ambitions – had been dismissed out of hand by Superintendent Leeyes, who had opted instead to blame the Kaiser's midwife for being responsible for the start of that war.

Leeyes had told the lecturer that in his opinion it was the midwife's carelessness in delivering the baby's shoulder at the time of the Kaiser's birth that had led to the Erb's palsy in his arm. And that permanently damaged shoulder and arm, Leeyes had asserted, had led to the grown man's notable inferiority complex – something he was sure was only ever to be compensated for in the German leader's mind by aggression. 'Like chips on the shoulder usually are,' he had said neatly.

The assassination of Archduke Franz Ferdinand of Austria and his wife at Sarajevo, advanced by the lecturer as another important factor in the start of the war, Leeyes insisted as having had nothing to do with it. That it was just one of your usual Balkan foibles was his parting shot to a bemused academic already considering giving up teaching in adult education.

'It's a case of knowing exactly where to start, sir,' Sloan admitted now. 'With a death or with the money.'

'Both,' said Leeyes, his usual bracing self. 'Now about the old lady who died . . .'

'The death of Mrs Susan Port might still have been a case of accidental poisoning, sir.'

'Not until you find out how she ingested it and who gave it to her,' said Leeyes flatly.

'We still don't know for certain that it was murder – only that she died from something that had ergot in it in some form or other. And that was nearly two months after the legatees had been told about the Mayton Trust.'

'No, not her, Sloan. I meant the very old lady who died in a care home, kick-starting the Mayton Trust off.'

'Clementina somebody . . .' He reached for his notebook.

'Dangerous places, care homes,' said Leeyes meditatively. 'The opposite of maternity ones. Ending-life ones, you might say. Some of them on purpose, I'm sure.'

'They're dealing with both ends of life, you might say, sir,' ventured Sloan, not sure where this was leading.

'I always think of care homes more as eternity ones,' said his superior officer. 'And as I said, dangerous. Very, because by the time someone's in one of them nearly everyone in sight wants the inmate dead.'

'The solicitors did say that they had checked Clementina's death out,' offered Sloan.

'*Nullius in verba*, Sloan,' said Leeyes unexpectedly.

'Sir?'

'It means "Take nobody's word for it" in Latin,' he said. 'It's what the ACC is forever banging on about. First principle of policing, he always calls it.'

'Of course, sir.' That explained it. The assistant chief constable was always quoting Latin. He was a man cast in a very different mould from that of the superintendent, who resented it. 'Simon Puckle is quite sure she died of natural causes,' he said, hastily adding, 'but we'll check it out ourselves, of course, sir.'

'And while you're about it, find out whether any of the legatees had any previous knowledge of the money coming to them when the old lady died.'

'Simon Puckle says that it was one of the conditions of the trust that Algernon Mayton set up that no one was to know in advance about it and he left strict instructions to that effect.'

'No flies on old Algernon, whoever he was,' said Leeyes appreciatively. 'Great expectations can do a lot of damage. You've only got to look at the children of the very rich and see what they get up to.'

'And can put others at risk,' said Sloan, mindful of two dead people on his patch. Already.

'What we need to know, sir,' he went on, 'is whether the inheritance has any bearing on Mrs Port's death or that of her godson.'

'Try drawing up a timeline,' advised the superintendent. 'Can be quite useful things, timelines.'

'In the beginning there was the money,' began Sloan. There was a saying about never asking a successful businessman how he made his first million pounds, but he already knew the answer to that in Algernon Mayton's case: faking a useless pseudo-medical product. 'And money makes money after that.'

'And usually marries it, too,' said Leeyes. 'Does that come into things?'

'No, sir. The solicitor said that all that mattered in the settlement of the trust was the direct descent from Algernon Mayton, male or female. Who the descendant had married had nothing to do with the inheritance. It was an absolutely straightforward case of father to child or mother to child, irrespective of whom they had married. The spouses didn't come into the trust.'

'Bully for them,' said the superintendent colloquially. 'That should make your enquiries simpler, Sloan.'

'I've looked at that family tree we found on Mrs Port's dining-room table and on her computer until I'm blue in the face, without seeing anything that looks in the least significant, except the question mark against the name of Tom Culshaw.'

Superintendent Leeyes leant back in his chair. 'It must mean something, Sloan. What about Tom Culshaw's war with his brother, Clive? Perhaps they aren't blood brothers after all? Had you thought about that?'

'Not in depth, sir,' admitted Sloan.

'You should. Suppose the mother had had Tom by a different father – perhaps she'd been raped and took against the child because of that? Or had an affair within marriage and the natural father had let her down. Or wasn't disclosed to her husband?'

'I have no means of knowing whether or not Simon Puckle had considered those particular possibilities, sir, but at least he'd had the birth and death certificates of all the legatees checked and found them to be in apparent order.'

'In my young day, Sloan, a child born within wedlock was deemed to be of that marriage and the birth certificate filled in accordingly,' countered Leeyes immediately, 'and therefore legitimate whoever the actual parent was, great Edwardian country house parties among the nobility notwithstanding.'

'Yes, sir,' agreed Sloan, who was familiar with the legend of children being known as 'of the house but not of the family' and of that historic one concerning a royal warming pan as well.

'These days,' said Leeyes, a man with never a kind thing to say for the present compared with the past, 'I suppose everything's hunky-dory unless proved to the contrary by DNA.'

'I'm sure you're right, sir,' said Sloan, before the superintendent could start talking about the good old days. 'You're suggesting, sir, are you, that Tom Culshaw doesn't have to be the child of his putative father?'

'It's quite possible.'

Detective Inspector Sloan gave thought to this. 'In his case, sir, it would matter since his inheritance comes through the father. The brothers could actually be stepbrothers.'

'And if it was proved that their father wasn't Tom's father after all – then the younger one – Clive, did you say his name was? – would collect both their shares of the dibs.'

'Yes, sir. If it could be proved, that is. There's another theoretical possibility, though.'

'Go on.'

'He might have been the father's love child born outside the marriage but brought into it and reared by the mother. I've known that happen, too.'

'That would explain Tom being excluded from his mother's will and his failure to get on with her,' agreed Leeyes. 'If she wasn't his mother, that is. If he was his father's son it wouldn't matter – he'd still get the money.'

'All we can do, sir, would be to try to persuade them both to take a DNA test.'

'Fat chance of that if they didn't want to,' responded Leeyes promptly, 'defence lawyers being what they are. All the same that tick of the deceased is our only lead in that family. She could have found something out. You'd better work on it.'

'And then there's still Daniel Elland on the loose, sir.'

'Find him, Sloan,' ordered Leeyes, adding ominously, 'and before anyone else does.'

TWENTY-THREE

D etective Constable Crosby was the unhappiest man of them all. He had waited until darkness had fallen and then slipped silently into what he had begun to think of as a commune. That he was wrong about this was made abundantly clear to him after he had selected a likely looking corner in which to sleep and sunk to the ground against a wall. He hadn't been there long enough to finish his first sandwich before a hoarse voice said, 'You there. Get out of it. You can't stay there.'

He scrambled to his feet, a hand descending on his collar as he did so. The voice said, 'That's my pitch, mate. Not yours.'

'My mistake,' mumbled Crosby, moving away, crab-like, as quickly as he could. He stood stock-still then for a moment, unsure where to go next. After a little while he set off again and wandered down the next street he came to, still searching for a likely looking doorway. There weren't many of them out of the wind, and those that there were all seemed to have someone huddled in them already.

Attracted by the noise, he then came across two men who appeared to be fighting over a bottle. He instinctively started to approach the pair to break up the disturbance but halted suddenly, remembering just in time that while he was a policeman, he wasn't meant to be one just now and here – especially here. Instead he had to school himself to watch a lawless activity he had been trained to deal with carry on regardless. It ended with one of the men caving in and uncertainly tottering away into the shadows. The other trium-phantly applied his lips to the bottle and then when it was finished, tossed it after the retreating man, muttering some-thing slurred, the only word of which that Crosby could catch being 'loser'.

The detective constable moved swiftly away himself, seeking another shelter against the cold. He had forgotten how very cold it could be out of doors in the early hours. He next came across a pile of cardboard boxes on the pavement at the back of a shop and made for them, hopeful that they might provide some protection against the increasing nocturnal chill.

He selected the largest and was making to lift the cardboard up and take shelter under it when someone from inside the box growled like a badger disturbed in his sleep and said, 'What the hell do you think you're doing?'

Taking this literally Crosby said, 'Looking for somewhere to sleep.'

'Not here, mate,' said the voice emphatically.

Crosby took a deep breath and added, 'And looking for a man called Daniel Elland.'

'You're not the only one,' said the man unexpectedly.

'Why?'

'What's it got to do with you?' bristled the man, instantly hostile. 'Get lost. Now, before I kick you out.'

'OK, OK,' said Crosby, starting to move away.

'But if you do find him, whoever you are and wherever the clever sod is, tell him that old Bert wants a word.'

Detective Constable Crosby, deciding that absence of body was better than presence of mind, left without opening his mouth any more. Fading silently back into the darkness, he stepped in another direction still. He was a bit luckier here in that there was an angle in the wall of a building created by the addition of an outhouse that was sheltering it from the eastern wind that was now getting up. Although there were already men trying to sleep there it looked to him as if there might be just room for him to tag on at the end of the row and out of the wind.

He lowered himself to the ground, careful not to disturb the man beside him. Not carefully enough, though, for a small terrier nestling against the side of the greatcoat of its owner. It aroused the man to his arrival who now turned a florid unshaven face in his direction, hiccupping the while. 'Got anything to drink?' he asked Crosby, raising himself up on one elbow and putting out a hand.

That was the moment when Crosby realised that the plastic bag containing his sandwiches and bottle of water had gone.

'No,' he replied, although from the smell of the man he deduced without difficulty that the drink his neighbour had in mind was not Adam's ale.

'Or anything else? I don't care what. Anything will do.'

'Sorry, mate,' said Crosby. 'I've only just left home.' He had carefully considered the choice of reasons for sleeping rough suggested to him by Inspector Sloan and decided that his story was that a wicked stepfather had thrown him out. He trotted this out now.

'Bastard,' said the man at once.

'I'll say,' agreed Crosby vigorously. 'An absolute bastard. I can't see what my mother saw in him.'

'Clink, clink, I expect,' said the man, sinking back, a tear starting to trickle from one eye towards his beard. 'That's all women ever care about. Money.' Another tear succeeded the first and made its way down a bruised and emaciated face. 'And more money.'

Crosby began to edge away from him and his dog, deciding that the man was best left to his own maudlin thoughts. As soon as he made the first movement, though, the little dog drew its upper lip back and bared its teeth.

'Quiet, Isaac,' commanded its owner. He put out a hand to restrain the dog and tried to struggle to his feet. He soon lost his balance in the attempt and fell back to the pavement with a loud cry of pain as his skinny body hit the unyielding stone. 'God, that hurt,' he cried aloud.

'I'm looking for a man called Daniel Elland,' carried on Crosby gamely.

'So what?' He rubbed his hip where it had met the ground.

'Do you know him?'

The man raised a head covered with long, unkempt hair and glared at him. 'Who wants to know?'

'I do.'

'What for?'

'That's my business.'

'Well, it's not mine so get out of it now.' He put a hand out to the dog and said, 'Go get him, Isaac.'

Detective Constable Crosby took the first opportunity he could to make his escape and slid off in yet another direction.

This one seemed a more hopeful one as he thought he could
see lights ahead. Attracted to them like a moth, he advanced a
bit further and found himself in the delivery area behind another
row of shops. Orienting himself, he realised that he was
standing at the back of Berebury's supermarket and thus near
their unloading bay. This had a canopy over it and showed
every sign of being as sheltered as possible. Slightly surprised
that it appeared to be empty – perhaps there was a caretaker
who did the rounds during the night – he hunkered down in
a corner as far away from the road as he could. He found out
the hard way during the small hours that a night sleeping rough
was a good deal worse than one on night duty. He did eventually drift into an uneasy sleep but awoke with a jerk a little
while later. He lay on the ground of the shelter as still as a
hunted animal but there didn't seem to be anyone about. Any
human, that is. His next thought was foxes: people were always
talking about the increase in urban foxes. Failing to spot any
foxes, his mind ran to rats, but he couldn't see any of those
scuttling about.

Something had undoubtedly woken him, though. Listening
intently he could hear – but not place – a low-pitched whine.
He tried to sit up to see if he could establish where it was
coming from but was immediately overcome by an attack of
nausea so acute that he straightaway fell back to the floor.
Quite disorientated now, he became aware that he was starting
to have a headache, too, even though the noise of the intrusive
whine seemed to be abating a little.

He tried to sit up again and promptly vomited. Dimly
recognising on its way back the half of the sandwich he'd
eaten earlier, he retained enough of a sense of humour to
realise the state of his clothes now could only reinforce his
pretence of being a genuine vagrant.

A bout of dizziness had succeeded the nausea and he gave
up any thought of standing. Instead he crawled out of the
loading bay and collapsed on the ground outside with the worst
headache he'd ever had in his life.

And knew no more until morning.

TWENTY-FOUR

S ister Samantha Peters sailed down the Accident and Emergency ward like the old wooden man-o'-war ship the fighting *Temeraire* in its heyday and on the offensive. 'Dogs,' she proclaimed thunderously, 'are not allowed in the hospital. You know that. You've been there before.'

'Sorry, Sister.'

'Go and tie him up outside at once.'

The man who had brought the dog in with him fumbled slowly and carefully with the string that was presently doing duty as a belt round his greatcoat and then equally slowly and carefully threaded it through the dog's collar. 'Come along, Isaac,' he said, leading the way to the door. 'You're not welcome here.'

'Nor are his fleas,' murmured Samantha Peters under her breath. She sat down at her desk and waited for the man to come back. As he did so she plucked a new form out of a rack in front of her and asked him his name this time.

'Still Little Sir Echo.'

She wrote this down without comment. She'd heard worse – much worse – from patients from the east side and wasn't disposed to argue.

'And I need some painkillers,' the man added.

'Oh, yes?' Painkillers were what everyone sleeping rough always asked for, being the nearest thing the hospital handed out to the addictive drugs they really wanted. 'And what is it that brings Little Sir Echo into the hospital at three o'clock in the morning asking for painkillers?' she asked without trace of sarcasm. Once upon a time she used to ask new patients what was wrong with them but had tired of the usual wisecracking response of 'That's for you to tell me' and had accordingly changed her approach.

'A fall.'

'How far?'

'Not far, Sister, but I really could do with some painkillers.' Samantha Peters sighed.

'I do think I've done myself an injury to my back, Sister,' he insisted.

'And did you fall or were you pushed?' she asked. That question was mandatory in the Accident and Emergency ward these days, since litigation usually followed hot on the heels of any injury the blame for which could conceivably be laid at someone else's door, especially those of either the victim or the hospital.

'I just fell back on the pavement when I was trying to get up,' said the old man simply.

'You'll have to let me take a look,' she said.

'Can't you just give me some painkillers?' he asked, his eyes beginning to fill with tears.

'Sorry,' she said, not unkindly, aware that he wouldn't want her to see the state of his threadbare clothes under the great-coat he was now so determinedly clutching round his thin, unwashed person. 'Not without examining you properly.' She waved a hand towards the couch in the corner. 'Can you get up on that?'

He tottered over to it and, aided by two steps, climbed on it. She drew the curtains round him and promised to return when he was ready. It was a while before she heard his call and stepped between the curtains. His spindly wasted flanks and undernourished back were now fully exposed to her view.

'I'm afraid you've got some trouble here, Mr Echo,' she said after taking a close look at his spine. No way was she going to address him as 'sir'. 'You've got a considerable haematoma – that's a blood blister to you – over your hip and a lot of swelling on the edge of the bone above it. You're going to need an X-ray of your hip and I'll have to get Dr Chomel to look at your haematoma and perhaps drain it. I think we should keep you in hospital overnight in case it bursts and goes septic.' That it would inevitably go septic in his circumstances she did not need to say. She pulled her watch up into view. 'It's three o'clock and I have to go on my break now, but I want you to wait here until Dr Chomel can get to see you. I don't think she'll be long.'

Pulling the curtains of the cubicle together behind her she set off for the staff canteen, even though she found food was seldom appetising at this indeterminate moment in the night that hung somewhere between yesterday and tomorrow.

By the time she got back to the ward, he who had called himself Little Sir Echo had got dressed and both he and his dog had disappeared back into the night.

'There's something very funny going on down by the Postern Gate, sir,' said a weary Detective Constable Crosby the next morning. 'Lovely and warm in here, isn't it?' he said, rubbing his hands and looking round the police canteen appreciatively for the first time ever.

'Go on,' said Detective Inspector Sloan, who was sitting across the table from him, having his own breakfast.

'Whenever I mentioned Daniel Elland's name to any of them, sir, they acted like they were sure he was there with them somewhere but that they didn't know exactly where.' Crosby had crept away from the east end of the town under cover of darkness and was reporting back, still unwashed and unshaven, to Sloan. There was a dark shadow on his chin now and another one under his eyes as well but for a different reason. 'Or exactly who Daniel Elland was. They didn't know that either. But they knew they wanted him. Funny that, isn't it, sir?'

'Not if he isn't using his own name, it isn't,' said Sloan. 'Down-and-outs don't always want you to know who they are.'

'But if they don't know who he is why should they want him so badly?' said Crosby, applying himself to the canteen's ever-popular all day breakfast.

'He might know something they don't,' suggested Sloan.

'Or someone,' said Crosby glumly.

'Unknown factors come into a lot of police business, usually at the beginning of a case,' said Sloan prosaically. 'You have to learn to live with them.'

Crosby hadn't been listening. 'I mean, what could they possibly want him for?'

'That is something we don't yet know.'

'But they must know all right,' he said, spearing a sausage. 'Why they want him, I mean.'

'I'm sure they do,' said Sloan warmly. 'But we don't and you haven't found out yet. Tonight, perhaps you will.'

He groaned. 'Must I, sir? Heavy rain's forecast for tonight.'

'Police work's never only "job and knock",' said Sloan. 'You don't just do what you choose to think is your job and knock off like ordinary workers can do sometimes when their work's done.'

'Yes, sir,' he said glumly.

'Besides, Crosby,' Sloan added, 'it'll be good experience for you, learning how the other half lives. It might even influence you when deciding whether or not to make an arrest.'

'How come, sir?'

'It's the small matter of their being fined for whatever they've got up to that they shouldn't have done, such as aggravated begging.'

'Even though they wouldn't be able to pay it?'

'Exactly. The Chairman of the Bench, the redoubtable Miss Hettie Meadows, is always saying that she has to take that into consideration when passing sentence. Or not.' Sloan took a mouthful of tea and said reflectively, 'You can be sent to prison for not paying a fine.'

'I do know that, sir.'

'It's nice and warm in prison in winter and I understand the food's not too bad, either.'

'I get you, sir.' Crosby attacked a rasher of bacon with some ferocity. 'My sandwiches got nicked in the night,' he said by way of explanation of his appetite.

'Tough,' said Sloan. 'It might have been your throat. You do realise that, don't you?'

'Yes, sir,' he said, shivering in spite of the warmth of the canteen. He turned his attention to the fried bread, demolishing it at speed. 'Sir, why are we looking for this man Daniel Elland like the people from Puckles are doing and some of the men down by the river, too? What's he done that he shouldn't have done?'

Detective Inspector Sloan pushed his plate away and sat back. 'Probably nothing at all. As far as we're concerned he's just one of the five surviving beneficiaries of the Mayton Trust and we only want to interview him in connection with the unexplained death of a fellow legatee of that trust.'

'Mrs Susan Port?'

'Who died in circumstances that are not entirely clear.' That went, too, for the death of he whom the police were fairly sure was Mrs Port's godson and heir, Terry Galloway. Where his death came into the equation Sloan still didn't know, Dr Dabbe not having been back in touch to date with any results from the forensic lab. 'And remember, Crosby, there may be no connection at all with whoever wants him among the dropouts, so beware of jumping to conclusions.'

'But,' Crosby objected, 'that only explains the other people – Puckles lot – they want him because of the money, don't they?'

'They want him for perfectly obvious reasons,' said Sloan, draining his cup. 'Financial ones. They can't get their hands on the dibs until Daniel Elland is found – the Mayton Trust can't shell out until then. That's why they want him, but why Clive Culshaw got clobbered down there for his trouble we don't know, and why anyone else down there should want him we don't know either.'

The constable nodded and said, 'Money talks, though.'

'It hasn't talked to Daniel Elland yet because he doesn't know about it,' pointed out Sloan. 'Can't have done because nobody can find him to tell him he's come into big money.'

Detective Constable Crosby downed the last of the tomatoes on his plate and gave this some thought. 'Suppose those guys in that squat there know about the money and he doesn't and that was why they were trying to find him?'

'A good try, Crosby, but unlikely. That Miss Fennel at Puckles didn't strike me as someone who'd rat on a client, let alone on the firm.' He found he could quite easily envisage Miss Florence Fennel going to the stake rather than break a professional confidence.

The constable sighed. 'Actually, sir, it wasn't having my sandwiches nicked that really got me.'

'Oh?'

'It was something that I didn't understand going on behind the supermarket.'

'What exactly?'

'That covered delivery bay. It looked quite all right, and I thought I'd be safe enough for the night there, seeing as it's so sheltered.'

'But you weren't?'

'You can say that again,' he said feelingly. 'I felt awful. First of all, it was this funny whine . . .'

'The air conditioning?'

'No, it wasn't like that at all. More like one of those insects in the jungle that go on and on in Eastern films.'

'Cicadas?'

'That's right, sir. The sound drives you mad in the end. It was something that I couldn't quite make out, however hard I listened. I felt as if I'd been concussed.'

'Nobody had hit you over the head, I hope.' Actually, if they had done, the police could have gone into the area with a vengeance looking for a policeman who had been assaulted in the execution of his duty.

'No, sir, but it upset my hearing for a bit – I went quite deaf – and then I was sick.'

'Even though you hadn't had anything to eat?'

'That's right, sir. It can't have been my sandwiches because I didn't have them.' He looked mournfully at Sloan. 'I did tell you that they'd been stolen, didn't I?'

'You did. Then what?'

'I was ever so sick again. I tried to get up, but I couldn't stand for quite a while and when I was on my feet again, I felt so dizzy I had to hang onto the wall. But that wasn't the worst of it.'

'No?' said Sloan, frowning.

'That's when the headache started. I've never had one like it, sir, and I don't ever want to again.'

'And then?'

'I came away from there just before it got light. The night duty sergeant let me have a bit of a kip in the custody suite.'

'Good. Don't wash or shave, though, before you go back there tonight. Are you all right again now?'

'Oh, yes, sir. Thank you, sir. Quite all right now that the headache's gone.' He paused and then said, 'Sir, that sausage you've left on your plate, would you mind if I had it, now that you don't want it?'

TWENTY-FIVE

'Oh, it's you again,' said Tom Culshaw. He wasn't particularly welcoming to the young man standing on his front doorstep that morning. He sighed. 'You'd better come in and tell me what you want this time.'

'Don't be like that, Tom,' said Martin Pickford. 'We're supposed to be family, remember?'

'So I have been led to believe,' said the other man. 'Well, if you ask me, you can keep your families. There's a famous poet who wrote about exactly what your mum and dad do to you and it's not nice. But now I come to think about it,' Tom added soberly, 'it's quite true.'

'I wouldn't know anything about that,' said Pickford, baffled, 'but I thought all the same I'd ask you about something very odd that's happened.'

'Ask me what?'

'Ask you if it was you who'd spilt the beans on me about what happened with Jim Stopford and the rugby club.'

'Certainly not. I wouldn't do a thing like that and you should know it. Why do you ask?'

'The police have been out to see him at his farm, that's why. Twice.'

'What about?'

'That's the funny thing. The first time they said it was because of that little tiff Jim Stopford and I had at the Bellingham the other night, though why that should interest the police all that much I don't know. That sort of thing must happen all the time.'

'Little tiff? That doesn't sound like an accurate description of the right good mauling Stopford gave you after he found out what you'd been up to. Not that I blame him myself. It was a rotten trick to play on him and just what you deserved.'

Martin Pickford ignored this jibe and went on. 'And then they went back again later with men in white overalls and masks and took some samples away with them from a field of rye on his farm.'

'Why on earth would they want to do that?' Culshaw frowned.

'Search me, Tom, but it turns out that Jim Stopford usually sells the rye crop on his farm to your sainted brother.'

'Does he, indeed?' remarked Tom Culshaw. 'That's interesting. Where does Mr Bun the Baker come into the picture?'

'What picture?' asked Martin Pickford, unfamiliar with the card game of Happy Families.

'The Culshaw picture or, rather, the Mayton one.'

Martin Pickford looked quite bewildered now. 'Don't ask me. I don't know.' After a long pause he said awkwardly, 'There is something about the Mayton matter, though, that I did want to ask you.'

'Like what?' Tom said discouragingly. 'And I'll tell you now that if it's anything like last time, I'm not going to do it.'

'It isn't.'

'I'm glad to hear it,' said Tom Culshaw, 'whatever it is.'

'You see, I'm a bit up the creek financially.'

'You mean you're having money troubles,' translated Tom. 'And how.'

'Why?' asked Culshaw bluntly.

'I've just got the push from my firm. Sacked. Actually, what they said was that I was being let go.'

'I do know what all those expressions mean,' said Tom.

'The same.' Martin sighed.

'So why – not how – were your employers prepared to manage without you?'

Martin suspecting – but not understanding – irony, rushed into an explanation. 'I didn't turn up to work on Monday morning for an important meeting and they didn't like it.'

'Overdid it at the weekend and slept in, did you?' suggested Tom solicitously.

'I got my place in the county team – thanks to you, of course,' he added hastily, 'and we won big time on Saturday.'

'And drank big time, too, I guess.'

'It wasn't only that.'

'No?'

'My face got a bit bashed in the maul and I didn't look exactly like the promising young businessman they wanted representing their firm.'

'I can well believe it,' said Tom, scanning the other man's still bruised face and missing front tooth.

'I was practically black and blue all over and could hardly walk straight.'

'So?'

'So, since your outfit Gordian Knots do jobs that other people won't do . . .'

'Can't do . . .'

'I was wondering if we could find this missing man called Daniel Elland . . .'

'I know what he's called,' said Tom.

'Then we could all . . .'

'All?'

'Well, obviously not Susan Port, but I'm sure the rest of us could then have some of the ready to be going on with. I could settle my money worries and so could anyone else if they've got them, too. And then it wouldn't matter if it took me a little longer to get another job.'

Tom Culshaw sighed and said, 'You'd better sit down.'

'I mean,' explained Martin, lowering himself carefully into a chair as if the rest of him hurt, too, 'we know roughly where he's hanging out because of that other down-and-out having a go at your brother.'

'But not the name Daniel Elland's using now. Remember, we don't even know that,' pointed out Tom, 'or what he looks like these days.' He didn't mention this to Martin, but he had already acquired a studio photograph of a business-suited Daniel Elland in his prime as chairman of his own company and persuaded a skilled techno friend to create a computerised picture of roughly what the man might look like suitably aged and ill-cared-for.

'People's faces don't change,' protested Martin.

'Unless they get damaged,' said Tom pointedly. 'Rugby boots don't do them a lot of good.'

'Being broke doesn't help how you look, either,' said Martin. 'I'm sure I've lost weight. My face is thinner already and I'll be totally skint in a week.'

'Why tell me? Are you hoping I'll do a second job for you for free, because if so, you're barking up the wrong tree.'

'No, no, it's not that.'

'What is it, then?'

'It's that two heads are better than one, especially if one of them's yours.'

'Flattery will get you nowhere, Pickford.'

'It's true, all the same,' he insisted. 'Brain is better than brawn.'

'Even for rugby players?' asked Culshaw ironically.

'Don't be like that. It's not funny.'

'Had it ever occurred to you, Martin, that since someone else is looking for Daniel Elland, too, that you or I might also be in danger if we tried to find him?'

Martin flexed his not inconsiderable muscles and said, 'I don't mind that – I like a good fight.' He put up his fists like a boxer and waved his left one at Tom. 'I call this one "Hospital" and the other,' he said, bringing up his right fist alongside the left one, '"Graveyard".'

Tom Culshaw sighed and shook his head.

'It's high time you grew up, Pickford. You're not ten years old any longer, you know.'

'What is it now?' asked Superintendent Leeyes irritably when Sloan appeared at his office door. 'I've got to go to a meeting of the Corporation's Watch Committee or what-ever it is that they call themselves now.' He scowled. 'They won't leave any names alone these days. You can't tell where you are.'

Detective Inspector Sloan knew better than to try and unseat his superior officer from one of his favourite hobbyhorses and so stayed silent.

'They think,' Leeyes grumbled, 'that if they can change an

outfit's name people will forget whatever mistakes they've made in the past but they won't.'

'No, sir.'

'And the press always puts the old name in as well as the new one so no one forgets, anyway.'

'Naturally, sir,' agreed Sloan, remembering somewhere to do with nuclear production in the north-west of England. Both its new name and its old one always came into his mind – and that of newspaper editors – concurrently.

'Anyway, Sloan, I've got to be there any minute now and you know what they're like.'

Sloan didn't actually know what the Watch Committee was like but he felt as if he did from listening to Leeyes' many animadversions about its workings in the past.

'Bunch of interfering old nonentities, with ideas well above their station, that's what they are,' declared the superintendent, 'and now they think that I can get rid of all our rough sleepers at a stroke.'

'Sir.' Sloan advanced a step forward and coughed. 'Dr Dabbe's report has just come through. He's heard from the forensic laboratory about that man Terry Galloway's post-mortem at last.'

'About time too,' said Leeyes testily.

'And the cause of death was poisoning. Not the head injury.'

Superintendent Leeyes, poised to leave, stopped in his tracks. 'Don't say he'd been taking ergot, too? Or,' he added an afterthought, 'been given it with malice aforethought?'

'No, sir. I understand that there was no trace of ergot in his body. He died from an overdose of a drug called Ameliorite.'

'And what, pray, might that be?' asked Leeyes, who every now and then took Winston Churchill's prose as his model.

'Dr Dabbe said that it's a powerful painkiller with very pronounced sedative side effects.'

'Not the original head injury, then?'

'It would seem not, sir.'

'Don't be so mealy-mouthed, Sloan. It either was or it wasn't.'

'It wasn't.'

'So someone had it in for him as well as for his godmother,' concluded the superintendent slowly.

Sloan nodded. 'First a blow on the head, which didn't do the trick . . .'

'Can't have been hard enough,' said Leeyes.

'. . . and then poison, which did do the trick.'

'And how, may I ask, did whoever gave it to him get hold of the stuff?'

Detective Inspector Sloan turned over a page in his notebook. 'I'm looking into that now, sir. The hospital seems the most likely source.'

'Go on.'

'A drug cabinet at the hospital was broken into last Saturday evening. I've seen the incident file now.'

'The night Galloway was killed?'

Sloan nodded. 'It was reported by the ward sister and the duty doctor who came across the damage when starting the drug round in the Accident and Emergency ward that night. They checked what had been stolen – quite a lot of the more addictive drugs had been taken . . .'

'And that one you mentioned?'

'Ameliorite? Yes, sir. Some but not a lot.'

'Saturday night, when presumably they are at their busiest,' nodded Leeyes. Saturday night was when the police were at their busiest, too. 'Good timing.'

'And they usually have plenty of experienced low lifes about in the department then.' Sloan snapped his notebook shut. 'Breaking into anything wouldn't have been too difficult for most of them. Been doing it for years, a lot of them, I daresay. And there would have been addicts among them, to be sure.'

Leeyes nodded. 'Bound to have been.'

'We're going back there next to take another look into it, now that we know about Ameliorite being used to kill Galloway.'

The superintendent nodded. 'And we still don't know the reason why the man was killed?'

Detective Inspector Sloan, a veteran of working under Superintendent Leeyes, was relieved to hear his superior's use of the plural pronoun 'we'. It was when Leeyes said 'you' and not 'we' that indicated that he wasn't going to share the problem with the force's Criminal Investigation Department.

'I'm afraid that we don't, sir,' he said, tacitly acknowledging Leeyes' stance in the matter. 'Not yet, that is.'

Leeyes grunted.

'All I think we can assume at this stage, sir,' hurried on Sloan, 'is that there is something in Susan Port's cottage that someone didn't want him to find.'

'Or perhaps had been there,' pointed out Leeyes, 'once upon a time but not by then.'

'And maybe that someone was there lying in wait for him,' said Sloan, mindful of a smashed kitchen window.

'Or was just seen by him and who didn't want to be seen by him, Sloan. Someone, at a guess, who shouldn't have been there in the first place.'

'But he'd only just arrived from Australia the day before. He couldn't have known anyone and they couldn't have known him.' He paused. 'There was quite a good photograph of Galloway on the sideboard, though, come to think of it. The deceased must have been very fond of him.'

'And why was someone there in the cottage in the first place?' Leeyes asked, ignoring sentiment. 'And what was he or she looking for, anyway?'

If Detective Inspector Sloan had been talking to a friend or colleague, he would have said, 'Search me.' Instead he said in quite a different tone that he couldn't possibly say, not at this stage of the investigation, 'Unless it was the deceased's computer.'

'If we knew that we'd know everything, Sloan.'

'Not quite everything, sir. We've got the computer here and that hasn't helped us so far.'

'If whatever it was he . . .'

'Or she,' said Sloan, ever mindful of Woman Sergeant Perkins.

'If that which he was searching for,' said Leeyes, rising above this, 'is in the deceased's computer, we still don't know what it was, do we?'

'No, sir.'

'But nevertheless, Sloan, remember that it might matter so much as to kill a man for.'

'The experts are still examining it for any sort of clue, sir. Apparently, it can be a long job.'

'So how did this other stuff . . .'

'Ameliorite.'

'Get into the godson?'

'We don't know that yet, sir, either. It's manufactured for delivery by both tablet and injection. Dr Dabbe said he would have to repeat his examination of the body before he could say which, the patient having had a number of needles stuck into him in the hospital.'

'As they do,' said Leeyes, never a good patient.

'The pathologist was happy, though, that it accounted for the liver damage that he found.'

'I'm glad somebody's happy,' said Leeyes morosely, 'because I'm not.'

Resisting the temptation to say, 'Me neither,' Detective Inspector Sloan murmured that he was afraid that they still didn't know who had administered the fatal dose of Ameliorite, or when or where, and that they were checking whether Galloway had been given an accidental overdose in the ambulance. 'The attendants could have thought that the patient might have been in great pain.'

'What about that man who was on bed watch? You've seen him, I trust.'

'He swears no one out of the ordinary came on the neurology ward all the time he was there – the patient arrived at nine o'clock from the Accident and Emergency ward – that's including the doctors and nurses on duty that night, and he checked them all out.'

'And he was there all the time, I take it?' said Leeyes.

'So he says, sir, and he's pretty reliable.'

'So I should hope,' said Leeyes absently. 'By the way, that field of rye that forensics was looking into? Anything back from them yet?'

'They said there had been a lot of rye growing in the field and subsequently sold to Clive Culshaw's firm but that they couldn't possibly tell whether any of it had had mould growing on it.'

'Mould?'

'On which ergot can grow.'

'Can?' Leeyes pounced. 'Did it?'

'Not that they could establish but, on the other hand, they couldn't swear that there hadn't been any either.' The phrase that had come most readily to Sloan's mind when he had read the report was 'Yes, we have no bananas'.

Superintendent Leeyes sighed heavily. 'I don't like it, Sloan. If you ask me this is a case where it's one step forward and two steps backward at every turn.'

TWENTY-SIX

'And what time was this break-in, Doctor?'

Detective Inspector Sloan and Detective Constable Crosby were at Berebury Hospital questioning the young house surgeon and Sister Peters about exactly when the drug cabinet had been smashed, the report from the original investigating officer in their hands.

Dr Chomel wrinkled her nose. 'It must have been sometime on Saturday evening, Inspector, but I couldn't say exactly when.'

'I can,' said Samantha Peters immediately. 'It's bound to have been when I was on handover just after eight o'clock, or I would have been around and heard it. You, Dr Chomel, if you remember, were dealing with that stabbing in Bay Five. We very nearly lost him.'

Dr Chomel nodded. 'That's right, Sister. So I was.' She turned to the two policemen and explained, 'Stabbings are always more serious than they appear from the outside. A blade can go through an artery before you can say—'

'Knife,' put in Crosby, smirking.

She looked at him in a calculating way for a long moment and then went on in an even voice, 'It's not necessarily that it does so – what really matters is that you can't tell whether or not the knife's severed the artery before the patient bleeds to death.'

'The hospital did inform the police of the break-in at the time because of the street value of some of the drugs that had been stolen,' said Samantha Peters. 'And we told them that a man from our ward had said that he'd got lost looking for X-ray, although it's quite clearly signposted. Where he got to, I can't imagine.'

'Do you know who he was?' asked Sloan.

'I don't know who he was, Inspector, only what he called himself, and that was Little Sir Echo, and he had a dog with him, in spite of our rules on animals.'

'So what went walkabout, then?' asked Crosby, peering at the newly repaired drug cabinet. He had been instructed to make a list and wanted to get on with it.

'Morphine, mostly, Constable, and all our stock of heroin as well as any other major painkillers that would have been in there, such as pethidine and ketamine – Dorothy, they call that,' said the nurse. 'Cocaine, too, although we don't use all that much of it these days.'

'Ameliorite?' suggested Sloan.

'Some, probably, but not a lot,' she said. 'It's not all that popular with the junkies – especially if they can get their hands on anything better.'

'Better?' queried Sloan.

'Ameliorite's a good enough painkiller, Inspector, but it's quite slow-acting and doesn't deliver any of the real kicks, which is what the druggies are after. Highs.'

'Besides,' supplemented Dr Chomel, 'it also sends them to sleep very quickly, their pain notwithstanding. You have to be quite careful with the dosage. Too much can quite easily damage the liver.'

'Amphetamines,' added Samantha Peters. 'There would have been some of them there, too, although we don't use them so much these days either.'

'They can help in some cases,' said the young lady doctor earnestly.

'Uppers,' remarked Crosby colloquially, making another note. 'And downers. Anything else?'

'We only record stocking in that cabinet those medications that come under the Dangerous Drugs Act,' said Dr Chomel.

'You don't count the aspirins, then?' said Crosby.

'Life's too short for that,' said the doctor, adding 'especially if someone's been stabbed.'

'I understand,' said Samantha Peters wryly, 'that the down-and-outs have been having a lovely time since Saturday evening with what has been taken.'

'Quite so,' said Detective Inspector Sloan, more mindful of a young man whose last evening it had been but whose assailant they seemed no nearer finding. He hadn't had a lovely evening at all.

Tom Culshaw, proprietor of the firm of Gordian Knots, would have been the first to acknowledge that a number of the homeless denizens of the Postern Gate part of the town were still showing signs of the consumption of noxious substances when he spent the night there a few days later. Like all young men of his generation he was able to identify the slurred speech, glazed eyes and the slow, almost mannered movements of the men as having their origins in drugs of almost any description.

Or a great deal too much alcohol.

Dressed for the part, Tom had insinuated himself seamlessly amongst the other men there, some of them already well away from the real world. Others, though, were obviously still in their customary state of cold, hunger and homelessness, their hopelessness apparent in their lassitude and malnutrition. Neither of these conditions of man deterred Tom from doing what he had come to do, which was to look for Daniel Elland. He was carrying a picture in his mind of an image created by a computer of what an older, raddled, unshaven and under-nourished Daniel Elland might look like ten years after that plump, well-dressed boardroom photograph had been taken.

Tom Culshaw's first encounter was with the burly leader of the homeless charity Latchless, John Holness, at his base in St Peter's Church in Water Lane. 'Daniel Elland? Never heard of him, mate, and even if I had I wouldn't tell you.'

'You could tell me, though, couldn't you if you'd seen him around here?' Before the man could answer Tom had pulled the computer-simulated image out of his pocket and held it up in front of him.

'I could,' said Holness, after studying it, 'but I'm not
going to.'

Taking that for a 'yes', Tom Culshaw shook his head.
'Pity that, because he's got a lot of money coming to him.'

'All that means, take it from me,' said Holness wearily, 'is
that he and his mates – that is, if he's got any left – will drink
themselves to death that bit sooner with it than without it.'

'The devil drink – that's what they used to call it, wasn't
it?' murmured Tom absently, taking back the picture and
stowing it away again. 'Never signed the pledge, did they, this
lot of yours?'

'There's plenty of other things around than drink these
days that these fellows have to worry about,' said Holness,
'including some that weren't discovered in the old times.'

'I can see that,' said Culshaw. 'Some of them look altogether
out of it now.'

'Break-in at the hospital last Saturday evening,' said
Holness elliptically. 'The drug cabinet was smashed in
Accident and Emergency. Whoever took the stuff sure spread
it around – and for free, too. They think Christmas has come
early. I don't know exactly what they're on now but most of
'em here have been half-cut ever since. Some of them couldn't
even tell you if it's Wednesday or Calleford.'

'What sort of stuff?' asked Culshaw curiously. He had no
idea what Daniel Elland's favourite poison was.

If any.

'Take your pick.' Holness waved an arm to encompass the
whole area. 'Heroin . . .'

'"The loving drug",' quoted Culshaw.

'If you say so, mate,' said Holness, 'but not from where I
sit. Give me alcohol any day of the week – you know where
you are with the drink, but not with some of the other fancy
substances.'

'Pethidine?' hazarded Tom.

'Anything you like as far as I'm concerned except K, if you
don't mind,' said Holness.

'K?' queried Tom Culshaw, more out of his depth in today's
drug scene than he had realised. He decided he must be
getting on.

'C is for the cat that sat on the mat all right, and K is for ketamine, which isn't all right.' He said sardonically. 'Special K they call it. The horse-killer.'

Culshaw frowned, the faint memory of a song coming back to him. He murmured, 'They shoot horses, don't they?'

'Not any more, they don't,' said Holness. 'They kill horses with ketamine these days. And people, too, if you're not very lucky.'

Tom Culshaw's next move was to try to take a good look at every face that he passed. This proved exceedingly unpopular with almost every man, especially with those whose faces were swaddled with tattered scarves or were patently on drugs of one variety or another. Whether this garment was worn against the cold or to hide the face of a man who didn't want to be identified he couldn't decide. His first thought was to emulate what his brother had done and ask for Daniel Elland by name, but this time that plan evoked no response from any of the men to whom he mentioned the name. Nobody now responded by saying that they were looking for him either.

A thinking man, Tom Culshaw could only assume that somebody had found Daniel Elland since. A resolute man, too, he concluded that therefore he ought to be able to do so as well.

And then it started to rain.

Really rain.

Tom turned up his jacket collar and made for the nearest doorway to shelter in but to his surprise he found he was alone there. The usual crowd that he had expected to be huddled under what cover there was to be had there was nowhere to seen. Instead, he was aware of a general slow movement in quite another direction. Curious, he followed a cohort of men shuffling through the darkness towards the covered loading bay at the back of Berebury's supermarket.

So did Detective Constable Crosby, there on duty.

'And I wasn't the only one looking for Daniel Elland, sir,' said the constable, reporting to Detective Inspector Sloan the next morning. 'That clever clogs from Gordian Knots, Tom Culshaw, was there, too. I saw him asking around and showing what looked at a distance like a photograph to everyone who would look.'

'He was, was he?' responded Sloan vigorously. 'We'll have to have a word with him about that. Elland's wife wouldn't give us one, remember?'

'I'm pretty sure, though, that he didn't have any joy in finding the man either because he stayed there a long time, asking around.'

'Go on.'

'All those old boys were crowded in there under that canopy out of the rain,' said Crosby. 'And the funny thing is that it wasn't at all like it was there last time when I got so dizzy. They weren't sick or falling about like I was then, sir.'

'None of them?'

'No, sir. Not even the dog that was there.'

'So, something had changed,' reasoned Sloan.

'Yes, sir, but I don't know what. It was quite all right under there last night out of the rain.'

Sloan frowned. 'Odd, that.'

'And I didn't get that dreadful headache this time either, thank goodness. It was just the rain that got me.'

'So what happened to you last night, Crosby? Were you really all right there?'

'Oh, yes, sir, thank you, sir. I squeezed in alongside a couple of grizzled old men – it was very wet and crowded – and a bit niffy they were, too, but I didn't feel anything at all last night. Not like before. That was awful,' he added, the unhappy memory still rankling.

Detective Inspector Sloan considered this.

Usually in a criminal case there was much evidence to be assembled, examined, tested and evaluated. In the matter of the deaths first of all of Susan Port and then of Terry Galloway there was an absence of firm evidence of any real value other than the causes of death. Mrs Port had undoubtedly died of ergot poisoning and Terry Galloway with a fractured skull but from Ameliorite poisoning. That, unfortunately, seemed as far as it went.

'There was something else, too, sir,' volunteered Crosby. 'I only got to the canopy out of the rain after most of the other men had taken cover there, but as I approached it, I heard a sort of cheer go up and a bit of clapping and shouting. Funny that, wasn't it?'

Detective Inspector Sloan nodded, his mind now elsewhere. It had rather belatedly occurred to him that a childless Daniel Elland dead was worth more than a childless Daniel Elland alive – that is, worth more to a particular small group of legatees.

And though they might want him alive to access their inheritance, they might want him dead that they might have it more abundantly.

TWENTY-SEVEN

'That is certainly true, Inspector, as far as Daniel Elland is concerned,' admitted Simon Puckle cautiously to the two policemen sitting in his office later that day. 'While it doesn't matter from the point of view of enacting the inheritance whether in the event Elland is found to be dead or alive, it would matter considerably in the distribution of the Mayton Trust.'

'All the more for the others,' said Crosby simply. 'Like when Susan Port was killed.'

'Obviously, Inspector,' went on the solicitor, 'I did not have any situation like that in mind when I used the expression "dead or alive" at my original meeting with the legatees.' He gave a little deprecatory cough. 'Perhaps in the circumstances it was a trifle too colloquial.'

'More of a figure of speech, you might say,' agreed Sloan, who had been something of an armchair cowboy in his school-days, reading as many of the works of Zane Grey and J. T. Edson as the library stocked. Posters usually had the heading 'Wanted Dead or Alive' over a picture of a fugitive from justice on the covers of the literature of that genre.

'I was, of course, Inspector, talking purely from the point of view of the conditions of the inheritance, which is my only remit.'

'I quite understand, sir,' said Sloan, whose own remit was wider and included the enactment of justice.

'And, of course,' pointed out the solicitor, 'at that stage Mrs Susan Port was still alive.'

'Hadn't been killed,' said Detective Constable Crosby insouciantly.

'Yes, indeed,' said the solicitor.

'Nor had Terry Galloway,' said Sloan, professionally concerned at what might just have been bystander bad luck.

Or not.

'Very worrying,' agreed Simon Puckle.

'That leaves four other legatees besides Daniel Elland,' stated Sloan.

Simon Puckle coughed. 'I'm afraid that is not theoretically correct, Inspector. You would agree, I am sure, that all possible outcomes have to be considered in cases such as this.'

'Four, Mr Puckle.' Detective Constable Crosby had been counting them off on his fingers. 'The two Culshaw brothers, Martin Pickford and the nurse, Samantha Peters.'

'That, Constable,' explained Simon Puckle, giving another little cough as a preliminary to delivering a legal point, 'is without taking into consideration the possibility – I trust only the very remote possibility – that one of the five remaining legatees whom you've mentioned could be indicted for . . . er . . . grave malfeasance.'

'Murder, you mean,' said Crosby.

The solicitor nodded in acknowledgement of this. 'In theory, should one of the other five be convicted of causing the death of Susan Port then they would be automatically excluded from their inheritance, as a murderer is not allowed to benefit financially from the death of his victim – in civil law, that is.'

'Or hers,' said Detective Constable Crosby, more afraid of Woman Sergeant Perkins than of anyone else in the force.

'Not criminal law?' said Sloan, surprised.

For a wonder Simon Puckle permitted himself a small smile. 'And you will well know, Inspector, the burden of proof in civil law is lower. You then only have to show that the person is guilty of murder on the balance of probabilities, rather than beyond reasonable doubt as in criminal law.'

'I didn't know that,' said Detective Constable Crosby, looking up, interested at last. 'That helps.'

'It depends,' said Puckle drily, while Detective Inspector Sloan privately marvelled at the capacity of all solicitors never to deliver an answer without a proviso. 'Muddying the waters' was what they called that down at the police station. The wider question of whether murderers could nevertheless benefit in other ways than financially from the death of their victim he left for the forensic psychiatrists to evaluate – revenge being high on the list.

'Back to the station, sir?' suggested Crosby hopefully, as the two policemen left the solicitors' offices.

'I'm sorry to disappoint you, Crosby, but the canteen will have to wait.' It wasn't the pound signs of the greedy that Sloan could see in the constable's eyes but mugs full of tea and perhaps a Chelsea bun. 'We need to go out Calleford way next to have a word with Tom Culshaw.'

'Yes, sir. Very good, sir.' He slipped the car into gear and swung it round, heading out of the Berebury traffic as swiftly as he dared.

'We need to find out what that legatee was doing down among the dropouts.' Sloan had strapped himself in the front seat of the car and now he took out his notebook. 'In my opinion, Mr Tom Culshaw is a great deal cleverer than he wants us to think. I'm not quite so sure about the abilities of his younger brother, Clive, though. Spoilt when young, probably. It sounds to me as if he'd been a right mother's boy in her day.'

It was one of the things that Sloan was determined on – that his own young son wouldn't ever become spoilt. Naturally it was a bit too soon now to start to toughen the boy up, so he'd have to wait a while before getting stricter with him. Besides, his wife wouldn't like it – probably wouldn't even let him, anyway – so perhaps he wouldn't try to make a man of him just yet. He was sure he'd know when to start, and in the meantime, it couldn't do any harm just to enjoy the boy, could it? This thought served to assuage the slight feeling of guilt he'd experienced that morning about the little toy truck he'd bought for his son on his way to work.

'Right, sir, we're on the Calleford road now,' Crosby said, bringing Sloan's mind back from childcare. The police car was nearly out of the town and the road less busy. The constable was keeping his eye on the speed limit, balancing it on the legal needle to a nicety.

'And, Crosby . . .'

'Sir?'

'There is no urgency about the journey. Remember that "softly, softly, catchee monkey".'

'Beg pardon, sir?'

'An expression that as far as the human animal is concerned means go gently if you want to catch someone out.'

'Drive ordinarily you mean, sir?' he said with a marked lack of enthusiasm.

'I meant drive as other people usually drive,' said Sloan, heavily ironic. 'Law-abiding people.'

'No blues and twos, then?' said Crosby, disappointed. He hadn't driven fast for days.

'Neither. We should keep everything as low-key as we can with this fellow. There are no flies on our Tom Culshaw, remember, which is how he is able to run a successful outfit such as Gordian Knots. I think it's high time we found out what he was doing down among the dossers.'

'Just following the crowd, Inspector,' insisted Tom Culshaw when the two policemen reached his house. He was sitting at his kitchen table playing with five metal balls. They were suspended by thin cords from a miniature gantry in a row alongside each other. 'My brother went there looking for Daniel Elland and got clobbered for his pains, so I thought I'd have a go myself and see what I could see.'

Sloan, policeman on duty, who hadn't for one moment discounted the possibility that in spite of all appearances to the contrary the two brothers might be acting in what the law called 'concert', merely nodded and said, 'I see, sir.'

'Brotherly love?' murmured Crosby almost – but not quite – under his breath.

'Professional curiosity,' said Culshaw, who had heard him.

On the other hand, thought Sloan, ignoring them both, that

the two Culshaws might each have had a different agenda was something that hadn't occurred to him before.

And it should have done.

Besides, for all he knew Tom Culshaw might be the murderer they were seeking. After all, somebody was and the man sitting across his kitchen table from him now was still in the running. All of the legatees were, although whether innate ability came into the picture he wasn't sure. He'd known some very dim murderers get away with it in his day. Mostly from keeping their mouths shut.

Tom Culshaw pulled back the ball at the beginning of the row of his plaything and then he let it go. It hit its neighbour but it was a different ball at the opposite end of the row that responded by moving forward to exactly the same degree. The middle ones didn't move.

'What are you doing with that thing?' asked Crosby, fascinated.

'Thinking,' said Culshaw.

Detective Inspector Sloan was anxious to pursue quite a different line of thought of his own. 'And what exactly came into your mind, sir, when you were down at the Postern Gate?'

'All I thought about,' interrupted Crosby by way of encouragement, 'was getting out of the rain.'

Sloan, qua mentor, made a mental note yet again to have a talk with Crosby afterwards, reminding him, once more, that policemen were there to gather information, not to dispense it.

'I did happen to see you there, Constable,' said Tom Culshaw evenly. He turned to Sloan and said, 'What I noticed first, Inspector, was that half of the men there seemed to be on something. Happy-baccy wasn't in it with a lot of them. I asked one of the younger ones who I could get it from for myself and he said "Father Christmas".'

'Really, sir?' said Sloan, unsurprised. No druggie that he had ever known would have given the name of his dealer to a stranger, who might have been a policeman and not seeking solace in the weed at all – if that's what druggies did.

'There's certainly something funny going on down there, anyway,' said Tom. 'I'm pretty sure that that man John Holness from Latchless knows more than he's telling. And that he

knows which of that bunch Daniel Elland is, too, although
he's not saying that either.'

That John Holness was next on the list of those to be interviewed in the case, Sloan didn't say.

'You may have ways of making him talk, Inspector, but I
haven't,' said Tom Culshaw, 'being a civilian, so to speak.'
Having thus impugned the integrity of the entire police force,
he reverted to pulling back one of the steel balls on his plaything and letting it go. 'Interesting this, gentlemen, isn't it?
It's called a Newton's cradle after the revered Isaac. Watch
how the impetus passes through the balls in between the first
and last ones and comes out at the end at the same strength.'

'Yes, I can see that, sir,' murmured Sloan. 'The knock-on
effect, you might say.' It was actually the apparent lack of any
knock-on effect following the murders of Sue Port and Terry
Galloway that he himself had to consider; it was something
else about the whole business that was odd. Two deaths and
seemingly nothing had changed – for good or ill – save the
abruptly curtailed lives of the two victims. Was there perhaps
something quite outside the circle of the Mayton legatees that
the police knew nothing about?

'And there's something else as well, Inspector . . .' Culshaw
was continuing.

'Go on,' said Sloan.

'Some of the men were moaning about the heavy rain,
all right, but nearly all of them were moving towards the
shelter behind the Berebury supermarket – you know, their
delivery bay.'

'That's where I came unstuck the first time,' contributed
Crosby, eager for sympathy from any quarter he could get it.
'I felt terrible while I was in there.'

'And after the crowd had got there,' went on Tom Culshaw,
'a sort of cheering went up. It was quite loud and I heard it
as I went that way.' He frowned. 'I can't understand that either,
and I've been wondering why ever since.'

'Very puzzling, I'm sure, sir,' agreed Sloan.

'I had a word with one of the more sentient ones, Inspector,
but he wouldn't say anything except that they were grateful
to be back under cover again.' He paused and added, 'Actually

now I come to think of it he put it a bit more forcefully than that.'

'But you didn't find out why?'

'No, but it's one of the things I've been thinking about ever since,' Tom answered him seriously. 'That and why anyone should want to kill—'

'Need to kill,' put in Crosby.

'All right then, Constable. Should have reason to kill anyone.' Tom Culshaw sat back in his chair and sent another metal ball pulsating through its neighbours.

Detective Inspector Sloan silently amended this in his mind from 'anyone' to 'someone', acknowledging that the man in front of him had put his finger on what was still unknown in the case and that was 'Motive'. Its companions in the usual triumvirate of successful murder – 'Means' and 'Opportunity' – had de facto existed in that murder had been done.

Twice.

'Especially one of us,' said Tom Culshaw.

Detective Inspector Sloan nodded. He had never thought that either death had been random and said so now.

'It can't be for money,' Tom Culshaw went on reasoning aloud. 'It sounded to me that what we were all going to inherit was quite enough, especially as we'd none of us had any expectations before Algernon Mayton came into the picture.'

That had been one of the things that had puzzled Sloan all along. Why kill two people if it wasn't for the money, in spite of Superintendent Leeyes saying he should follow it?

'But I'm blessed if I can think what else it could be,' said Tom Culshaw, his words meshing with Sloan's unspoken ones.

Detective Inspector Sloan, experienced police officer, could run through a whole litany of the customary motives for murder – blackmail, greed, revenge, dynasty, jealousy – had indeed already done so in his mind in this case – and answer had come there none. Apart from the two brothers, none of the legatees had even known of the existence of the others before being summoned to the solicitors' offices that day. Simon Puckle had been sure of that – Miss Fennel had been equally certain that, except for the two brothers, they had met as strangers.

Or had they? It was something else that he would have to check on, should have checked on before now.

This time Culshaw picked up two of the nearest metal balls and set them off together, one behind the other. Obedient to some force Sloan didn't understand two balls at the other end responded by swinging out together to exactly the same degree. 'Newton's cradle,' said Tom Culshaw, indicating it, 'demonstrates his third law of motion: "For every action there is an equal and opposite reaction".'

'Really, sir?' Detective Inspector Sloan didn't have time to play with desktop toys. What the opposite reaction to murder was he didn't know. He would have liked to think it was justice but he had been a policeman too long to be sure of that.

'You hit someone on the head and they die,' suggested Crosby brightly.

'I think that might be cause and effect,' murmured Tom Culshaw, 'which is rather different.' Detective Inspector Sloan's mind, like the action of the balls in the Newton's cradle, had gone on moving until it, too, produced a reaction. He decided that since he hadn't been told anything that wasn't patently untrue, that which he was dealing with in the case was an absence of information instead.

'Back to Berebury,' he ordered Crosby as they left Tom Culshaw, 'and the drawing board.'

TWENTY-EIGHT

Tom Culshaw's next visitor was Martin Pickford.

'Well?' asked that young man who, like John Bunyan's pilgrim, Christian, took his scars with him. 'How did you get on then at the Postern Gate? Did you find Daniel Elland?'

'Not exactly.'

'What does that mean?'

'It means that I'm pretty sure that I know where he is but not who he is.'

Pickford, no great shakes intellectually, had some difficulty in working this out. 'So you can't put your hands on him?' he said eventually, that being the thing that mattered to him most.

'Not yet. I'm getting there, though.'

'Just sitting here and doing nothing like this?' If nothing else, Martin Pickford had always been a man of action.

'On the contrary, I've been thinking deeply ever since I got back from the Postern Gate.'

'And playing with those little balls?'

'Working things out, that's what I've been doing.'

Martin Pickford looked distinctly sceptical.

'I'm getting there, man,' Tom Culshaw assured him. 'I think I know now what Daniel Elland has been doing at the Postern Gate, too.'

'So? Then tell me.'

'I'm not going to because I can't prove it. Not yet. Daniel Elland is over there, all right, which is very useful to know.' Tom Culshaw drew back one of the balls in his Newton's cradle and sent it on its way. 'It's a start.'

'But you can't tell me which of all the men there he is? Is that it?'

'Roughly.'

'Is it because most of them look very much alike – old and grey and dirty – so that you can't work out t'other from which?'

'No, it's nothing like that.'

'Then it's not a lot of good to me, Culshaw. I need Elland properly found and pronto – we all do. Don't you understand? I need some money and I need it soon and none of us can get at it until he's been got hold of.'

'Oh, I understand all right. Don't make any mistake about that. But let me put it this way: I've picked up the ball, but I haven't run with it yet.' He regarded the rugby player with something like amusement. 'You do understand that, don't you?'

'So why don't you get on with it?' said the other man. 'If I get my hands on the ball on the field I don't hang about just thinking and pushing other little balls about like you're doing now.'

'Because I haven't worked out how to get the man to show his hand yet, that's why,' Tom Culshaw said. 'But I have worked out what he did when it rained.'

'What on earth has the rain got to do with it?'

'Everything,' said Tom Culshaw gnomically. 'But whether that's any help in finding out who killed that woman out at Bishop's Marbourne, I couldn't begin to say.'

Detective Inspector Sloan wouldn't have been able tell Martin Pickford that either, even though he was equally aware that Daniel Elland must be down by the Postern Gate among the other vagrants. What he was afraid of now was that the man might be in the same sort of danger as that which had over-taken Susan Port and Terry Galloway. The fact that Elland was being so actively sought by some of the other Mayton claimants was no comfort to a police officer dedicated to the safety of all members of the public, winos or not.

'Where to next, sir?' asked Detective Constable Crosby, ready by the driver's door of the police car.

'To the church by the Postern Gate, Crosby, to see what that Latchless man has to tell us about Daniel Elland. It's high time I had a look at the place myself.'

'You want John Holness, sir,' said Crosby, setting off as fast as he dared. 'He's the one who Tom Culshaw showed his photograph to and swore he'd never seen the man.'

'Him,' agreed Sloan. 'Culshaw said he was certain John Holness knew which of that bunch of raddled old destitutes is Daniel Elland, remember, but he wouldn't tell him, no way.'

'Can't have that, sir, can we?' said Crosby, subconsciously stepping up the car's speed.

'Certainly not, Crosby. And we'll soon see about him not telling us,' said Sloan, setting his lips in a firm line. There was such a thing as assisting the police in the course of their enquiries, which it behoved all good subjects of the Crown to do. 'And we can't go on assuming that Elland's quite safe down there in the meantime just because he's still unknown by anyone else. Somebody could easily push him through the Postern Gate and into the river one dark night.' Nobody had expected that Susan Port or Terry Galloway had been at risk and that hadn't saved either of them.

'Perhaps he'll be in more danger if we find him than if we don't,' suggested Crosby brightly. 'After all, if nobody knows who he is then they can't kill him, too, can they, sir?'

'Ah, but that happy state of affairs might not last for ever, Crosby,' Sloan pointed out, 'and we may not know when it doesn't. Always think long term when you can.'

'Yes, sir,' said Crosby to whom the thought of the following week was usually virgin territory.

'Besides, not finding him might mean not finding out who killed Susan Port and Terry Galloway, Crosby, which is something we must do. Had you thought of that possibility either?'

'No, sir,' admitted Crosby.

'Who?' asked John Holness, looking up at the two policemen from his table in the nearby church where he was sitting studying a bunch of forms.

'Daniel Elland,' said Sloan.

'That man's Mr Popular all of a sudden,' said Holness, 'although he's usually Billy No Mates. You're not the only ones looking for him, I can tell you. The fellow that owns the bakery was here the other day asking for him too, and someone else showed me his photograph.'

'And you said you didn't recognise him,' said Sloan, 'but we think you did, Mr Holness.'

'Our policy at Latchless,' declared the man stiffly, 'is not to disclose the names or whereabouts of any of the men we are helping.'

'Not even to the police?' said Crosby, jumping the gun.

'Oh, that's who you are, is it?' Holness put his pen down. 'I suppose you're after whoever it was who broke into the hospital drugs cabinet? Well, I don't know who did that, but I can tell you that this place has been awash with the stuff ever since Saturday night. All of them are controlled drugs, too – none of your home-grown illegal substances. Not surprising really, I suppose, since they must have come from the hospital in the first place. The men all insist they found them in their pockets when they got back.'

'A likely tale,' sniffed Crosby.

'No, it isn't,' said Detective Inspector Sloan, light dawning with a sudden flash, a completely new vista now opening up in his mind. It was a very different crime scenario from all that had gone before, and he needed time to think about it. He took a deep breath and made himself carry on with an enquiry that suddenly seemed mundane now. 'They shared the drugs out afterwards, I suppose, or sold them,' resumed Sloan, as if he hadn't reached the conclusion that he had done.

'Or those that did have them had their pockets picked,' said the manager of Latchless, worldly-wise in spite of being dedicated to good works. 'Nothing's really safe round here for long.'

'What we would really like, Mr Holness,' said Sloan, producing his warrant card and laying it on the table in front of him, 'would be to fingerprint everyone here until we find him.' Locating Daniel Elland was still important, but he had no time to waste now.

'You must be having a laugh, Inspector,' said Holness, picking the card up and reading it. 'Try it on the first one and you won't see the others for dust. They'll melt away like snow in summer and you'll never see the going of them. And I won't see them back again for yonks.'

'Pity, that,' said Sloan, 'since we really do need to talk to this Daniel Elland and fingerprinting your – er – clients would have been one way of finding him.'

'He wanted for something, then?' asked Holness.

'Yes, but not in the sense you mean,' said Sloan.

The man from Latchless looked at him suspiciously. 'It isn't a wife after him, is it?'

'Certainly not,' Sloan assured him.

'Cause us terrible trouble, do some wives,' said the other man. 'Mind you, as often as not, meeting their wives explains what brings a man here in the first place.'

'Quite so,' said Detective Inspector Sloan, a happily married man, letting his mind dwell briefly on the image of his own wife, not the sort of woman to drive a man to drink. Mentally much refreshed, he got back to the job of finding Daniel Elland, still his job.

'I must remind you, Mr Holness,' he said at his most formal, 'that obstructing the police in the execution of their duties is a criminal offence, and I shall have no hesitation whatsoever in charging you with so doing if you fail to tell me which man here is Daniel Elland.'

'The one with the dog,' muttered John Holness, 'but for God's sake don't let on that I told you.'

But there was no sign anywhere to be seen near the Postern Gate of a man with a dog.

TWENTY-NINE

Superintendent Leeyes was sitting at his desk when Sloan got back to the police station. He was waiting for him like a hungry spider waits for its fly to come within range of her web and pounced.

'There's been a message for you,' he growled, 'from one of your precious Mayton legatees.'

'Sir?' Sloan stiffened – which one of them it was could make a big difference at this stage.

'Someone called Tom Culshaw rang, asking for you . . .'

Sloan breathed out a silent sigh of relief and waited for Leeyes to go on.

'He said that the man who you should be looking for down by the Postern Gate is the one who's just disabled the sonic deterrent in the loading bay behind the supermarket.'

'We already know which man we want, thank you, sir.' It was very seldom that Detective Inspector Sloan – or, indeed, anyone else on the strength – had a chance to upstage the superintendent, and Sloan was human enough to enjoy the fact. 'Daniel Elland used to own a firm called Berebury Sound and so he knew how to deal with that sonar system. That's why the men there were looking for him.'

'And,' went on Leeyes, ignoring this last, 'he says no one hit him – this Tom Culshaw, that is – on the head while he was there.'

'There was no need for that by the time Tom Culshaw got there, sir. I guess his brother, Clive, got clobbered when he was down there because he'd announced that he was looking for Daniel Elland, too, and they wanted to find him first.' He coughed. 'But it's helpful to know what Elland's done there now and that he hasn't lost his touch after so long.' He didn't know what life after Mayton would hold for Daniel Elland but something good, surely? Better than life by the Postern Gate, for sure.

Leeyes swept on. 'Apparently, like you said, the man's old firm were sound engineers and Tom Culshaw said to tell you that Elland must be the only man there who would have known how to disable the nuisance and therefore it must be him who neutralised the effects of the sonic waves under the supermarket canopy.'

'That must have been what the cheering was all about the evening Crosby was there,' said Sloan.

Leeyes scowled. 'Crosby should have found that out for himself. We'll never make a policeman of him, you know.'

Sloan hurried on. The wider question of the competence of Detective Constable Crosby would have to wait for another day. 'We already have the man's name and photograph and his last known whereabouts,' he said, although Sloan would have been the first to admit that this last was stretching it a bit, since the man had disappeared back into the crowd. He added that it should only be a matter of time now before they picked him up.

'For murder?' asked Leeyes hopefully.

'No, sir,' he said, 'but to claim a healthy inheritance.'

'That, may I remind you, Sloan,' said Leeyes at his most crusty, 'in case you should have forgotten, is not the object of the police investigation. We have two unsolved murders on our hands and I want to know what you propose doing about it.'

'I'm going to go to Kew, sir.'

'What? Kew, at this time of the year? And what on earth for? I know you fancy yourself as a gardener, Sloan, but you especially should know that there won't be any flowers left there by now.'

'Not to the gardens, sir, to the National Archive, which is at Kew.'

'To do what?'

'To look for something that I think isn't there.'

'Even you, Sloan,' the superintendent said testily, 'should know that you can't prove a negative.'

Sloan hastily amended this. 'I need to go there to confirm that something that should be there isn't there, sir.'

'And might I ask why I have not been privy to the outcome of these investigations so far?'

'That's because, sir, I haven't had any real information to give you to date.'

'The absence of war isn't peace, Sloan,' pronounced Leeyes enigmatically.

As far as Sloan was concerned the absence of war was usually armed neutrality but he held his own peace. 'As far as I could see, sir, until very recently no one had told me anything that appeared on the surface to be untrue or at least not verifiable.' This not so subtle distinction was lost on the superintendent. 'What I am hoping to do next is to confirm the absence of certain information, not its presence.'

'I wish you wouldn't talk in riddles, Sloan.'

'Sorry, sir.'

'But perhaps, Inspector,' Leeyes said, heavily sarcastic now, 'when you do reach any conclusions you would see fit to apprise me of them.'

Sloan's promise to this effect was delivered in a studiously neutral tone as he made his escape.

In the event he didn't go to Kew but rang the National Archives instead. The official there took his time to carry out Sloan's request but when he got back to him he was quite definite. 'No, Inspector,' he said, 'we can't trace anything to that effect for the years you mention or, indeed, for five years on either side of the date you gave us, which we have also checked to be on the safe side.' He gave a little hortatory cough. 'You will understand that we can't be too careful in our line of work.'

You couldn't be too careful in the police force either, thought Sloan to himself. He didn't like to say to the man at Kew that it had been that sort of detailed checking by a retired civil servant that had led to all the trouble with the Mayton legatees – let him keep his ideals.

'And the death certificate?' Sloan asked.

'To all outward appearances it is quite unexceptional, Inspector. It was all in order except, of course, for what you are suggesting. That is,' he added meticulously, 'if what you are postulating is actually the case.'

'And the birth certificate?'

'Similarly apparently quite straightforward. At first sight, that is.' He coughed again. 'Obviously some amendments might be called for in both instances in future. Naturally, I would have to look up the proper procedure for that.'

Revised birth and death certificates did not figure in Sloan's priorities.

'I take it, Inspector,' the official was going on, 'that you will want certified copies for whatever legal action you will be taking?'

'In due course,' replied Sloan. The law could afford to take its time.

The police couldn't.

THIRTY

'**N**o, I'm afraid not,' said Simon Puckle with every appearance of genuine regret. He sounded every bit as professional as a doctor did when delivering bad news to a patient. Sympathetic and concerned but at the same time detached. 'The terms of the Mayton Trust are quite specific in the matter.'

'I'm sorry to hear that,' said a dejected Clive Culshaw, his shoulders sagging perceptibly.

The solicitor did, however, contrive to still sound sympathetic towards the worried businessman sitting across his desk, clutching an untidy file of papers. Not that that helped the man opposite. 'I fear, Mr Culshaw, that the inheritance is only to be distributed – and I may say accounted for, too – when all the legatees are in a position to receive it at the same time.'

'So you can't help me at all, then? I was wondering if you would just consent to my having a loan from the money coming to me. Short term, of course.'

'I'm sorry but any premature distribution of the capital might make for uncertainty. And it could also perhaps complicate the furtherance of a theoretical claim against the trust by or on behalf of some or of all the other legatees, you understand.'

Clive Culshaw's shoulders sagged even further. 'I can't say that I do understand, Mr Puckle,' he said. 'After all, my having an advance on what is coming to me anyway can't possibly make any difference to any of the other legatees.'

'There could be a challenge to the whole estate from others who might even at this late stage consider themselves interested parties,' said Simon Puckle, before quickly adding, 'although we have naturally taken every precaution we can against such a contingency.'

'Naturally,' said Culshaw, struggling to keep a note of sarcasm out of his voice. The last person he wanted to upset at this particular time was the solicitor.

'We could postulate other difficult circumstances too but the main fact to bear in mind is the provision against what you are proposing contained in the terms of the trust in relation to anticipating any capital from it before its distribution.'

The solicitor had never – could not ever have – met the long-deceased Algernon Mayton but having had the trust under his care for so many years he felt he knew the old man's mind by now. Anticipating money would, he was sure, have been anathema to a man who had made so much of it in his time. It would have been a dangerous practice in Mayton's day and it was a dangerous thing to do today.

'Surely it couldn't do any harm . . .' Clive Culshaw began in a persuasive, salesman's voice.

The solicitor hadn't finished. 'There is the added complication of our inability to find Daniel Elland. You do realise that if he cannot be found it could conceivably be seven years before we could make a claim for presumption of death?'

'I don't believe it,' howled Clive Culshaw. 'It can't be.'

'Every possible contingency has to be taken into consideration.'

'Except my urgent need for money,' said Culshaw bitterly.

'There is also,' continued the solicitor, sounding sterner now, 'the added consideration of the . . . er . . . unexplained – the unresolved – death of one of the other legatees as well as the aforementioned unavailability of another, both of which understandably preclude a speedy settlement.'

'The law doesn't make anything easy,' muttered Clive Culshaw sourly, 'although you'd think it should.' He shifted tack a little. 'If it isn't legally possible for me to have an advance on my share of the Mayton money, then would there be any objection to my using the fact of my eventual inheritance as collateral for a loan?'

He pointed to the file in his hand. 'As you can see from these papers, Culshaw's Bakery . . .'

'Your firm,' Puckle reminded him gently, 'of which you are the sole owner.'

'My firm which is in financial straits.'

'Dire financial straits,' said the solicitor, who had been shown the papers.

'And is in great danger of going under,' conceded Culshaw. 'Some of my creditors are getting very pressing.'

'Word does tend to get around,' murmured Puckle.

'Vultures looking for pickings,' said Culshaw, 'that's what they are. Well, at this rate they won't be fat ones.'

'Smaller firms are always at risk from bigger ones,' observed Puckle in a detached way, forbearing to say it was how the world of business worked or that this factor applied in the animal kingdom as well.

'It's all very well for you to say that, Mr Puckle, but it's not only my livelihood that's at risk but that of my workers, to say nothing of my family's well-being as well,' responded Culshaw haughtily. The fact that the game of bridge cost almost nothing to play wasn't likely to compensate his wife for losing a standard of living that she had got used to.

'True,' nodded Simon Puckle, refraining from passing any opinion on the matter. 'Very true.'

Clive Culshaw got straight back to the matter in hand. 'So, then,' he asked directly, 'can I borrow what I need to keep going on the strength of this inheritance, using the promise of the Mayton money to come? That's what I need to know now if you won't advance me any of it.'

Simon Puckle, senior partner in the long-established firm of Puckle, Puckle and Nunnery, Solicitors and Notaries Public, and an experienced operator, said, 'That, Mr Culshaw, is entirely a matter for whomsoever you are able to secure a loan from.'

THIRTY-ONE

'Are you quite sure, Sloan?' Superintendent Leeyes had started to pace up and down his office, never a good sign.

'Quite sure, sir.'

'Both deaths?'

'Both murders, sir,' said Sloan, greatly daring. He didn't often correct anything his superior officer said.

'Beyond doubt?' asked Leeyes. 'You know what the press are always like if we drop a clanger.'

'Yes, sir,' said Detective Inspector Sloan, answering both questions at the same time.

'Even Terry Galloway being killed? Don't forget the newspapers always come down on us like a ton of bricks before they ask for our side of the story.'

'Yes, sir,' said Sloan, searching his memory for the military term that covered the unintentional killing of the innocent. 'I'm afraid that was collateral damage.'

'In the wrong place at the wrong time,' said Leeyes, putting it in his own way.

'It was purely fortuitous, sir, that he should have been there and then. Terry Galloway shouldn't have been in the picture at all. He couldn't possibly have known that the murderer was in the house when he arrived on the cottage doorstep at Bishop's Marbourne.'

'But the murderer could have recognised him all right,' concluded Leeyes. 'You said there was a large photograph of him on Susan Port's sideboard.'

'That's right, sir. So far, we only know that the deceased was his godmother and, having no children of her own, fond enough of him to leave him all her worldly wealth.' Christopher Dennis Sloan, husband and father, was content to know that he himself had a proper heir of the body male, not a contrived one. He hastened on. 'What we don't know yet, sir, is whether the deceased's own solicitors – PC York found out that they were in south London somewhere – had got round to letting Galloway know that he'd come into all Susan Port's worldly wealth before he set out for England or not. We're trying to find that out at this end.'

'Then you'd better get on with it, Sloan.'

'It's already in hand, sir. We've also asked the Australian police to try to establish at their end whether or not Terry Galloway knew about Sue Port's death before he set off for England. It's quite important for us to know. If her solicitors had advised him of the fact, then he would have known that there shouldn't by rights have been anyone in her cottage when he went there.'

'As by rights it would have been his own cottage by then,' reasoned Leeyes.

'Exactly, sir. Presumably, if so, it would explain why he went out to Bishop's Marbourne to take a look at it – I mean, that he didn't actually hurry over there to see her as soon as he got to Berebury.'

'And what was anyone doing in her cottage anyway, might I ask?' asked Superintendent Leeyes heavily.

'Trying to remove incriminating evidence, at a guess,' said Sloan.

'Such as?'

'A computer full to the gunnels with Mayton family history for starters.' Sloan didn't know if that was the right way to describe all the information contained in that small machine, but it would have to do since nobody could know, except in a month of Sundays, how much was actually in one. If he hadn't known exactly where to check, then he wouldn't have done either.

'But why the long delay in trying to get hold of it?'

'Friday night was the only night of the week that the murderer could be sure the Dysons would be out. They played cribbage at the local hostelry every week.'

'It was the computer, not the ergot, then?'

'The ergot had only been there from time to time when she was visited by the murderer. I daresay a few tablets would have been handed over each time in the guise of painkillers.'

'Tablets?'

'Something called ergotamine tartrate.'

'I suppose it makes a change from arsenic, whatever it is.' There was only one thing worse in Sloan's book than Leeyes being sarcastic and that was Leeyes being facetious. 'They say that's usually a woman's favourite weapon – there was that well-known Scottish woman . . .'

'Madeleine Smith, sir.' There were some names that stood out in the memory.

'And do we happen to know what this stuff ergotamine tartrate is?'

'Oh, yes, sir.' Sloan had already had a rapid lesson in pharmacology from Dr Brooke Helston over at Calleford. That slip of a girl had told him all about ergotamine tartrate, and when he had asked why it was given to patients if it could be poisonous, had quoted some ancient called Paracelsus at him: 'It's the dose that makes the poison.'

'Well?' asked Leeyes impatiently.

'It's a tablet used routinely in hospitals in obstetric departments – I am told that forty milligrams given over a five-day period has been known to cause impending gangrene in all four extremities. We don't know yet how much was given to Susan Port, but if you remember, sir, Dr Dabbe reported on the gangrene in his post-mortem report on the deceased.'

'A hospital drug, then.' Difficult he might be, but nobody had ever called Superintendent Leeyes slow on the uptake.

'Usually, sir. It's obviously one containing ergot from its name and it's prescribed as part of the childbirth process,' said Detective Inspector Sloan, carefully avoiding the medical specifics. The doctors would have to do that later. It was just the maladministration of ergot that came into the police orbit.

'So . . .'

'That's what clinched it, sir. At one time she'd worked in midwifery. She'd even told Tom Culshaw so but I'm afraid I didn't take the fact on board soon enough when he told me. I'm sorry about that. I should've done because the drugs expert at the hospital in Calleford did mention at the time that there were therapeutic uses of ergot, too,' Sloan said, standing by for a reprimand.

'Information overload can hamper an investigation,' quoted Leeyes unexpectedly. It was a sentiment that he usually expressed when being requested to spend more from his budget than he was prepared to do on something he didn't approve of.

Sloan breathed again. His mea culpa had done the trick. This time but not always.

'So what put you on to her, Sloan?'

'Something that Detective Constable Crosby said.'

'Crosby?' harrumphed Leeyes sceptically.

'After the break-in at the hospital's Accident and Emergency Department, most of the drugs taken needed putting somewhere in order to make everyone think that they'd been taken by an outsider who had smashed the drug cabinet to get at them.'

'So where does Crosby come in?' asked Leeyes.

'I'm coming to that, sir,' said Sloan. 'She very cleverly slipped them into the pockets of all the men from the Postern Gate area who came into her department that Saturday night.'

'Why on earth . . .'

'She only needed the Ameliorite from the drug cabinet herself – by the way, she'd done the smashing as she went to the handover in the sister's office – to kill Terry Galloway. That was after that young African doctor examined him in the Accident and Emergency ward and said that she was sure he was going to come round in time and live.'

'So?'

'So she decided she had to make sure he didn't because he might have seen her.' Sloan hesitated. 'I suppose that she'd worked out that if he did happen to come round on her ward, he'd recognise her.'

'I can see that, Sloan,' Leeyes waved an arm dismissively.

'What I still don't see is exactly where young Crosby comes into all this.'

'When the men told John Holness from Latchless that they had found clinical drugs – and only clinical drugs – in their pockets but didn't know how they got there, Crosby didn't believe that that was a credible story. He was scornful, saying that was a likely tale – he actually meant it was an unlikely tale – and I suddenly realised it wasn't and went looking for evidence to prove it.'

'And found it, I take it?'

'Oh, yes, sir, once I knew where to look.'

'Kew?'

'Yes, sir.' Detective Inspector Sloan didn't approve of toadying to the superintendent but there were times when he could do it with a clear conscience and he decided this was one of them. He mustn't give Crosby too much of the credit: Leeyes wouldn't like that either. 'But, sir, it was something that you yourself said that helped clinch the matter.'

Leeyes looked up, visibly pleased. 'Really? What was that?'

'It was when you said that whoever had hit Galloway on the head hadn't hit him hard enough to kill him.'

'Ah, yes,' said Leeyes, preening himself. 'So I did.'

'I ought to have known then that the blow was too light. The killer must have had what you might call a woman's touch, sir.'

THIRTY-TWO

One thing that could always be said about all the members of the healing professions was their higher realism and Detective Inspector Sloan was grateful for it now.

'I didn't know myself until my mother was dying,' admitted Samantha Peters. 'She only told me then.'

'Told you what?' asked Sloan, although he thought he had a pretty good idea by now.

'That she had never been married,' said the nurse.

Detective Constable Crosby sat up and said indignantly, 'Being illegitimate doesn't stop anyone inheriting their parents' money these days. It's not like it used to be.'

She gave Crosby a look that Sloan was to remember for a long time afterwards. 'I was my mother's daughter all right, Constable, but I was not the child of William Charles Peters, the descendant of Algernon Mayton. Actually, he never knew anything about me at all.'

'But—' he protested.

'In fact,' she said, 'he didn't even know that my mother was having a baby. Not ever.'

'I don't get it,' said Crosby.

Detective Inspector Sloan did.

'She was pregnant when William Peters died, that's all,' said Samantha Peters.

'All?' echoed Crosby.

Sloan said, 'What you are saying, miss, is that at the time your mother was pregnant she told everyone else . . .'

'And me as a young child,' she interposed swiftly.

'That she had been married to William Peters,' said Sloan, nodding his own understanding. It wouldn't be the first time a girl had come back home from the city to the country with child and pretended to be a young widow. And it wouldn't be the last either.

'And that he was my father. She told them that, too,' she said.

'But what did William Peters say to that?' persisted Crosby.

Detective Inspector Sloan said gently, 'He didn't say anything, Crosby. He couldn't because he was dead.' He looked across at the woman sitting at the table opposite to him in the bleak interview room at the police station. 'That right, miss?'

She nodded. 'My mother was his housekeeper and he didn't have any relatives or many friends. He'd always been in bad health and when he died suddenly at home – it was from the asthma he'd always suffered from and not a surprise to his doctor or anyone else – she filled in all the paperwork and registered his death as his widow. She had him buried, shut up the house – it was rented because he'd never been well enough to get a mortgage on account of his long-term chest condition – and came back to her parents' home in Ornum village, with a baby on the way.'

Crosby opened his mouth to say something. 'Me,' she said before he could speak.

Detective Inspector Sloan made a note.

'There was no rent on his house owing,' she went on, 'and anyway the landlord didn't know anything at all about my mother – probably not even that she'd been there at all, let alone her name, seeing as it wasn't anything to do with him in any case. Neither was where she went to after William Peters died. She told me she only brought her own things back with her and took care not to leave any clues as to who she was or where she had gone.' She looked down at her hands and said wryly, 'Finding missing people wasn't as easy in those days as it is now, Inspector. In any case, there was probably no one around who needed to.'

'It's not always that easy finding people now,' blurted out Crosby, still brooding on his own broken nights. 'Look at Daniel Elland.'

'That poor man,' she said compassionately, the nurse in her seemingly rising to the surface notwithstanding everything else. 'I heard they'd found him at last among all the dropouts.'

Sympathetic she might sound but Detective Inspector Sloan reminded himself that nevertheless it was the woman before him who had tried to implicate the man with the dog, now duly identified as Daniel Elland, in the theft of the drugs at the hospital. There had been cold calculation, not compassion, about that.

And of the killing of two innocent people.

'Tell me,' he said curiously, because it was something that didn't fit, 'why it took you so long to try to retrieve Susan Port's computer from her cottage.'

'Two reasons, Inspector,' she said as calmly as if they had been discussing the weather. 'The next-door neighbours . . .'

'The Dysons . . .' put in Crosby.

'They only went out on Friday evenings.' Crosby, who had remembered that much, nodded.

'And,' said Samantha Peters, 'because I was almost always on duty on Friday nights. Besides, I had to wait until the evenings drew in and it was dark enough for me to get there unseen.'

'A window of opportunity,' nodded Sloan.

'It was a kitchen window,' said Crosby, who hadn't understood.

'So nobody in William Peters' old circle knew who your mother was or where she had gone after he died,' concluded Detective Inspector Sloan, sticking to what mattered in law. 'And if anyone there had started looking for her they wouldn't have been able to find her.'

'Or you, miss,' put in Crosby, cottoning on at last, 'after you were born.'

'That right?' Sloan asked her.

She nodded her head again. 'They wouldn't have known where to begin to look. They probably didn't even know my mother's surname – she was only the housekeeper there and things were rather different in those days. Servants – what you might call the below stairs people – weren't thought of as real people then.'

'Other days, other times,' said Sloan. Every policeman knew you couldn't correct the past.

'She didn't tell anyone in London where she'd gone or anyone in Ornum where she'd come from. And that's where I was born, in her mother and father's old home at Ornum here in Calleshire. She told everyone at this end that she had come back home to have her baby because her husband had died.'

'So who was your father?' asked Crosby curiously.

'I have absolutely no idea,' she said, flushing, 'and after she died I never had any desire to find out either. All I know is that she put me down on my birth certificate as the posthumous daughter of William Peters. He'd never married nor had any children of his own – not that she ever knew of, anyway.'

'So he didn't have anyone else's and not really you, either,' pointed out Crosby, only just beginning to appreciate the whole situation.

Samantha Peters shook her head. 'He didn't ever have a

great deal of money either because he hadn't been able to work for years, but he wasn't well enough to manage without some help. My mother told me that much.'

'A story good enough for everyone except Susan Port,' divined Detective Inspector Sloan, 'who presumably had left no stone unturned in her family history researches.'

'She was one of these pedantic civil servants who liked everything checked and checked again,' Samantha Peters said with some heat. 'It's the nature of the beast, I suppose.'

'I thought solicitors were supposed to check on everything with a fine toothcomb,' grumbled Crosby, who had never liked the extent that defence counsel went into detail in every case he'd ever been involved in. 'Puckles never found any of that out, did they?'

'They had all the beneficiaries' parents' death certificates and their children's birth certificates checked, as well as their family trees all the way back to Algernon Mayton,' she responded dully. 'They didn't really need the marriage certificates of everyone as well.'

'They only thought they didn't,' said Crosby triumphantly, pleased to find a fault in the work of a profession he didn't like.

'And I didn't know anything about it either until my mother told me just before she died,' said Samantha Peters. 'She said William had been a good man and she was sure he wouldn't have minded if he had known.' She gave an ironic laugh. 'So I put her down as his widow on her gravestone in Ornum churchyard when she died. I thought she'd have liked that.' She gave Sloan a quizzical look, half amused. 'I take it, Inspector, that there's no law against uttering a false statement on a gravestone, is there?'

'If so, it is not in the same league as murder, Miss Peters,' he replied gravely.

'So nobody ever knew?' said Detective Constable Crosby, anxious to get everything clear.

'Except me, of course,' she said. 'And I only knew eventually.'

'But nobody else?' asked Crosby.

'Not until Susan Port started to do her family history research on all the descendants of Algernon Mayton,' explained the woman. 'For her own interest, she told me.'

'Civil servants like to be meticulous in dotting their "i"s and crossing their "t"s in their daily work,' said Sloan. He thought of adding, 'Like the mills of God, they grind exceeding small', but he decided against it. This was no time for any Biblical quotation save 'Thou Shalt Not Kill'.

'That was when I knew that I had to kill her,' said Samantha Peters with a detachment that was frightening in itself.

'Before she found out about you?'

'Oh, yes, Inspector, long before. That was when I first started bringing her the tablets from the hospital. I told her that they were much more effective than the ones the doctor there had given her. I brought her a few each time we met – in my handbag, not in a bottle.'

That figured, thought Sloan, making a note.

'Susan Port obviously couldn't trace my mother's marriage certificate to William Peters when she tried,' she said.

'Because there wasn't one to find,' said Detective Constable Crosby.

'Of course not. I've told you that already and you've written it down,' she snapped.

'Then what?' asked Sloan, detective first and foremost. The interview with the woman – properly, now the suspect – was being recorded too, for the benefit of the Crown Prosecution Service as well as the defence.

'Then,' said Samantha Peters, 'she began to drop little hints to me that she'd been looking for it and the next time I saw her she said it again. At first, she was quite sure that Tom Culshaw had been born outside of marriage in some way or another because of the way his mother treated him, but I'd worked out that it was just a case of mother and baby failing to bond.'

Detective Inspector Sloan never failed to marvel at the way the medical profession could reduce domestic disaster merely to a question of diagnosis.

'The heirs,' put in Detective Constable Crosby suddenly, light dawning. 'You wouldn't have been in the running for a handout if you weren't really William Peters' daughter, would you, miss?'

She shook her head. 'No.'

'And then?' asked Detective Inspector Sloan. 'After she discovered your mother hadn't been married to a Mayton, and let you know what she had found out, what did you do next?'

'Everything about our relationship changed after that,' said Samantha Peters sadly. 'Including her behaviour towards me.'

'Blackmail?' suggested Detective Inspector Sloan at once. Those who went in for blackmail were always at high risk of being murdered themselves, although they didn't always take that fact into consideration before they made their demands.

'Worse than blackmail,' she said, tightening her lips.

'What on earth could be worse than blackmail?' asked Detective Constable Crosby, who still had a lot to learn.

Sloan waited with close attention for him to be enlightened.

'Susan Port wasn't interested in having more money herself and said so,' said the nurse. 'She told me that she'd got all she wanted now and would be getting the Mayton money in due course as well, which she said was more than I would.'

'Nasty one,' said Crosby.

'But true,' she said.

'So?' persisted Crosby. 'What was worse than blackmail?'

'Sanctimoniousness,' she said tersely.

'Come again?' said Crosby rather too informally for Sloan's liking.

'She went all prim and proper on me, Constable. She insisted her attitude wasn't anything to do with the money at all but that she had a moral duty as a good citizen to tell Simon Puckle that I wasn't really in line for the Mayton money.'

In spite of himself, Sloan said, 'Holier than thou?'

She gave him a wan smile.

'But surely it wouldn't have mattered if she had, would it?' said Crosby, frowning and trying to think like a policeman. 'You hadn't actually had any money from the trust yet, had you? None of you had because of not finding Daniel Elland. You couldn't have been done for anything, miss. You'd have just lost out on your cut of the kitty.'

Detective Inspector Sloan took a deep breath, reminding himself that this was not the time or the place for reprimanding a constable for a degree of partisanship incompatible with his role as an upholder of the Queen's peace.

She sighed and reeled off a litany of potential offences. 'False pretences, masquerading as someone I wasn't, making a claim on someone's estate to which I wasn't entitled – I know in the event I hadn't actually done so but I had acquiesced in potentially committing fraud.'

Detective Constable Crosby began to say something, but she interrupted him and carried on quite angrily. 'You don't understand, Constable. Even knowingly making a false declaration on my application for a passport when I went on holiday is a criminal matter and would have made me liable for prosecution.'

Detective Inspector Sloan understood all right. 'Your job . . .'

She turned to him. 'I would have lost it, Inspector. The General Nursing Council doesn't like nurses who commit fraud.'

'Or who go to prison,' agreed Crosby, at last getting the full picture.

She said savagely, 'I was damned if I did anything and I was damned if I didn't.'

'So you chose to do something and killed Susan Port,' summed up Sloan starkly.

She fell silent.

'And you also killed an innocent young man called Terry Galloway,' Sloan pointed out.

She didn't deny it. 'He saw me at the cottage. He would have recognised me,' she said, much too matter-of-factly for Sloan's liking. 'Especially if he had come round in the hospital while I was on the ward. Don't you see? I had to do something about that even if he was a patient. So I gave him the Ameliorite from the drug cabinet and put the rest into the pockets of the patients from the east end.'

There had been an occasion in the past when those on duty at the Berebury police station had had to respond to a major local disaster, leaving several officers quite severely traumatised. The force had employed a professional counsellor to talk to them afterwards who had spoken of the need sometimes not to care too much.

Her declaration that Samantha Peters had chosen not to care was now safely enshrined not only in Sloan's notebook but on tape.

He began to caution her, conscious that although she had some of the characteristics of the trained nurse, she most certainly didn't have them all. Killing two people in cold blood for gain, nurse that she might be, was as good an example of not caring as he'd come across in a long time.

THIRTY-THREE

D etective Constable Crosby turned the police car back in the direction of Berebury from Bishop's Marbourne and asked if it was all the same with Inspector Sloan if he went off duty at five o'clock now that everything in the case was all tied up.

'Sure,' said Sloan after a glance at his wristwatch. He added without thinking, 'Something on?' His wife, Margaret, would have said he shouldn't have asked, that the boy might have been going to meet a girl as he went off duty.

'We've got a beef tea in the canteen this afternoon, sir.'

'A beef tea? I thought beef tea was something you cooked for old invalids with weak stomachs.' It wasn't a girl, then.

'Not that sort of beef tea, sir,' said the constable earnestly. 'It's when we meet to have a beef about Sergeant . . .' His voice trailed away. 'Better not say, sir, who.'

'No, you better hadn't,' said Sloan warmly. Not that Crosby needed to name names. He knew without being told which sergeant it was who made the lives of all the young constables at the station such a misery.

'No names, no pack drill,' said Crosby, who had never been near a parade ground in his life. He added gloomily, 'Walls have ears, too.'

'Very true,' said Sloan, finding himself quite curious. 'Tell me, what has occasioned this – er – particular beef?'

'Sergeant – the one I said, sir . . . .'

'Shall we call him Sergeant So-and-So?' suggested Sloan.

Crosby brightened. 'Very clever, sir, because he's a right so-and-so.'

'What's he done?' said Sloan, ignoring this last, in spite of the interests of discipline in 'F' Division of the county force.

'He sent me and my mate, Fleetwood . . . you know PC Fleetwood, sir, don't you?'

Sloan admitted to knowing Constable Fleetwood, an unimaginative young ox of a man.

'Well, he sent Fleetwood and me to look into a theft . . .'

'An alleged theft, I take it,' cautioned Sloan. 'Unless you've made an arrest?'

'Fat chance of that,' said Crosby richly. 'An alleged theft then, from the garden of a Mr McGregor.'

'Apples?'

'No, sir. Lettuces.'

'Lettuces?'

'Oh, and French beans and some radishes.'

'A vegetarian thief, then.'

'That's what Sergeant So-and-So said.'

'People don't usually steal lettuces.'

'We should have known that, shouldn't we, sir?' said Crosby bitterly. 'Apparently the theft – the alleged theft, that is – had been witnessed by this Mr McGregor who was working in his garden at the time. All the sergeant told us that he knew about the theft was what this Mr McGregor had told him. Oh, and he said that the thief was called Peter O'Hare.'

'So Mr McGregor knew him?'

'Sounded like it, didn't it, sir? We thought – Fleetwood and me – that the sergeant might have known him as a regular offender because he said he came from a fatherless family and was well known as a young tearaway. Besides he left his shoes behind when he ran away.'

'Anything known?'

'We couldn't find any record at all, even though the sergeant said it had all been written up, big time.'

'Really?' Sloan frowned.

'But we couldn't find out anything about him, sir, could we?' He sniffed. 'Even after the sergeant told us that the mother had always found her Peter a proper handful, which fits young tearaways.'

'Strange, that,' mused Sloan, an unworthy thought beginning to cross his mind. He, too, knew the sergeant in question.

'So, like a couple of ninnies we went out to the address we'd been given, didn't we?'

'And?'

'And nothing, sir. There was no Mr McGregor there and no sign of this Peter O'Hare either. All we found was just a garden full of vegetables.'

'Including lettuce?' said Sloan, his suspicions now thoroughly aroused. There had been a time when his infant son had liked being read to at night and, in the way of small children, liking to be read the same book over and over again. And then, equally in the way of small children, suddenly deciding he'd heard it enough times, pushing it away and never listening to it ever again. There had been one such tale much favoured by his son and it came into his mind now.

'Yes, sir,' said Crosby. 'But it seemed at first from what this Mr McGregor had said to the sergeant that nothing else except vegetables had been taken.' He sighed. 'At least that's what the sergeant told us.'

'Ah,' said Sloan.

'Perhaps we should have guessed something was up then, sir. Or even when he talked about this Peter having three well-behaved sisters.'

'Possibly,' agreed Sloan, 'although I don't think you could have known what it was all about at the time.'

'We didn't. Not then.'

'When?'

'When we got back to the canteen with our report. That was when the sergeant told us he'd made a mistake with the name and it wasn't Peter O'Hare after all but Peter . . .'

'Peter Rabbit?' suggested Sloan gently.

Detective Constable Crosby nodded. 'And then he told us that Peter's sisters were called Flopsy, Mopsy and Cottontail.'

'Then everybody laughed, I suppose.'

'I'll say they did. The whole canteen roared. Ever been

had, they said. You guessed, too, didn't you, sir?' said Crosby sorrowfully.

'My whiskers did twitch at one point,' admitted Sloan.

'I suppose we should have known we were being taken for a ride.'

'You will find, Crosby, that that goes with the territory. People,' he said bracingly, 'are always trying to lead the police up the garden path.'

'I know, sir, but . . .'

'When you win, you party,' said Sloan. 'When you lose, you learn. Don't get caught again, Crosby.'

'No, sir.'

'And remember,' said Sloan, unconsciously emulating Oscar Wilde, 'the good things that happen become happy memories . . .'

'And the bad ones, sir?'

'You're a police officer, Crosby, so you put them down to experience.'